Doctrine of Indecency:

18 Coveted Tales of Lust

Kyle Perkins

Virginia Lee Johnson

Brianna West

Lila Vale

Taylor Rose

Mia Sparks

Erin Trejo

Samantha Harrington

LJ SeXton

Katherine Mizera

AR Von

CeeCee Houston

Crystal Dawn

EJ Christopher

TL Wainwright

Eden Rose

Tiffani Lynn

Amanda O'lone

Editing

Virginia Lee Johnson
(Formatting)

Kat Mizera

A Cabin… Somewhere.

By Kyle Perkins

I wake up to the sound of ringing in my ears. A deafening sound making logical thought impossible. I shakily rise to my feet and take in my surroundings. The air is frigid, like a cold day in January. I take a few steps and the carpet makes a sloshing sound as I move.

Where am I?

The wooden paneling on the walls are bare, and the furnishing seems old, but placed here. Everything is neat and tidy, from the crimson silk curtains to the picture frames housing stock photos of smiling people that I don't recognize. I must be in some type of cabin, but how did I get here? Moving through the living room, I find the old stone fireplace, with embers still burning.

Did I light that?

The smell of burning wood clings to the heavy air, every breath seems to get harder and harder, almost as if my lungs won't expand. I move from the living room down the darkened hallway. I flip the switch on the wall but it is unresponsive. I feel utterly fatigued, every muscle in my body sore to the touch. Everything feels all wrong, out of place. I go into the bathroom and stare into the mirror. My face looks worn, almost as if it has aged since the last time I looked at it. The dark circles under my hazel bloodshot eyes stick out like a sore thumb, but more curiously, I have scrapes and cuts all over my head and chest. My hair is soaked and sticks to my skin, I must have been out for hours. I run my fingers through my jet black hair to try and get some of the knots out, but when I bring my hand back down level with my eyes, it's covered in blood.

None of this makes any sense.

Panic begins to surface and I start to hear myself breathing rapidly. I continue to stare into the mirror and watch as my pupils contract and dilate at various speeds. My hands and fingers feel like they have fallen asleep, the tingling sensation creeping from my extremities to the rest of my body the more I focus on it. I need to get out of my head.

"Pull it together, Dillon," I say out loud, which was barely audible over the ringing in my head.

I turn on the old copper faucet and water sputters out onto my hands. As it runs over my skin and between my fingers, the dirt and blood mixes with the water at the bottom of the sink. I splash some on my face and turn, leaving the bathroom. Out of the corner of my eye I see a figure at the end of the dark hallway, but when I turn to face it, it disappears in my peripherals.

Now I'm seeing shit too?

I walk to the end of the hallway to a set of two identical wooden doors. I open the door on the right as it creaks loudly. Inside the room is a large pine desk, pictures and a king sized bed with crimson colored bedsheets. The pictures on the wall upon closer inspection reveal old family photos of my wife and son. He'd be nine, today. If their pictures are here, that must mean that this cabin is mine, but I've never seen this place in my life.

The desk is barren; without anything a desk would normally have on it. I run my fingers across the surface and find there to be no trace of dust, none. The drawers are empty except for a single notepad with the words "Pine Bluff" written across it. I slide the notepad into my pocket and leave the room.

In my peripherals, I see the same figure again, but again, I turn my head and it vanishes. I can't help but feel like I am being watched and the hairs on my neck stand up. I move across the hall and try the door but it's locked. I slam my shoulder against it, but it won't budge even an inch. Giving up, I return to the living room. The fireplace remains unchanged and the smoke continues to rise from the ashes.

The kitchen is decorated like a fifties style ranch house, and the linoleum flooring is sticky, gripping my foot with each step. I open the pine cabinets to only find cobwebs, but no food. The cast iron stove looks like it hasn't been touched in years, but that would be impossible, considering the pictures on the wall. I feel my stomach begin to turn as the unsettling vibe of the cabin really begins to set in.

I walk over to the couch and take a seat, immediately placing my head in my hands. As I close my eyes, I hear whispers from every direction, filling my mind with nonsense that I can't decipher. Lifting my head from my hands, I see the same shadowy figure off in my peripherals. Everything I know about the world is telling me that the figure isn't really there, but how can I deny what I see with my own two eyes?

I have now been through the entire cabin, and I am none the wiser for it. I stand up from the couch and walk over to the window for the first time. Beautiful lush pine trees dot the landscape, along with a crystal clear lake and my jeep. The windshield is smashed and the front end looks severely damaged. The jeep is totaled, and probably the reason I don't remember much. Certainly would explain all of the blood.

I hear a sharp knock at the door and jerk my head towards it. The sound tears right through me like a buzz saw. Do I answer it? I don't even have any answers as to why I am here, covered in blood. Furthermore, how can I even be certain it's all mine? Obviously this person knows I am here already.

Another round of knocks threatens to rip the door from its hinges. I nearly jump out of my skin as my eyes seek for a place to hide. However, if this person knows I'm here, there is nowhere to hide. Nowhere to run at all. I slowly walk over to the door and quietly press my ear against it. All I can hear outside are the howling winds cutting through the trees. I pull my head back and take a deep breath.

"Yeah? Who is it?" I say trying to sound confident as I cower behind the door.

There is no response, just the howling of the wind.

"Get off of my property before I call the Sherriff!" I bluff, hoping that would be enough.

Again, there is no response. Not even footsteps.

I shuffle quickly to the kitchen and pull one of the drawers off of its track, then return quickly to the door.

Still nothing.

"You have until the count of three to announce yourself!" I say out loud, possibly to no one at all.

I pace in front of the door readying my drawer as some type of makeshift weapon, as if it would cause anyone any real harm.

"Hehehe," An otherworldly giggle is heard through the thick door.

I jump back a few feet and stare at the door unsure of what to do. On one hand, there could be a kid out there that needs help, but on the other, why in the fuck would a kid be out there?

I slowly move back to the door staying completely alert, but again, there is no sound. I grab the door handle and begin turning it slowly. I try to pull the door open, but it's impossible. It's almost like it is boarded shut from the other side. Moving quickly across the living room and through the kitchen, I make my way to the back door. I give it a few good tugs and realize that I am trapped inside.

The feeling of panic returns and I start biting my nails, regardless of the heavy copper taste from the blood under them. As I move through the kitchen back into the living room, I am stopped in my tracks by the photos in the picture frames... Did they always look terrified in them? The people in the photos all look like they are mid scream, or cowering in terror.

Quickly, I move from the living room back into the bedroom with my family photos.

"What in the fuck is going on..." I trail off as I see a photo of my boy and my wife, both with dread etched across their face.

I know I took this photo, and that isn't how they were that day. The reason I remember that day so clearly is because that is the day they died. Funny how one wrong turn can change your life like that. Not funny like a comedy special, funny like "life is meaningless and we're all fucked in the end."

The pictures are not only unsettling because of their expressions, but because the pictures technically shouldn't exist. Again, nothing makes sense. I reach into my pockets to search for any relics from the night before that I may have left behind, something to piece this together. In my pocket I only find a wallet, spare change, and an envelope with '*Open Me*' written on it.

I check the wallet for cash, but it's empty. As I open it the rest of the way, I see pictures of my family and I, all with faces twisted in horror. I drop the wallet and it makes a splash on the carpet. I back away sluggishly, beginning to feel a little faint. As my feet hit the edge of the couch, gravity and shitty balance forces me to sit down. I put my head in my hands again, and hear the cryptic whisper screams inside my head. Something doesn't want me to shut my eyes.

I open the envelope and pull out a neatly folded piece of paper. Pulling together what nerve I have left, I open it and read the single word written on it in crimson ink… Or blood.

"Intrare," I say out loud.

Suddenly there is another loud knock on the door, only this time it seems even more urgent. I stay on the couch, choosing to ignore it, the door doesn't open anyway.

The door swings open with such force that it is ripped from the hinges, flying to the other side of the room before smacking against the kitchen counter. In a moment of shear reflex, I jump out of my seat and land behind the couch. I crouch low to the ground and peer over the edge towards the door, but no one is there. My skin begins to crawl as fright engulfs me. I look over at the coffee table and see the pictures in the same place, but the people in them mouthing the words, "help me."

That was the final straw, something fucked up is happening here, and I want no part in it. I make a mad dash towards the door, but I am paralyzed in my tracks when I see what is waiting for me on the porch.

A woman, maybe eighteen to twenty years old stands on the porch, sopping wet. Her skin is a pale white, almost translucent. Deep purple spider veins are covering face, all leading to her pitch black eyes. Snow white hair hangs from her head in thick tangles down to her waist; she is beautiful, but clearly ill.

All fear vanishes from me as I move closer to her; like everything is going to be okay. There is a warmth to her, a disarming aura.

"Ma'am, are you okay?" I ask as I extend my hand out to her.

She says nothing as she walks past me onto the soaked carpet. Standing there perfectly still, she eyes the photos in the corner of the room, causing the people in the picture to cover their eyes and turn away.

"Look, what is going on?" I say to the unresponsive woman.

She moves over to the pictures and lays them face down, then walks back over to stand right in front of me.

"You've been a naughty boy, Dillon." She says in an ethereal voice that sounded like the combination of both man and woman.

"How do you know my name?" I back away.

"I know everything about you," she says moving towards me.

I move all the way back until I'm forced against the wall. She closes in, standing just inches from me.

"What are you here for? What do you want from me?" I probe for answers.

"In due time, Dillon." She says as she drags her charcoal black nails over my chest.

I make a bee line towards the open door as the woman watches on. As I make contact with the threshold of the doorway, I am thrown back onto my ass by some invisible force compelling me back inside.

The woman watches on as I try this a few more times without moving even slightly. It was almost unnatural just how still she could be. Giving up, I walk back over to the center of the room where she is standing.

"Dillon, come with me. I have a surprise for you," she hisses as she travels down the darkened hallway.

"Not until you tell me what is going on."

"Oh, Dillon. You will like this one." Her voice resonates in my head, almost like she is right beside me.

I follow her down the hallway and stop at the end. She has her hand on the doorknob to the door that wouldn't budge.

"Dillon, have you been inside of this room yet?" She asks with a smile, showing off her sharpened white teeth.

"Something tells me that you already know the answer." I guess.

"How very observant of you, Dillon. Now stand back." She says as she gently opens the door.

To my absolute horror the room is covered in blood, and in the corner, my wife and kid have the same look of terror as in the pictures. My wife runs toward me from across the room in a panic as she sees me.

"Dillon!" She screams.

"Erica! Zach!" I scream back as I try to rush into the room.

I am thrown back by the same force as before and the door slams shut. As I hit the door opposite of the room, I look up to see the woman is gone. I scramble to my feet and start kicking the door and throwing my weight against it, but nothing affects it.

"That won't work, you know." The woman's voice calls out from the living room, but manifests in my head as well.

"You're going to tell me right fucking now, what will then," I say as I charge the woman, only to be stopped by her hand on my chest.

"There is a way." She says as she moves her hand to my head and forces me to my knees with unhuman like strength.

"What do I need to do?" I plead.

She then casually lifts her dress up to reveal that she is not wearing any panties. Her pussy, though pale, is absolutely gorgeous. I can visibly see her clit throbbing and it completely disarms me. I suddenly have an overwhelming urge to obey her, even though my wife that I haven't seen in years is just in the next room.

"Eat it, Dillon," she commands, her two toned voice deeper this time.

I bring my lips to the edge of her pussy and begin kissing it. Her skin is cold to the touch, but her scent very pleasant. I slide my tongue across her clit, and her taste instantly reminds me of honey. Why am I doing this?

I pull her dress over my head and lick her clit faster, gripping her tight ass with both hands. She writhes against my face with every pass, wetness clinging to my lips. I bring my hand up her thigh slowly, and slide a finger inside of her. She lets out a loud moan as she grips my hair and forces my face against her. With her clit pulsating against my tongue, I squeeze her ass hard, helping her put more pressure on my face.

She slowly backs away and lifts me up to my feet by my arm before chains appear out of thin air and wrap around both of my wrists, holding me in place. Hands rise out of the floor and grab my feet, anchoring me to the ground with my legs spread.

I don't say a word as I look into her cold, black eyes. I just stand there, unsure of what I could do even if I wanted to. Whatever is happening is not of this world, I have figured out that much. I need to do whatever she says to get my wife and kid, and get back to my jeep. As long as I can reach the jeep, I can get home.

"Dillon, I want to play a game. Do you like games?" She asks.

"How are my wife and kid alive? They died years ago."

"That was not a correct response to my question." She replies as she rips my clothes from my body, leaving me standing there naked.

"Yes! I like games!" I scream out loud.

"Great, I'll ask you a question, and you'll give me an honest answer." She says.

"Okay, if I play this, can I leave?"

"Enough questions, Dillon." She smiles.

I stand there naked, with nowhere to run, wondering how in fuck I'll get out of this.

"If you answer correctly, you get something nice. If you lie however, you get something... Disagreeable."

"Understood," I say.

Hopefully this game will allow me to buy some time while I think of a way out of this.

"Question one, have you ever cheated on your wife?"

"No," I reply.

"Wrong answer." She says as a large whip appears in her hand.

She slings the whip across my body with such force that it tears the skin from my ribcage.

"Fuck! Yes, I mean yes!" I say as my knees buckle under the pain.

"Next question. Have you ever used a mind altering substance?"

"Yes. Alcohol." I say wincing from the pain.

"Good. That is correct, Dillon." She says as she gets on her knees in front of me.

As she moves eye level with my cock, I start to get as hard as a rock. I don't want to do this, but my body is forcing me. Poor Erica...

"Well would you look at who showed up to the party." She says licking her lips.

"Please don't do this." I say, thinking of my wife.

"You did this, you agreed to the game, Dillon."

She slides out her long serpent like tongue and moves it up and down my shaft, before bringing her lips around the head. I try to close my eyes, but the hushed screams return inside my head, forcing my eyes back open. I watch as she bobs up and down on me, forcing more and more of my cock down her throat. It doesn't even seem like there is a bottom to her throat, or any type of normal gag reflex. I have never had a woman that was able to fit it all in, but she is doing it with ease. The woman cups my balls in her cold hand and uses the other to stroke the shaft.

My entire body begins to spasm as her tongue rolls around the head inside her mouth as she sucks me in even deeper. She opens her mouth wide to an eerie size and slides my balls in along with my cock as he stares up at me with those vacant eyes. Just as I'm about to cum, she pulls away.

"Dillon, do you recognize the people in the photos on the coffee table?"

"I've never seen them before in my life."

"That is another lie, Dillon." She says shaking her head as she moves behind me.

She places her hand on my back and forces me to bend over with such force, that the chains tear out of the ceiling. The chains move with a mind of their own, wrapping around my arms and cutting into the same cut in my ribs that the whip left behind.

I feel a sharp pain as she quickly enters me from behind and I let out a horrified gasp. I struggle to breathe as she starts sliding in and out of me, rapidly. The pain is almost unbearable, as I feel myself stretching from whatever she has inside of me.

"Please... Stop..." I say in between breaths.

"Oh, Dillon. Isn't this what you always wanted? You've always wanted a little pegging, haven't you?" She asks.

"No, please." I beg.

"That's another lie, though I won't count it as it wasn't one of my official questions. You will have to suffer a little though for lying. I hate liars, Dillon."

She grabs my hips and shoves the full length of the device inside of me. I fall to my knees from the pain, but she lifts me right back up and keeps thrusting.

"Didn't you ask Erica for this on several drunken occasions?"

"Yes, but it was just a fantasy. I would never actually want her to do it," I say as she tears into me some more.

"Then why did you hit her, Dillon?"

"I was drunk, it was stupid, and I have lived these last couple of years in regret."

"That excuse isn't good enough for me." She says as she picks up the pace.

"Please… I can't… Take anymore…" I say through gritted teeth.

"You're almost there, quit whining," she says as she angles herself differently, causing the shaft to penetrate deeper.

I can feel my cock begin to tingle with every thrust, almost like I'm going to cum, but how? It's not even being touched.

"Just a few more." She says against the back of my neck.

With just a few more thrusts, cum starts leaking out of the end of my cock, and drips onto the floor below me. A flood of endorphins rush through my body and I feel myself growing tired.

"See, I told you that you liked it." She says as she pulls out and walks in front of me.

A huge strap on, the size of a forearm is in her hand as she comes into view with a huge smile on her face.

"You sure know how to take a cock, Dillon," she laughs.

I curl into a ball on the floor instinctively, shamed and embarrassed. I feel warm liquid running out of me and down my legs, and I'm certain it's blood.

"We aren't done with our game, Dillon." She says as she walks over and lifts me to my feet again, strapping me back up to new chains hanging from the ceiling.

"Can I ask your name?" I ask.

"I have been called many things, none of which are your concern at the present. Next question. Have you ever gotten so drunk, that you hit your son, Dillon?"

"Yes." I say with deep shame in my voice.

"Good boy." She says as the chains disappear, causing me to collapse onto the floor.

While I lay on the floor, in a puddle of my own blood and cum, the woman walks over to me and sits on top of me. I can already feel my cock getting hard again, and it's again completely out of my control.

"Now you get something nice." She says climbing on top of me and sliding my cock inside.

All of the fear drains from me again, and all I can think about is her. I want her, every inch of her body for myself, regardless of the pain she has caused me. She begins moving her pussy around my cock, sliding it in and out with her hands on my chest. As she stares at me with those dark black eyes, I can only feel the absolute love you would feel for a soul mate. Something infinite, unshakeable.

"Erica, come in here." She says as I hear the door open down the hall.

The door quickly slams back shut, and Erica appears from the darkness.

"She is going to watch." The woman says smiling over me.

"Okay." I say, unable to fight it.

Everything in my head is telling me that this is fucked up, but I cannot resist this woman. She owns me, and she knows it. I feel my cock swelling to capacity as she grinds down hard, pressing me further inside. Erica watches on, with tears streaking down her face. I want to console her, to tell her everything will be alright, but I am compelled to keep fucking this woman.

"Have you ever driven drunk?" The woman asks.

"Yes..." I say as lust courses through my veins.

"Good." She says as she begins to fuck me even harder.

I look past Erica out the front windows to see thick ashes raining down from the sky onto the green landscape.

"What about with your family in the car?" She asks.

"Absolutely not, I always had someone else drive. I would never drive drunk with my kid in the car."

"That's another lie." She says as she punches me in the face so hard that I hear my nose crunch.

Bright lights flash in my eyes as my head is jarred by the punch, and I lick my top lip and taste the familiar copper taste from earlier.

"Want to know a secret?" She asks as she slides my cock in and out hurriedly.

"Sure," I say, panting from the pleasure.

"You have driven drunk with your family in the car, ironically, on the day they died."

A flood of images flash into my head... The crash, the ambulance, the surgery that didn't save her.

"What have I done?" I say out loud.

"Oh, you know what you did, Dillon."

"Erica, I'm so sorry." I say as I feel myself closer to cumming.

"You killed us, Dillon. You killed Zach and I. I begged you not to drink that night. I pleaded." Erica says by the doorway.

"Baby, I'm so sorry. I'm so incredibly sorry."

"How could you forget us?" She asks.

"I never forgot you. I just forgot the accident."

"Dillon, do you recognize the people from the pictures on the coffee table?" The woman asks again as she places her hand around my throat and fucks me even harder, almost to the point of breaking my hip.

Another flash of memories fills my mind... Me standing over their lifeless bodies, the paramedics trying to revive the family, the body bags being zipped up.

"Oh, God no!" I cry.

"Oh, God yes." The woman smiles.

The family from the pictures appear in the hallway and watch on as the woman continues giving me the best fuck of my life. As she continues bouncing on top of me, the paint on the walls begins to chip and the air smells of sulfur. The family's expression changes to one of loathing, along with Erica. The door at the end of the hall swings open and Zach walks to the middle of the living room, eyes as black as the woman.

"Tell him." Zach says with a look of revulsion on his face at my presence.

I look up to see everyone in the room has these eyes as black as a void. They begin circling in around me as the woman grips my throat with both hands. I feel myself so close to cumming, right there in front of all of them.

"They weren't the only ones that died on Old Pine Bluff Road, Dillon." She says as she holds a mirror in front of my face.

My eyes are pitch black, and my face covered in blood.

"I'm fucking dead?!?!" I scream.

"As dead as a doornail." She replies.

"Am I in Hell?" I say as I feel my cock begin to spurt, a tidal wave of euphoria rushes over my body and cum begins torrenting inside of her.

I moan loudly and grip her thighs and as quickly as I came, disgrace comes over me as my entire family, and the people I've killed are all watching me. The woman broke her spell and suddenly there is no lust for her, just sorrow and grief.

The woman just smiles as pulls her hand back and drives it into my stomach, pulling out my intestines and stomach, then throwing it beside me.

The family, along with my own begins to smile down at me, as they watch me in pain. My vision begins to blacken and the world around me starts to grow smaller.

"... I love... You... I'm sorr-" I trail off as everything goes white.

▪▪

I wake up to the sound of ringing in my ears. A deafening sound making logical thought impossible. I shakily rise to my feet and take in my surroundings. The air is frigid, like a cold day in January. I take a few steps and the carpet makes a sloshing sound as I move.

Where am I?

Check out my current releases -

Reddened Wasteland – released January 2016

Monte – released February 2016

Ecta:The Divide – released February 2016

Coming Soon - 2016

Bait, Brutes, and Bullets: Tales from the new Biloxi

Humanity's Ark: Kepler

Follow me

Amazon -

http://www.amazon.com/Kyle-Perkins/e/B01BO9SYUI/ref=sr_ntt_srch_lnk_1?qid=1460003160&sr=8-1

Goodreads -

https://www.goodreads.com/author/show/14924560.Kyle_Perkins?from_search=true&search_version=service

Facebook -

https://www.facebook.com/KylePerkinsAuthor/?fref=ts

Revenge

By

Virginia Lee Johnson

I slow my speed as I enter yet another small town covered in dirt and horse shit. This is becoming the norm on my road to the new life I am desperately in search of. As I cross the city limit I am greeted with an aged sign, crumbling at the base from the wear and tear. The weather has obviously had an impact on the peeling paint and rotting wood.

"Welcome to True Lake," I read the words that were vaguely written across the sun bleached relic.

Where in the hell have I ended up?

The sun is beginning to set as I make my way to the center of town. As I reach my first stop sign since I exited the freeway miles back, I am met with the sounds of deep bass and melodic tempos. The bright strands of lights decorate every pole, dangling from one another across the street creating a web of lights above the heads of the locals.

"Every person in this town must be here." My patience wears thin as I see hundreds of people crowding the street.

"Ma'am, you need to keep moving. You can't get through tonight. You either have to turn around, or stay for the Centennial Street Party. It should all be cleared up by morning." The deep voice radiates through me as I consider glancing in the direction of the person delivering the demand. No-one tells me what to do. I'll be damned if a rookie traffic cop is going to dictate whether or not I am going to plow through the swarm of people without regard for their lives, or listen like a good girl and lay low as I make my way through the detour that is offered. Centennial, huh? That explains the rotting city limits sign.

"Thanks." The word slipped through my lips, laced with sarcasm and irritation. Turning right, I am able to avoid human interaction today. There are few parking spaces open away from the street party that interrupted my drive. I guess if I am going to be stuck here for the night, I should find a place to sleep.

As I shift in to park, the music from the street picks up its pace and people start flooding the main stage. I have heard this song before, but the obvious cover-band licks make me roll my eyes in disgust. *I need a drink.*

Pulling my dark hair in to a clip and reapplying my lipstick, I am ready to go. Crawling out of my car with my wallet, I easily spot the beer gardens not far from where I am. The short distance from my car to the – barely old enough to check my ID much less drink – security guard at the gate, allows me time to scan the area for any possible threats. I hand the underage kid my ID and wait for him to slide the gate open for me.

"Hello, Aspen, is it? Aren't you a pretty thing." His words are less of a question and more of a statement. As my eyes meet his, I can tell this line has worked for him before. I move closer to him as his eyes widen, "Yes, my name is Aspen, and has that line worked for you before?" I rip my ID from his hands, "Are you going to let me in, or you going to spend all night staring at my tits?"

His sudden movement to open the gate causes me to chuckle at his embarrassment. I do have nice tits and I use them when I need to, but right now the only thing I want is a beer. With the gate open enough to slip through I attach the wristband I was given by the kid, and head for the tent after collecting a necessary amount of tickets.

"What can I get for you?" The petite girl behind the make-shift counter leans in close to hear me over the bass of the kick-drum on the stage.

"I'll take whatever you have in a bottle." I hate tapped and canned beer. The only way I'll drink it is in an ice cold bottle. I drop five tickets onto the counter as she hands me the bottle. "Thanks."

The girl eyes me for a moment, but I have learned to not react. With the smile I forced across my mouth, I decide to stay a while.

Scanning the crowd for a place to blend in, I notice a group of women off to the side gathering their things to leave the bench the are occupying. I make my way in their direction and I am forced to linger as they bitch about some guy. I really don't mind a little man-bashing, but the girl taking her sweet ass time putting her shit in to a bag, has me growing more and more irritated with each passing minute I am forced to listen to her.

"What about Ethan? That man is fine as hell and I have never been with someone so good with his tongue." The only girl with dark hair has gained my attention. "I have never been with someone that I wanted to keep around another night."

"Are you kidding me, Anna? He just broke up with Kim." I am hiding my chuckle behind my bottle as I realize the blond girl is Kim. "Sorry, Kim. You know Anna has no filter." I am mentally encouraging them to hang out a little longer. I am torn between the hurt in Kim's eyes and the sudden rush of blood to my clit as I listen to Anna continue on about the experience with this Ethan guy

"Don't even start pointing fingers at me, Sara. All of us have enjoyed a lick or two and I know damn well you enjoyed it. It was your constant ramblings that led me to his bed anyways." Anna has a thing for pissing people off. I really like this girl.

"Will you two stop!" Kim isn't having a good time. I notice the tears in the corner of her eyes, causing my eyes to roll. Is this girl for real? All of her friends just admitted to riding Ethan like the fucking pony ride and she is going to try to gain empathy from them. *Oh, for fuck sake*.

I can only take so much, "Excuse me ladies. I am sorry for being forced to hear the entire conversation you are having, being I was five feet away and none of you obviously care about who hears, but can I offer up a suggestion? Actually that wasn't a question. Will you please hurry the fuck up so I can continue to enjoy my evening without wanting to find Ethan and have my way with him, too? That would be great."

Tact is something I have learned to disregard when dealing with catty bitches with a victim complex. Although Kim seems shocked by my comment, her tears have ceased to decorate her cheeks, so I consider that a win for both of us.

Anna, on the other hand, doesn't seem as shocked by my forwardness as the others, "Who are you?"

"Oh, me? I am just the person that you have managed to piss off and turn on. I strongly suggest you move on to wherever you were planning to go. Not sure you would want to be embarrassed by the amount of gossip that could be made very public if you continue to fuck with me. See, I have nothing to lose here. How do you feel about your slutty reputation?" My mouth always gets me in to trouble, but right now I know damn well, the information that I just overheard may get me the bench that I have been waiting for.

"Anna. Sara. Let's go." Kim begins herding the girls away from me as I stand there with a very pleasant smile across my face. I finally have a place to sit and calm down. I tip the bottle back, allowing the cold liquid to flow across my tongue and cool my throat as I crave the loss of inhibitions I need. I toss the empty bottle in to the recycling can, not far from where I am seated. *I am stranded in a small town, what could happen?*

It never fails, as I lay my head back against the hard wood of the bench and allow the liquor to seep in to my blood stream, I hear someone clear their throat. Opening my eyes against my better judgement, I am greeted with another group of people. This group is a much better looking mass. "Can I help you, gentlemen?"

"I noticed you finished your beer. Thought you might like another." His forwardness is appreciated being I am thirsty, but I never take a drink from a guy. I learned that lesson the hard way. I haven't been the same since.

"Well aren't you a sweetheart. I have an idea. How about you keep my bench warm while I buy my own beer? Then, I will come back and you can give me your best shot at getting into my panties." I don't even wait for an answer as I stand and push the two men onto my bench. With a wink and a quick turn on my toes, I am back in line for a beer.

The pitiful lives of the small town folks are wearing thin on my patience. If I am going to be stuck here for the night, I may as well have some fun. The line isn't moving as fast as it was the first time. I notice Kim in the corner of the garden staring off into the crowd like a sad dog. I follow her gaze hoping for a little more excitement. The line is full of drunk girls trying to get someone's attention.

This is ridiculous. All I want is a roofie free beer and my bench back when the conversation behind me grabs my attention.

"There he is. Can you believe he broke up with Kim?" Huh… I knew about this fifteen minutes ago and now I am slightly intrigued with the infatuation with this Ethan character.

"There is no way he will be single for long. I mean, look at him now. The dance team can't keep their hands off him." Another girl starts drooling as I begin scanning the crowd for a bunch of horny teenage girls with a daddy complex. Kim was at least twenty-five. He can't be any younger than her, that would be fucked up.

That is when I see him, Ethan; definitely over twenty-five. He has to stand at least six feet tall; his dark 'fuck me' hair is an invitation and his eyes just locked on to mine. That is exactly the fun I want to have tonight. Even with the herd of girls surrounding him, his height makes him easy to notice.

He nods to me with a glimmer in his eyes and a smirk on his face. Returning the attitude with a wink and a nod, I stay where I am for the moment. Considering there isn't anywhere I need to be, I decide to let him sweat it out. Maybe I won't have to piss off his girl quite yet. I find myself squeezing my thighs together as I think about the strong muscles outlined by his white t-shirt and the low rider jeans clinging to his hips. If he is as good as Anna said, I will be using his hair to hold him tightly in place while I ride his tongue.

Fuck this, I need to get laid.

Leaving the endless line, I turn to the reason for the wetness slowly dripping down the inside of my legs, becoming noticeable to anyone paying attention to my shorts. He still hasn't looked away from me as I confidently push my way through the crowd of women pining for his attention. His stare is predatory as I stalk towards him. He turns more towards me and disconnects the redhead from his arm as I make my way through the final circle of horny women.

"Hey, I've heard a lot about you." He needed to know why I was here and what to expect.

The corner of his lips lift to the left letting the humor reach his eyes as he processes what I just said, "Yeah? You're hot enough, come on over. I got beer."

I reach for his shirt with one hand, balling it in my fist as I grab him with the other by the neck and drag his lips to mine. The need for him, for anyone, is enough for me to publicly do what no other girl in this town would ever do. His mouth quickly opens to my tongue as I dominate the motion of our dance. His hair feels exactly as I thought it would as I pull it, hard, forcing him closer. His hands circle my back slamming me in to the erection that is obviously ready for me.

His fingers glide beneath my cami as he reaches for my ass. I pull away from the intoxicating kiss, "Not here, pretty boy."

Knowing he will follow me if I walk away, I turn towards the exit and wave to Kim. That bitch doesn't know how to treat her man, of course, I will teach him how to treat a woman. If not, he will deserve what's coming to him. I need to be alone with him, now.

I make it past the juvenile pervert at the gate and continue to the parking lot. "Bye, Aspen." I can't believe the little fuck remembered my name. That's not the best news today.

I stop at the large oak tree and wait. It's only a matter of time before he acts as every other human sporting a dick. Leaning against the rough bark, I kick my foot up behind me as Ethan makes his way past the boy. He may be alone, but I clearly see Kim making her way through the crowd towards me.

"Aspen, is it?" His voice is alluring. The way the bass of his vocal range vibrates through my body is enough for me to continue my assault.

"Ethan, is it?" Returning the answer as a question goes unnoticed as he moves closer in long strides until he has me pinned against the trunk of the tree. He's strong, but I can outmaneuver him. *Let's see how far he's willing to go on his own*.

He wrenches on my hands, bringing them above my head. He releases one hand slowly running his fingertips against my sensitive skin at my wrist. Continuing the torture his hand glides over my elbow; along the inkless skin below. His breath hitches as he wraps his fingers around my neck, forcing the back of my head to drag against the rough bark behind me as he lifts my chin in a quick movement.

"Aspen. You have no idea what I am capable of." His eyes narrow as he leans in closer. I can feel his breath against my cheek as he cages me in. "I know exactly what you want from me. The same thing every girl in this damn town wants from me."

A smile creeps across my face as I consider my next words, "Ethan, please. If I wanted to be licked like a prom date, I would have gone to prom. If I wanted to be fucked with a flaccid dick, I would have saved my last boyfriend." He backs away slightly to attempt an intimidation technique I know so well. "Of course, if I want someone to eat pussy like dessert and fuck me like a purebred, then you might have to point me in his direction."

Neither one of moves to break eye contact. The fire that ignites catches quickly. Before I know it, Ethan has one hand in my hair, pulling the clip out painfully, replacing it with his fingers. His mouth devours mine as I reach for the button of his jeans, pulling him closer than he was. As he continues to prove to me he is capable of satisfying me, I see Kim.

I offer my neck to him as he sucks the blood to the surface, bites down on the sensitive skin and licks it to relieve the sting. *Christ! He is that good.*

He continues the series of mating bites, causing me to lose sight of what I need to do. I feel my clit pulsate with every lick of his tongue. Squeezing my thighs together to relieve the pressure isn't allowed with Ethan as his knee slams between my legs, forcing his thigh to hit exactly where I needed it. The moans I hear could be escaping either of us. Aware that Kim is watching only makes me hotter and more in need of his tongue on my pussy.

"We need to get out of here." My voice, barely over a whisper, invites myself to his place.

He pulls my long hair, hard, straining my neck to look up at him. "Follow me."

He grabs my hand and pulls me in the opposite direction of the party. I can't help myself as I glance over my shoulder to find Kim making her way closer to us. I wink to her, hoping to really teach her a lesson and encourage her inner demon to break through and see this piece of shit for who he really is.

We walk past a few houses before we turn to a small white house with a large porch. He takes the stairs two at a time, forcing me to follow in step while he impatiently drags me up the stairs. He releases me as we reach the porch. The door opens without the use of a key. *Go Figure.*

I kick the door closed with my sandal as I pass over the threshold of, what I can only guess, is his house. He stops as soon as the door slams shut. His voice deepens as he makes his demand, "Come here, Aspen."

I am well prepared for whatever he has in mind, but I would like a mind-blowing orgasm before I have to head out of town. That will make for a much more comfortable drive to my next destination. Confident in my decision, I move slowly and calculated with each step.

I kick my sandals off as I move towards him. Backing away from my prowl, he moves down the hallway away from the door. With every step I take, he mimics the movement in the same direction. I decide it's time to play his game. I want him, all of him. Reaching for the hem of my cami, I stop pursuing him to tease him a little. Pulling slowly, I reveal just enough skin to entice his sexual nature.

"Maybe you should come here, Ethan." I reach down to the button of my shorts, sliding my fingers in to the waistband. The summer warmth and the tension between us has moistened my skin to the touch. The button of my shorts springs open revealing the placement of my fingertips. I slide them further down, pressing hard on my clit as my head rolls to the side. "Are you going to just stand there or are you going to show me how accurate the things I've heard about you are?"

He pleases me, closing the gap between us, crushing his lips to mine as he forces me against the wall. Grabbing my thighs, he lifts me, effortlessly wrapping my legs around his waist. I grind against his hard cock while his tongue slides against my mouth begging for entrance. I don't realize we have moved until he rests me on the dining room table. He rips my cami down the front exposing the black lace separating his want from my pleasure. He releases my bra with ease, sliding it down my arms.

"I don't know who you are or where you came from," his hands grip my tit, rolling my nipple between his calculated fingers, forcing me to lay back on to the hard wooden table, "after tonight, you will never forget me." His statement is meant to be a promise. What he doesn't know is that I have never forgotten a man I've been with.

A moan escapes my lips as he drags his tongue along my stomach, painfully slow. He nips and bites his way to my nipple, causing my hips to roll against him, begging for the friction I need. His warm mouth on me makes me wetter as I crave the release I have been pining for. His hands continue to roll my other nipple making me arch into his mouth. I wrap my legs around his waist, forcing him to slam against my wet shorts.

I need him, now. I grab hold of his hair and pull hard causing him to make eye contact with me. The color of his eyes has darkened to a deep blue and the dilated pupils are a telling sign that he is ready for me. "Fuck me with your mouth. I want you to make me cum."

"I am going to make you cum more than once, little lady." As I release my hold on his hair, he reaches for my remaining clothing, ripping them down my legs in one swift movement. I am left bare to him and I can feel my clit pulsate as he watches. The moisture builds between my legs, dripping slowly down my entrance and falling to the table. "Fuck me. You are ready, aren't you, Aspen?"

I don't have a chance to answer him. He grabs my legs, pulling me to the edge of the table allowing him full access to the meal I am willing to serve him. He teases my clit with gentle licks. His tongue slides over my entrance before continuing his assault on my nub. The power of his rapidly moving mouth has me on edge quicker than ever before. The urge to release is becoming so intense that when he slams two fingers inside of me; *I need more*.

He is pulling and pushing me closer to the explosive orgasm I have been craving all night. His thumb replaces his tongue as his fingers curl into the wall of pleasure within me. Reaching for his hand, I force him to move faster and harder. I reach down, begging for more, and join his fingers with one of mine. The fullness forces my hips to roll in to him uncontrollably.

"Christ, woman!" His breathless excitement makes me contract around us as we increase the movement, making my cunt wetter with the pleasure I have demanded. He leans in, sucking my clit into his mouth. My orgasm rips through me sending explosive shudders through my body. His fingers slow as I come down from my high.

Pulling my hand away he wraps his free hand around my wrist, bringing my dripping finger to his mouth. His moan sends vibrations through my body readying it for another go. He pulls me to a sitting position, him tightly pushed between my legs.

"You taste like fucking candy." His eyes darken with the scent of the hand he's bringing to my mouth. I suck my juices from the tips of his fingers, "I want more." The growl of his words and the swiftness of his movements, he lifts me, releasing sounds from my lips that I am not even sure were mine.

Holding me with one arm, he effortlessly takes the stairs two at a time, reaching a room to the right. I continue devouring my sweet juices from his fingers as he collides with the bed, slamming me down and covering me with his muscular body. I can't help but arch into him as he pushes his jean covered cock against my wetness.

"Are you just going to continue to tease me, or are you going to fuck me like the rest of this god forsaken town?" My time is limited and I need him inside me like I need air to breathe. A deep growl vibrates against the sensitive skin below my ear causing my pussy to clench with desire and anticipated release.

He braces himself within the space between my legs, tearing off his shirt in one swift movement. The button of his jeans pops open with ease, allowing his hard cock to escape. It is so close I can feel it against my moist folds. *Fuck this.*

I instinctively grab hold of his shaft, running my fingers along the underside of him while his tip teases my entrance. The promise of one hell of an orgasm is within my hands. I can barely wrap my small hand around the girth of his cock as my mouth waters for the taste of my slick pussy on his tip. I pull myself up moving to the edge of the bed, directly in front of him.

"Suck it, Aspen." There is no option in his demand and I find myself questioning his tone.

"What if I say, no?" Of course I am going to do this, but his reaction is exactly what I need to feed off of. His eyes darken as he glares at me with pure power. Apparently, Ethan doesn't like to be told, no.

He reaches for my chin, forcing me to look him in the eyes, accept my fate as the next girl he is going to have his way with and dispose of like a paid hooker. "I don't think you understand me, Asp. You got yours. Now, you are going to do exactly as I say." His strong grip is sure to leave a bruise along my jawline. "I said, suck it."

Although my tough exterior has created the monster in front of me, my craving for him is undeniable. I circle the tip of his length with my tongue, wrapping it around the tip and tugging forward. Teasing him is as pleasurable for me as it is for him. His hands wrap tightly within my hair, forcing my lips to spread as he pushes deeper into my throat. With quick thrusts of his hips, he fills my mouth with the promise of a night to remember, and I plan on him remembering me for as long as he lives.

Taking him to the base of his cock, I flick my tongue against his balls causing a guttural growl to reverberate through my body. My clit pulsates with every hiss and moan that passes through the quiet room. He finally releases my hair, pulling me off his cock. I breathe deeply, unaware of the air I was desperately missing. A mixture of pre-cum and saliva strings between us before separating and falling to my taught nipple.

As I bring myself to my knees, I caress my body with slow hands, guiding his eyes to the glistened nipple begging to be pleased. His cock twitches as my finger rolls over my tit and he knows I noticed. Before he can speak, I need to gain control again, "I am willing to bet you have never been with someone like me." His lips smirk to one side as his brow lifts, accepting my bet.

"Woman, you have no idea how many 'someone's' I have been with. You are just another one of those tramps, marching their pretty little asses around just begging to be fucked. Some of them are even lucky enough to get their petty little heart broken." Oh, this couldn't have come at a better time as the soft gasp echoes through my ear. *It's time.*

"I want to prove it to you. You think I am just another fuck and I promise I am anything but." I move off the bed looking up to his amused expression as I use his words against him, "You got yours. Now, I want mine."

His chuckle strikes me in a place deep within my body. That's my trigger; my switch is flipped and there is only one way to satisfy that craving. I have done this before; I will do it again. Poor Ethan.

"I'll bite, show me." The humor in his voice only feeds the fire I am so desperately trying to control. My last boyfriend won't recover from the pain he caused me and Ethan just fueled the monster inside.

The look on his face when I begin laughing can only be described as confusion. I lift my hands to his chest, turning him until he is facing the door. With a light push, he lands on the bed allowing me to occupy the space between his legs. Straddling his lap, I am fully aroused with anticipation of what's to come. I easily cover the tip of his cock with my pussy while his eyes roll with the movement. Grabbing his hair and refusing to move another inch, I make my demands, "I am not fucking you until you tell me about Kim."

He opens his eyes, both confused and surprised by my statement, "Why do you want to hear about that cunt?"

"Oh, Ethan. I don't think you understand. What I understand is that she loved you and you fucked around on her. Isn't that what happened?" I slide down an inch or so, stretching to fit him inside me.

"Yes...," Hissing passes through his teeth as I lower myself slowly down his shaft. I stop my decent, encouraging him to continue, "she wasn't shit. I only wanted her around for the image. Pretty piece of ass on my arm made for one hell of a pussy parade."

His admission was more than I asked for, allowing him more pleasure. I lift off him slowly, watching his mouth drop open with the absence of warmth. "Did you love her?" I begin to line up with him again, awaiting the answer

"Fuck... No. I didn't love her. If I did, I wouldn't have banged her best friend, Anna, every night for the last week." *This is going better than I could have hoped for.*

My pussy drips on to his shaft as my body awakens to a heightened state. I slam down on to his thick cock releasing a scream from my chest as I begin rocking my hips back and forth. The lack of condom doesn't bother me as I can't have kids anymore anyway. The faster I move the tighter the grip on my ass becomes. His strong hands guide me to an increased pace. I am so close. He removes one hand, trading it for my clit. He pushes down, hard. My body responds as it should, sending shudders through my body. Noticing the irregular movements, Ethan reaches around with the other hand, sliding it down my ass until he finds what he was looking for.

Sliding his finger inside of my ass, I know to relax to his touch. As he begins moving his hips, he pushes down against his cock with his finger. He slams in to me, filling me to the hilt with pleasure. Penetration has always made me cum fast... well, the first time. My orgasm rips through me as he continues to fuck both my holes. The contractions of my inner wall pulls him closer to his release.

Coming down from the feeling of pure ecstasy, my body begs for more. "No, you don't get to finish. Not yet." He struggles to stop moving within me and complies with my request.

""Lay down, Ethan." He reluctantly slides to the headboard with a cocky smile plastered to his face. *I will remember him*.

I reach for his discarded t-shirt and begin tearing it in to strips while he watches without interrupting. I notice a few other things that will be of great use to me. A detailed piece on the night stand catches my eye. For now, I want him begging for more.

I crawl to him, sliding my pussy along his cock as I slither up his body. His eyes close in anticipation as I fasten the cloth to the headboard. With one quick motion I reach around, putting the noose over his head. It easily tightens as he struggles to pull it away, "I wouldn't do that if I were you, dear Ethan. The more you fight it, the tighter it pulls."

He loses the battle with the restraint as he slips in and out of consciousness. I make sure he's alive; wouldn't want to cut my night short. But I know now, I call all of the shots.

The movement in the hallway isn't a surprise, she's been whimpering since I sucked him off. "Kim. Don't be a prissy bitch and don't act surprised by the shit that spewed out of this worthless piece of shit." The door swings open and there stands a very upset, very sad girl that just watched me fuck her ex. *I am humored by this, because I knew she would follow me.*

"You have no right to talk to me that way, you bitch!" Her mouth is going to land her on her ass if she keeps it up.

"Oh, please. I knew you were there the whole time. You needed to see for yourself that there isn't a damn person in this town you can trust. Not those catty bitches you call friends. Not the True Lake pussy filler, here. Christ woman! When were you going to open your eyes and see this asshole for what I saw in twenty minutes?" After loosening the ties and ensuring his life was safe, for now, I stalked towards Kim.

"Why are you doing this to me?" Kim plays the victim role so well.

Her whole body is trembling and her glossy eyes begin to widen as I reach her. Standing only a breath away, I inquire impatiently, "Are you going to be hysterical all night, Kim?"

Her lips are quivering with fear as she realizes she can't handle the situation. Tears escape her lids, her cheeks redden and her frantic nodding tells me she's a liability. I can't have that right now. I turn to the night stand, where I know I saw the badass blade. I quickly with my arm extended drag the etched designs across her neck causing her lifeless body to collapse to the floor. Grateful that I am naked and completely enamored with the sharpness of the blade of this knife, I pursue the bed.

I spread Ethan's legs apart, allowing me better access to his cock. I drag the bloody blade up the inside of his leg as he begins to stir. I love the feeling of a cock growing and expanding in my mouth. He is going to be mine. I am leaving town in the morning, so he won't be mine for long.

"Ethan. Wake up, we have to talk." His eyes begin to flutter as he comes to.

"What the fuck? Why are you still here? Why is Kim..." He notices the blood pooling on the carpet and the body of his girl, lying soulless on the floor. His life will end, it's inevitable. He is no different than Chris. The only difference is that I should have killed Chris sooner.

Holding the blade against the thin skin above his heart I ask, "Ethan. How quickly would you like to die?"

To be Continued – Maybe?

Current release –

Soulless Nights – February 2016

Coming Soon –

Humanity's Ark: Kepler 2016

More from Aspen? Tell me on Facebook!

Soulless Days - 2016

Follow me -

Facebook –

https://www.facebook.com/AuthorVirginiaJohnson/

Goodreads –

https://www.goodreads.com/author/show/14849135.Virginia_Johnson

Pleasure Bite

by

Brianna West

~~***~~

I adjusted the length of my dress, surprised by no means when it only shifted down a centimeter more. I hated wearing these hussie dresses, but this was work. Good paying work. The same work that fed me on ramen noodles and made sure I was only two weeks late on most of my bills. I sucked in my lower lip, nibbling it as I sashayed my bare legs to the door. My 'fucking freezing until I couldn't feel them' damn legs. I'd left them bare tonight for a reason.
I was playing bait.
"Hey, Devon," I greeted the tall giant at the door. His all black attire barely concealed his heavily muscled chest—a chest that was as wide as the door he stood in front of. His head twisted my way, lips upturned at the sight of me. "Molly. Business or pleasure?"
I scoffed. "You know it's always business, Devon."
"In that dress, I'd wonder how it couldn't be pleasure," he remarked as he unhooked the small rope blocking the entrance and allowed me inside. "Make sure you clean up the mess."
"Don't I always?"

"No," came his swift reply as I slipped past him and ignored the crowd of awaiting men inside the rope line as they drooled at the sight of me.
Men were so easily enticed. A bit of leg here, some cleavage there; it's all they could do not to throw themselves bodily at you.
My dark hair was styled around my blue eyes, my lips painted red, and my entire body encased in a dress that covered just enough that I wouldn't be arrested for indecent exposure. Not that any police officer could catch me. The twelve-inch blade strapped inside my thigh was cool against the flesh as I navigated the heavy swarm of intoxicated bodies. I didn't bother to conceal it since most of the people that stared at me weren't looking down at my legs; they were looking at my ample and ill-covered breasts. And that suited me just fine. I got a night's worth of drinks when I wore this outfit, and after taking out a hit, I was always in the mood for a drink.
It was Friday night at *Bite*, and the club was overcrowded with just-barely-of-age teenagers and oversexed, underdressed women that were being led astray by the many gym-obsessed, heavily cologne doused pretty boys that were buying them drinks with their daddy's money. I was far beyond my years of being enticed by pretty boys looking to add another sparkling notch to their ever-lengthening belts.
I was here for one thing.
I scanned the room, shoving away a persistent bastard that had followed me all the way from the door. His complaint was drowned out by the

pounding tempo as I pushed my way through the crowd and pinned my target with my gaze. The slithery bastard was hugged up in the middle of the dancing sea of bodies, circled like prey by five women all vying for his attention.

His pale-blonde hair and vivid green eyes were only two of the many features that made him incredibly delicious, especially to the boy-crazy girls frequenting this club tonight. He was a rare specimen of the male sex. Completely ripped with solid muscle that was bare up to his wide shoulders and clothed in a tight black tank all the way down to the hard angle of his waist. A self-assured smile hung on his lips as his emerald eyes found their way to mine and narrowed in on me. Almond eyes and puckered lips, that were perfectly illicit in nature, mouthed something that I didn't bother to make out. His strong jaw was smooth and caught one of the lights from above, revealing the near white of his skin.

That was definitely my high hitter.

I pushed my dark hair back and away from my eyes, lifting my head and exposing my long, pale neck to him. When I felt like I'd effectively ensnared him with the action, I pivoted and headed towards the stairs leading up to the second floor. My heels clicked along the tile as I made my way slowly up the flight of stairs, evading a few perverts and their wandering eyes along the way.

I could feel him. I could feel the subtle electric heat of his presence as I reached the second floor and turned the corner. This hallway led to the V.I.P. rooms, which my group had on reserve during our *shops.* Shopping in my world was when we were assigned a hit—a target we were meant to either capture or kill. In many cases, like at this club, hits were delivered either on a one store basis or a shopping spree. Meaning we could be taking out hits along a block of businesses or have several hits at one business to take out. Depending on your level, you would be assigned three or four hits in an evening. However, despite my high return and skill level within the group, tonight's hit was my only one. He was a high hitter. A hard catch. A skilled target, and I had to be on my 'A' game.

I slipped into the room with the door left open, bending over and retrieving the small box from the floor. It was a sedative. It would afford me nearly ten minutes of advantage as it dramatically decreased their speed and hindered their ability to fight back. I didn't like to use it, since I could easily match their movements and take them out, but it was a last ditch effort if I was in a bind. I tucked it away in my cleavage—one of the many advantages of having a large chest.

His presence washed over me the second my hand slid away from the low dipping collar of my dress. I smoothed over the material on my stomach and glanced over my shoulder. He stood in the doorway, eyes trailing from below and slowly up my body in no real hurry, and certainly without shame.

Troy Bates, head vampire of the northern region. A high hitter that I should have enlisted back-up for, or at the very least a partner, but refused. My boss was sweet enough to fill out my death certificate

information *before* I left tonight. You know, just in case.
"Like what you see?" I asked, baiting him.
Troy's green eyes flashed with amusement. "Might explain why I followed you up here." The heavy husk of his voice was inviting. It sent shivers down the full length of my spine as I shook away the beauty of his face.
Best not to get distracted with this one. He could easily end me, and I wasn't about to die that effortlessly.
I'd never struggled with my shops. If anything, most were too easy. I'd hit them and go; that was my way. Chit-chat was reserved for the high hitters, like the man before me, but I never faltered. Never hesitated when I had them where I wanted them.
But even when he headed slowly towards me, the low sound of his expensive Louis Vuitton shoes scraping against the granite floor and echoing off the walls, I didn't reach for the weapon concealed inside my thigh. Instead, I found myself watching him, almost as if I'd been caught in a trance. His beautiful green eyes sparkled in the low light, the door clicking closed as the heel of his foot kicked back and shut it. The sound startled me, enough to cause me to take a step backwards.
Troy's eyes had gone predatory as he easily closed the distance between us, his six-foot-five-inch frame easily dwarfing my barely five-foot-seven one.
"Hello, Molly."
Wait, what?!
My eyes jerked upwards, catching sight of his smug smile before he dipped forward and brushed the dark

hair from my neck. "I've been waiting a long time to get a hit from you."
What was going on?
Words had fled me as his silky fingers skimmed over the line of my shoulder and pushed the fabric of my dress strap away, slipping it over the soft curve of my arm and tugging it down. A fear I've never experienced built up inside of me like a fast burning brush fire. It spread through my stomach and chest, and then all the way up through my throat and into my face as his perfectly shaped mouth neared mine.
"I wonder if you taste as good as you smell," he commented huskily as his fingers weaved through my dark hair and then pulled, angling my head backwards and exposing my neck again to his bewitching eyes. "You were much easier to catch than I expected."
As if those words had been the trigger to get my mind working again, I twirled out of his hold, evading his fingers and pulling the hidden dagger from my thigh. My strap had fallen down my arm and exposed part of my upper breast, but I was able to ignore it, entirely focused on the tall form of the vampire standing before me.
His body moved, but I didn't see it until he was in front of me, slamming my smaller frame up into a wall with my armed hand pinned into the surface. The strength of his hold caused me to release my weapon, and I threw my head forward and knocked it hard into his face. In spite of the dizzy sensation whirling through my head, I dodged his attempt to grab me after he'd recovered from his injury, tumbling to the other side of the room and retrieving

my dagger, ready to strike out at him. My voice erupted from my throat in surprise as I was thrust up against the wall again, neck pinned with a strong hand and air flow efficiently cut off.
"There's that fire I was waiting for!" he cried out in elation. The vampire's green eyes were brightly illuminated and bored into my own with rapture. "That dangerous look in your eyes, it's quite alluring, little Molly."
I struggled against his hold, attempting to free myself and kick him anywhere my legs could reach. I'd been stupid to let myself get caught by him. This wasn't who I was. I never failed. Why did my stomach burn and fizzle like the very sight of this man brought about a dormant desire I never knew was inside me to emerge with only a few words? Why did I desperately hope he would pin me down to the floor, strip me of my clothes, and press our mouths together, thrusting his hot heat all the way inside of me? The desire to feel him was so strong it was causing me to tremble, near violence, beneath him.
"Oh, there it is. You feel it, too, hmm?" His voice was provoking as he released my neck and instead pinned me in one fluid movement to the floor. His large thigh spread my legs, forcing the material of my dress to bunch up and expose my lower lace-clad half to his all-seeing stare. "Your blood is calling to me, sweet Molly, as mine is calling to you."
"Get the fuck off of me," I bit out, jerking my arms and trying desperately to free my hands, of which he only had pinned with one of his. The knowledge that

I was so easily restrained made my throat burn with spite.
He leaned forward, pressing his nose to the throbbing jugular of my neck and smelling me deeply. Body-wide trembling suffused my form with the illicit act. "Your natural aroma is intoxicating. I've thought of little else since the first time I caught scent of you all those months ago."
I was struggling still, but it was weak. Completely unlike me. It was as if every part of my body was yearning for him. Desperate for him. Begging for him. I fought the desire to wrap my legs around his hovering form and paint myself up against his incredible body—a body that was roped with corded muscle that I could see as it strained to hold his position over me. And to my dismay, it was becoming increasingly more difficult to deny him the longer he held me down to the floor.
When he pulled away, his fangs were visible, green eyes radiant with 0ethereal light. His pale hair was covering patches of alabaster skin that was practically glowing in the dim light. And I was mesmerized, immersed inside those gorgeous greens that regarded me with the same desire that was answered, no doubt, in my own eyes.
"That's it," he whispered sensuously, dipping down and sliding his plump lips along my jaw. The touch enflamed my desire as I fought back a shiver when he breathed into the shell of my ear. "No need to fight it, dearest Molly. You were always meant to be mine."
My eyes shuttered closed the moment I felt the scrape of his fangs against my thudding pulse. His

tongue tasted up the protruding surface of it before he was trailing his hand from arm to breast. His finger hitched underneath the other strap of my dress, sliding it over my shoulder and dragging it down to expose my breast to the cool air. His face drew away, gaze sliding down to the area where his hand rested. He kneaded the soft mound, eliciting a heady moan from my throat. My legs quivered, tightening around his thigh and rubbing against it as he dipped down and suckled my perked nipple into his mouth.

His fangs nicked the flesh, causing me to gasp sharply. But my brain was muddled and my body was yielding to him almost entirely as he mouthed my sensitive nipple and licked a pathway up to its previous spot along my jugular.

"I need to taste you," he growled, a carnal sound that reverberated in the place our bodies touched. "And then I'm going to claim you. Fuck you. Take you with your legs spread and your hips riding the intense pleasure I give you, until your cries can be heard by all the mindless humans on the dance floor."

In spite of my desperate need to do what I came to do, to kill him before he could kill me, to take his life and leave him as ash, everything inside of me refused to listen. Refused to deny him. Couldn't find the strength to deny him, or to cease this profound desire to have him.

So when his fangs pierced into me and Troy took his first taste of me, I'd yielded to him wholly. The pleasure ripped through me as his solid body weighed me down to the floor. My neck was ravaged by a tantalizing tongue before Troy was throwing his head back, blood spilling down the side of his mouth and body going rigid as he savored the taste of me. It was the most beautiful and undeniably dangerous image I'd ever been made privy to. All of my training had warned me against this very scenario, and yet I felt nothing but indescribable lust from the sight of him with my blood on his lips.

My blood looked good on him.

His hand dipped between us, twisting the lace of my underwear around his fingers and ripping it, like it was a thin sheet of tissue paper, from my body. His rough fingers spread the wet lips of my sex, swiping across them and causing my spine to arch upwards into a sharp curve as a low moan escaped my lips. Troy's fingers penetrated me deeply in one strong movement, scissoring inside and forcing more unbidden moans from my throat. His other hand pressed down on the space between my hips, intensifying the sensations.

"You're hot and wet for me, aren't you, sweet Molly," he whispered lowly, hoarse voice penetrating me as deeply as his fingers did. "Want me to taste you here?" His fingers curled, triggering my hips to roll down and seek more pleasure from his touch. "Do you want me to suckle your sweet juices and pleasure you in a way no mortal man can?"

Oh god. I wanted him so badly. Needed him desperately. Wanted him to taste me with his mouth. Fuck me with his mouth. Make my body numb with the pleasure and heat from his mouth.

"Yes," I whispered, hips gyrating wantonly as he knelt closer to where his fingers pleasured me.

His green eyes glowed brightly, enchanting me from where they hovered over my trembling body. "Beg me for it, sweet Molly. Beg me."
"Please," I pleaded, utterly lost and incapable of modest thought or rationale. All I knew was that right now I needed him.
The pale-haired vampire smiled in triumph before he lifted me from the floor and sat me down on the couch. He pulled at the bunched up material that I wore, discarding it to the floor and leaving me bare from head to calf, only my several-inch-high heels left on. He knelt down before me, hands spreading my legs to expose my wet desire in a way that made my cheeks flush with heat. He leaned forwards, kissing his way along my pale thighs to the sharp triangle of my sex, swiping his tongue lightly over my wet core, and then pressing forward with more intent. His guttural growl caused my head to fall back into a pleading moan, hips thrusting against his scorching mouth as it sucked and licked roughly at me.
Pleasure washed over me in powerful waves, forcing my legs wider and my moans to grow crazed, unhindered. My hands held tight to the back of the couch to keep me upright against the ecstasy of his mouth as it teased me between my legs. I was slowly riding the edge of my orgasm before Troy was pulling away. My hand shot out, grabbing his shirt and trying desperately to draw him back in.
"Eager little one, aren't you?"
He chuckled, lifting his shirt and exposing raw, deeply grooved muscle to my hungry eyes. His fingers unhooked the buckle of his pants, drawing it

out of his pant loops and into his hands. Troy maneuvered me to my feet, wrists out in front of me, as he took the belt and tightly secured it around the pair of them. He turned me around to face the wall of glass, brushing the hair from my shoulder and forcing me to bend forward with my bound wrists anchored to the back of the couch, my eyes overlooking the pulsating crowd beneath us.

I heard the subtle scrape of the material of his pants as he eased in closer. His hand came down hard on my ass, surprising a cry from my throat as the hot sting of his hand seared across the afflicted skin. The pain intermixed with pleasure as the fading heat remained.

"I want you to see how utterly desirable you are when you've given yourself over to me completely." Our forms were mirrored in the glass, the low light illuminating only parts of our bodies as Troy hovered from behind me, halfway masked in shadows. "I want you to see yourself as you betray everything you are by having me inside of you."

His voice was so low that it sent warning shivers to splay out over my exposed body, igniting every part of me with anticipation as his hands grappled my hips and drew me back, spearing his large, hot erection all the way inside me. The wide girth and length of him fully sheathed shot blazing heat into my quaking legs.

It felt fucking incredible.

"You're so fucking tight," he groaned behind me.

I gasped sharply as he withdrew slightly and slammed back into me, the loud slap of flesh echoing inside the small room. I closed my eyes to the image of the two of us. It was one that made my stomach coil with guilt. The bright illumination of his eyes; the flash of his fangs; the clenching and unclenching of his defined abdominals and pectorals as he thrust inside of me. It was all enough to make me come right there.

It was wrong. It was criminal. Dangerous. Forbidden. And yet, all I wanted was more of it. More of the pleasure. To feel his heat fill me again and again in a way that no one's ever had. I wanted to break every vow to have him. And I was. Every single vow was broken the moment I let him taste me. Drink my blood. Fuck me.

Troy bent with his forehead pressed between my shoulder blades, his hips snapping forward and dragging a strangled cry from my throat. He fucked me hard with his fingers intertwined tightly within my dark locks and forcing me to lift my gaze and look at our joined bodies as they hovered over the gyrating, pulsating, swarming crowd below. No one could see us, not with the windows blacked out from the other side, but it still made my body shiver with mortification when any of them looked up towards us.

It was that fear that lent to the ultimate sensation of his touch as he jerked me backwards with his unyielding hands and drove into me again, making me moan out in a voice that I didn't recognize.

The overwhelming pleasure as he slammed hard into me over and over was enough to make my vision speckle and my arms to shake violently as I endeavored weakly to keep my body upright with their hold. My voice was uncontrollable and breathless inside the room as the rough vampire penetrated me deeper with each sure thrust. I was barely holding up to his treatment, and I clutched the couch tightly, hands going visibly white and struggling inside their binding when the rush of pleasure overtook my body, causing me to stiffen against the vampire impaling me and cry out as the waves of my orgasm flooded through me.

Troy's hold on me tightened, hand following my curved spine up to the dark hair that flowed over my bare shoulders. His hand grasped a large chunk of it, tugging me backwards as my legs faltered beneath us. His other arm encircled me beneath my chest, pressing me up tightly against his taut torso. His lips kissed over my shoulder as the moving body of the unsuspecting club-goers continued to pulse and throb to the changing rhythm through the thin layer of glass.

But all I could feel, see, sense, or comprehend was Troy's dangerous touch.

"Come away with me," he said in a tenor so deep it crawled over me as if he'd physically touched me with it. "Be mine alone. Forsake everything you are and give yourself to me, to the pleasure, and become a creature of the night, my sweet little vampire hunter."

My breathing was haggard as my back melded up against his cool flesh and fused. His fingers danced over my belly and down over the tops of my thighs, teasing along the surface as the vampire's mouth trailed from ear to the soft curve of my neck and shoulder. Fingers released the binding around my wrists, which were raw and red from the friction of our lovemaking. The belt fell to the floor with a loud clang, startling my head clear. Troy nipped the flesh along my shoulder gently, hitching my breathing as the fingers in my hair dragged my head to the side and exposed my neck once more to him—the very same place where he bit me before.

I was trembling in anticipation as his searing breath bathed over the expanse of flesh, and I found only one response lodging inside my throat when I realized that Troy expected me to answer him. Give in to him. Surrender myself to the pleasure he'd give to me should I say yes.

I was trembling, quaking with yearning as I glanced around me with the little movement I was afforded with his hands in my hair. I found the small box that I'd previously hidden in my chest laying haphazardly on the floor. And with every bit of remaining speed I owned, I escaped his hold, grabbing the box and taking the small needle from it. I stabbed it into him without a pause in between. His vibrant emerald eyes widened as his reflexes slowed.

I redressed in an instant, shrugging away the residual pleasure still rolling through my body. I only had a short time, but with it, I leaned forward and pressed a small kiss to the vampire's smooth cheek. "As thanks for the pleasure bite, I won't kill you tonight," I said into his ear, sheathing the blade back inside my thigh and fixing my tangled locks. "But I'm not so easily caught, vampire boy."

I splayed my hands over the heavy rise and fall of his chest, marveling at the musculature that warmed beneath my touch. There was no thudding heartbeat; there wasn't even a flush to his skin or a sheathing of sweat to give away what had previously transpired. The only thing I felt as I touched him was the electric spark that resulted from this intense connection we shared. It wasn't enough, though. I was a vampire hunter, and he was a vampire. Regardless of the connection and obvious sexual chemistry we shared, it would never be worth disregarding all of my beliefs for a single night of incredible passion.

I just didn't roll that way.

A smirk tilted my lips as I headed for the door. His body was starting to show signs of returning strength and agility, so I left without another word. I navigated the sea of perspiring bodies and reached Devon just outside of the club as I searched for a nearby cab.

"Have a nice shop?" he asked, glancing towards me.

I fixed my dress, attempting to regain the calm thud of my heartbeat. "Out of stock," I replied coolly. "I'll have to come back."

"Tough break," Devon said, flagging down a taxi. "The high hitters are never easy."

I grinned at the large man as the cabbie pulled up and idled in front of us. "Neither am I."

Amazon: http://www.amazon.com/Brianna-West/e/B016APSN6Q

Facebook: http://www.facebook.com/authorbriannawest

Blog: briannawest.wordpress.com

Twitter: https://twitter.com/bwest0426

Goodreads: https://www.goodreads.com/briannawest

Newsletter: http://eepurl.com/bTxG9z

Suicide Mission

By

Lila Vale

My heart is pounding and I'm beginning to get lightheaded with every thump that reverberates off my eardrums. I don't scare easily, it's just that there is so much at stake. Human life on Earth, in fact.

A year ago, if you'd have told me I'd be fighting for the survival of the human race like some heroine from a sci-fi flick, I would've laughed in your face. That was before our 'friends' arrived. Before then… well, it was a complicated time as always on Earth, but immeasurably simpler than what we face now.

A real life alien invasion. Who would have thought?

I try not to dwell on the disbelief of it all. I haven't for a long time. I was one of the first of the civilians to volunteer for training when the extra-terrestrials – ETs for short, because it's easy to remember. I'm bummed that they've tarnished the name of one of my favorite childhood movies – cut through wave after wave of human military forces. Even the combined efforts of countless countries are having trouble holding them off.

If something doesn't happen soon, it's going to turn to nukes. I'm honestly kind of surprised it hasn't, already. And if this plan fails, you can bet that's exactly where it's going to go. There's a glimmer of hope that it won't get that far… Somehow, through a bizarre chain of events, I've become humanity's Hail Mary pass. A last-ditch effort to end this thing without burning the whole place to the ground.

I think we've got a good plan, and I think I have a fair shot if everything plays out how we need it to. Then again, a year ago I thought we were alone in the universe. So what the hell do I know?

Right now, my main objective is to get captured. Accomplishing that without getting myself killed is the tricky part.

I steady my breathing and press my back so hard against the wall behind me that I wonder if my shoulder blades will bruise. My hands are going numb from anxiety and I trade off shaking them out, balancing the rifle with one hand as I curl and uncurl my fingers on the other.

The shots that have been steadily cracking through the night slow, then eventually stop. I know this means that my comrades have fallen.

And although this is just what we planned, and exactly what they volunteered for, my heart is heavy. I mourn, and then I remember it will be my turn to greet the grim reaper, shortly. I'll see them again, soon. Hopefully not *too* soon. I have some business to take care of first.

Even if I fail, I'm totally coming back to haunt these motherfuckers. ETs have slaughtered everyone I've ever cared about and millions that I never had the chance to know. If they kill me now, they'll get a heavy dose of poltergeist hellbitch that they never saw coming.

I strain to hear over my pulse as I listen to the eerily quiet battlefield. I start to hear noises in the distance, boots prodding at fallen bodies and the sounds of corpses being dragged through the dirt. I visualize the scene in my mind and I feel like I might vomit, but I hold it in.

Get it together, Maci. You prepared for this. You expected this. You cannot fail.

The footsteps draw closer and I can tell the moment that the soldiers register my heartbeat because they pick up the pace. The foreboding sound slows as they near the wall and I brace myself. It's time to put my acting skills to work. I *want* to be captured, but they can't know that.

The soldier rounds the corner and I pretend to aim at him as I lunge and roll to the left, allowing the battered rifle to fall from my grasp. It's all intentional. I am to appear as an untrained, terrified civilian who just happened to get caught in the crossfire and pick up a gun. It's pretty close to the truth, anyway. There's a reason this plan doesn't rely on my skills in combat; even with intense training the past few months, they might as well be nonexistent when we're facing the staggeringly advanced ETs.

I hear the shot from his gun and I feel particles of shattered concrete spray against my face, but I don't think I've been hit. I've never been shot before, so I have nothing to gauge it off of, but I'm assuming it hurts like a bitch. I feel no pain, aside from where I scraped against the ground, so I think I am probably alright.

I have no time to appraise my body. I still have a performance to execute, after all. I lock my gaze with his uncomfortably human eyes; they appear black in the shade of his helmet. I cower and raise my hands up in surrender, holding my breath for the few moments that stretch for an eternity while I wait to see if he's buying my little charade.

Full disclosure: I'm unarmed, I don't want to die, and I'm absolutely fucking terrified. At this point, it's really not an act.

Finally, the soldier steps forward and although he roughly twists my ponytail in his gloved fist to yank me to my feet in a painful manner, I am relieved. I'm alive. I'm captured. I've succeeded... so far.

The soldier drags me out onto the battlefield and I hear noises and grunts coming from some of the others. I avert my eyes from the carnage, unwilling to let emotions distract me from my task.

Abruptly he stops, pulls my arms behind me, and secures my wrists. I can't see it, but I know it's alien tech and it glows a pretty shade of blue. I've seen as much in the briefings on what we know about the invaders.

We start moving again and I look forward through the brunette strands of hair that have fallen loose from my ponytail. We're almost to the transport ship, the iridescent doors are a physical barrier between the known and unknown. Everything so far has been expected, predictable. As soon as I step through that entrance, all bets are off. We know nothing about what happens in those vessels, nothing of what happens on the mothership that looms up above.

I volunteered for this suicide mission, but panic still infects my mind and I fight the impulse to flee. I know it would do no good – I'd be shot down the second I projected anything but passive defeat – but my self-preservation instinct still makes the idea incredibly tempting.

We wait at the door and the soldier speaks something in a tongue my ears can't process, then the doors slide open and we step through. He eases up a little as we walk down the white hallway, apparently my complacency has relaxed him. We stop at a room and he fiddles at my wrists before pressing on my back to guide me inside, then sliding the door shut behind me.

I hear a beeping sound and then the static of an intercom, "Wash and change."

I frown and look for the source in the stark white room, but can't find a speaker. "Hello?" I ask, wondering if they know our language or if a captive has been coerced to give orders.

The static goes silent, and I am left to my own.

I comply with the commands of the disembodied voice with great reluctance; it feels like I'm being watched the entire time. I bathe in the white tub and dress in the puffy white robe. I feel an odd weightlessness after a while and I realize we must've lifted off.

There's a mirror in my room and I glance at myself, surprised at how healthy I still appear. Then again, I haven't been infected with the virus for very long, it's not very surprising that my gaze is still bright and clear and my round cheeks haven't hollowed yet. The long incubation period for this strain is one of the reasons it was chosen.

That, and it's relatively easy to transmit. Body fluids of any kind may work, but sex or blood will ensure that the other party is infected.

Tests have been done on the few measly captures that the humans have made. It progresses much faster in the alien system. If I take the less-violent route and I work quickly enough, I may be able to know if I succeeded before I die. I also will know if it works like we suspect it might. Optimally it will spread from the main ET out to all of the minions.

We know they are all connected somehow, though it's unclear just how strongly linked they are. I could be cutting off the head of the snake, or I could be taking them all down. It's a tossup.

So basically, all I have to do is find the big boss and fight him or fuck him before my symptoms start showing. I'm sure it'll be a piece of cake.

The disease will kill me eventually, I know that. I'll never return to Earth. All I have driving me now is the need to take as many of these fuckers out with me as I possibly can.

***

"I am not sure about this bunch. Especially this one. I don't think he likes the ones with blue eyes."

"I agree. At this rate, we won't be home in time for the—"

"Quiet! It is stirring."

I crack my eyelids open and immediately regret the decision as my retinas are assaulted by a powerful light. I blink several times as I try to orient myself, and the light suddenly dims.

"Apologies," one voice says. "Can you understand me?"

I turn my head to find the source and a spike of fear pierces my chest. A raven-haired ET is looking at me, his brow furrowed as he awaits my response.

They're unsettling, the ETs... and not for the reasons you might think. At a glance, they all could pass as human. It's only a trained eye that catches their slightly larger eyes and the faint point to their ears.

Almost like elves, funny enough, but not nearly as friendly as the ones from the movies.

Their complexion is pretty pale and they're also larger in stature than average humans. They're built like soldiers but not so large that they appear freakish. It's as if you took an athlete and just clicked the "enlarge" button on them a few times. Not giants, but never under six and a half feet.

The ones that we've seen have all been male. They might be considered attractive, if they weren't absolutely terrifying. The fact that this one just spoke to me in plain English… it's too close for comfort; I'm thoroughly freaked out.

He narrows his eyes at me and then looks to the identical ET to his right, "Perhaps it did not take…"

"It always takes when I do it."

"Then how do you explain this?"

"You must've done something incorrectly."

I clear my throat and they stop their argument to whip their focus back to me. "I don't understand. You all know our language?"

"Brilliant!" one shouts and claps his hands together.

"Told you," the other says.

"Why am I strapped to this table?" They still haven't answered my first question, but I might as well try another.

"You've been implanted so that you can understand us. The belts are to keep you from harming yourself during the procedure," one of the ETs begins unfastening my straps. Once I'm freed, he helps me off the table and guides me out of the room and down the hall.

I reach back and gingerly feel my scalp, wincing when my fingertips brush across a scabbed wound. *Strange. That wasn't there before, but it feels like it's been healing for weeks.*

"What do you mean… so I'm understanding alien-speak right now? Am I talking in alien? How long was I out? How long have I *been* here?" the questions flood out.

He doesn't answer, he just guides me into a large room. The floor is a flood of white-robed, cross-legged humans. They all look complacent and their attention is focused on a large, clear panel on one of the walls. I shuffle over to a young blonde woman and crouch beside her.

"What is going on? Why is everyone sitting?" I whisper.

She whips her head over to look at me, "Hush!" she hisses, then looks back towards the front.

Well alright then, indoctrinated cunt! I sneer to myself before finding an open space near the back of the room and sliding to the floor with my back against the wall. After a few moments, the panel lights up as crisp and vivid as if it were real life. Sound floods the room, and although I am disturbed by what I see, the images and videos hold my attention hostage.

It's a reel of the most violent, terrifying, and tragic moments in human history. Some of the footage predates any authentic photography that I've ever seen. Scenes that took place long before humans had the ability to photograph or film are shown in incredible detail with vibrant colors as if they were captured with a state-of-the-art HD camera. I have no way of verifying, but somehow I know that these aren't scenes from a movie. They're real events, just as they happened.

They've been watching us for a while, it seems.

I don't know how long we sit there; I am too transfixed on the images to register the passing of time. When the film shuts off and the lights in the room brighten, I get to my feet and realize my muscles are stiff. The blonde from earlier approaches me, and I notice there's a telltale roundness to her robe.

"Sorry about earlier. I didn't want to miss anything," she shrugs.

"It's alright," I say, too disoriented by what I just watched to be upset about being shushed. I frown as I look down at her stomach, my temper flaring at the monsters who took a pregnant woman hostage, "How far along are you?"

"Oh," she beams and rests her hand on her stomach, "One week, thank you! Anyway, I'd better get going. Duty calls, you know," she giggles, then frowns when she looks towards my flat abdomen, "Oh… Don't worry, I'm sure one will choose you, soon."

I blink as I watch her walk away, thinking I must've misheard her. *One week?*

I follow the mass of white robes and it's then that I realize several of the women have distended stomachs poking their robes out. No telling how many more aren't pregnant enough to show. A sickening feeling turns my gut at the implication.

ET guards stand at the end of the hall, sorting us. The pregnant ones go one way, and the rest of us go another. I hate following a crowd like a lemming, but I don't really have much of a choice. Besides, my objective is to blend in.

We enter a large hall and another ET starts lining us up, shoulder-to-shoulder, in a tight formation. There's enough room between each row for a person to walk. Dread paralyzes me and I wait with the others; I don't like the vibe of this.

A door at the opposite wall slides open, and all the tiny background noises in the room simply cease to be. I've never heard such a pure silence.

From the doorway emerges a towering ET clad in a uniform that is entirely black. Up until now, all the ETs I've seen have been in white. Everything is white here. This guy – whoever he is – must be special.

He marches towards us and begins a slow perusal of the first row. I allow my eyes to look him over, though I am careful not to move my head and draw attention to myself. I'm in the third row, so I have a little time to observe.

Scary as he is, he is by all accounts incredibly attractive. I find myself getting excited that he could potentially be my mark. His dark brown hair is trimmed neatly and his eyes are a shade of green that I've never seen before, like glittering emeralds. He has a strong, chiseled jawline and his presence screams pure power and authority.

He moves to the second row and my pulse accelerates, though I don't know if it's fear or excitement triggering the response. He stops in front of the second girl, and a flutter of disappointment crosses my mind. *Why?*

He doesn't look at her, though… he does a slow pivot, looking directly at me. I can't help it; I turn my head to be sure. He raises a brow and I don't know how to respond to whatever unspoken question he's trying to ask. A wicked smile curls the corner of his lips and he parts the crowd of women to stand in front of me.

"This one," he barks out, his voice loud as it bounces off the bare walls in the room. It's immediately followed by a chorus of disappointed sighs from the women and surprised gasps from the ET soldiers.

"What do you mean?" I ask.

He doesn't answer, he just grips my arm and pulls me towards the door on the other side of the room. I struggle to keep up with his long strides.

When we reach the end of the hall, a door slides open to reveal a large room. Everything is polished and crisp and clean, though there are shades of blue and grey in the décor, unlike the rest of the ship. It looks like a bedroom, with a few odd gadgets here and there that I don't understand the function of.

The door closes behind us and he releases my arm, standing a few feet away from me as his eyes scan over my body. I'm not sure what he's looking for; the robe doesn't cling or hug anything significant. His eyes meet mine again, and he stares at me for a moment before speaking.

"Do you know why you are here?" he asks.

"I think I missed the orientation meeting," I let out a short laugh.

I realize I have a choice to make, and I need to make it soon. *He's obviously somebody important... possibly the exact guy you're looking for. What's it gonna be, Maci? Fight or fuck? Flight isn't really an option, here.*

"Ah, so you are a new guest. Then you do not know the honor you have just received..." he turns and walks towards a deep blue chair and begins unfastening the buttons on his coat.

"Guest, or prisoner?" I snort, "Spare me the honor bullshit."

He looks at me with an amused expression, "I forgot how argumentative humans can be before they are fully enlightened... You'll understand, soon enough."

"Don't hold your breath. I'm not drinking the Kool-Aid, Jim..." my eyes dart around the room, searching for anything I can use as a weapon. My eyes land on a decorative looking crystal that is resting on a table. I start inching towards it, hoping he doesn't realize my intentions.

"You are drawing parallels where there are none."

"I don't know, buddy..." I swallow hard as I casually rest my hand near the base of the crystal, "The robes, the propaganda movie time, the unusually high ratio of knocked-up women. All seems pretty cult-like to me."

"You're curious as to why so many of our guests are pregnant."

"I have a guess..."

He drapes his jacket onto the back of the chair and turns towards me, holding my gaze as he moves across the room. He bends his neck to whisper in my ear, and the feel of his breath on my skin sends goosebumps all over my body. My mind is temporarily lost and I forget my intentions.

"We are stronger, we are more intelligent, we are more graceful and we are more attractive than anything the human race has to offer. We can fuck for hours and we are more attuned to a lover's wants and desires than any human is capable of being. We are superior in absolutely every perceivable way. The appropriate question would be; why wouldn't they be pregnant?"

"Oh," I swallow hard, then I remember my original plan. I grip the crystal with my hand.

"I wouldn't..." he warns, leaning back to give me a hard look in the eyes.

How the hell did he see that?

I feel the fabric of my robe moving and I realize he is undoing the belt. I have less than a second to decide, and I make my choice. My hand relaxes. I don't even know if this is the head of their operation, and truth be told, my extra-terrestrial friend is getting me pretty worked up.

Nobody said I couldn't have a little fun with this mission, right? I've already sacrificed myself, might as well go out with a bang...

I hold still as he slides the robe off of my shoulders. My stubborn side doesn't want him to know that I'm actually getting kind of excited about this whole thing.

He steps back and watches me as he slowly removes the rest of his clothing. His naked form is breathtaking, all toned muscles and smooth skin without any visible imperfections at all. And everything – yeah, I mean *everything* – is so similar to a human that I start to wonder if they have some way of mimicking our physique.

"Is this what it's all about, then? You just travelled across the universe to fuck up our planet and get some strange?" I ask as he starts to move towards me.

"Do you really expect me to answer that?"

"Was worth a shot..." I breathe, right before he reaches me. His powerful hands grip my waist and he lifts me effortlessly, moving us around the table and pressing me against the wall. I instinctively hook my legs over his shoulders and ball my fists in his hair.

"Despite the typical shortcomings of your species, you are remarkable," he hisses before he slides his tongue in long, slow strokes along my pussy.

"Thanks, I think..." I pant. I try to fight the moans that want to escape, but I fail miserably and he quickly has me singing the tune his tongue is demanding with every pass.

"That's it, Maci..." he says with his lips against my clit, the vibration of his voice wracks my body with pure electricity, "Let go. There is no point in fighting. We are both going to cum a lot tonight, I promise you that."

His words push me deeper into my frenzy and I writhe into him as I open my legs wider to give him better access. I arch forward and his hands slide up to support my back before he carries me to the bed and slams me down.

The question of how he knows my name nips at the back of my mind, but I'm too far gone to care.

He grips my thighs firmly and spreads them farther apart, almost to the point that it's painful. "Don't move," he demands.

I obey because I want him to keep going... I am so wet and the need for release is so intense that it's starting to get painful. I look down at him and his eyes are fixed on me intently. He slides one arm across my hips and presses down, locking me in place so I can't squirm.

The control he has, the weight and restraint of his arm... it intensifies everything. I try to buck against him but he's strong and determined. His tongue relentlessly massages my clit as he slides a finger inside me. He moans when my body responds to him and he starts working another finger inside.

"So fucking tight..." he growls, thrusting his fingers inside me with increasing intensity. "Cum for me, little human. I want to feel it around my fingers, and then I want to feel it around my cock."

His words send me over the edge, every muscle in my body tenses as he works my pussy, guiding me through the most intense orgasm I've ever felt. It feels as though every nerve in my body is electrified, my head is fogged with euphoria.

After the final wave passes through me, he rises from the side of the bed. Even in my post-climax stupor, my eyes widen in surprise. His cock is fully erect now, and it is both impressive and intimidating. He must notice the uncertainty in my eyes, because a smug smile crosses his lips.

"You can handle it," he answers the question on my face, "Just do yourself a favor and get it wet."

He kneels on the bed and I crawl to him. He rests a hand on the back of my head as I run my tongue over the length several times before gripping and working him in my hand. I tongue his balls while I slide my hand back and forth, working his cock in my hand.

The sharp breaths and moans that my motions elicit start building that pressure inside me, again. I feel powerful as I manipulate this intimidating being with just a flick of the tongue. He grows even harder in my hand, I feel his cock pulsing in my grip and I need to feel it inside me. I watch his eyes roll back as I slide my tongue around the head of his cock before welcoming him between my lips.

I take him as deep as I think I can go, but he shoves himself even further down my throat. His fingers knot in my hair and he works himself in and out of my mouth. I use my slippery hands to massage the rest that won't fit and he lets out a satisfying groan, sliding his free hand down to squeeze my breasts and tease my nipples.

His thrusts increase in speed and his breathing grows ragged. I feel his cock pulsing between my lips. I know what is coming, and I want it more than I've ever wanted anything. I increase speed, demanding his cum with my lips and hands, begging for his release with my tongue.

His body stills and he moans, flooding my throat with wave after wave of cum that I suck down greedily. I've never been so eager to swallow in my life, and part of me knows I'm not behaving normally, but I don't care.

He withdraws from my mouth and I realize he's still just as hard. He just grins in response to my confused expression.

"We're only getting started, human," he grabs me and lifts me again, and I'm in such ecstasy that I just relax and let it happen. He carries me to a low table and I'm positioned on all fours, one by one he secures each of my limbs with those blue, glowing restraints.

"Why the shackles?" I whisper, "I'm not exactly fighting any of this..."

"Because you like it," is his matter-of fact response.

He has a point. It's hot as fuck, relinquishing all control to him.

He presses his wet cock against my ass as he leans over me, and runs his hands along my body, setting my hyper-sensitive nerves on fire. He massages my tits and pinches my nipples, then runs a hand down my stomach and between my legs. His fingertips find my clit and he starts rubbing slowly, torturing me as my anticipation reaches a maddening level.

"Please just fuck me..." I choke out.

He chuckles, then moves his hands to my hips and anchors his fingers before pressing the head of his cock against my pussy, easing himself between my lips. There's a stinging pressure as he stretches me well past my limit, and I find it strangely intoxicating.

"More," I pant, "I thought you said you guys were good at this."

He responds to my teasing challenge with a laugh, then holds my hips steady as he buries his cock completely inside me, laughing again at the involuntary yelp I let out in response.

"How does it feel, Maci?"

"Good... Overwhelming..." I whisper.

"You'll get used to it." He slams into me, connecting so hard that I'm sure my ass is going to be bruised. "Though, I understand. You're so... unbelievably tight..." he hisses the words through gritted teeth.

The room is filled with a symphony of moans and smacks as he drives into me harder. I cling to the edge of the table so tight that I feel like I might break my fingers and I notice that the restraints are rubbing my skin raw. None of it matters to me, though... I'm maddened with the need to cum, with the need to make him cum.

I feel him throbbing inside me and I know he's close. He reaches between my legs and starts working my clit again to the rhythm of his rapid thrusts and I lose it.

"That's it, that's what I wanted to feel..." he purrs as I spasm around his cock. I moan at the satisfying warmth that spreads inside me as he finds his own release.

The room is quiet aside from our labored breathing as we both struggle to catch our breath. He lingers inside me for a few minutes, then pulls out and walks around to where his cock is at my eye level.

My brow furrows; he's still fully erect. *I guess he wasn't kidding about the stamina thing.* Impulsively, I flick my tongue out to collect the milky bead that has collected at the tip. He groans and leans into me, forcing himself between my lips again.

This cycle continues for a while. I'm utterly exhausted, but he has some sort of spell over me... I lose all concept of time as he fucks me again and again, more times and more ways than I even thought possible. He eventually lets me out of the restraints which gives way for even more ways to explore and please him and more hours of intense, uninhibited fucking.

I'm a mess when it's all said and done. He and I lay next to each other on the floor in silence. In my euphoric and sleep-deprived state, my guilt starts to get to me. Thoughts of my mission return, and it finally hits me that I've definitely just infected him with the virus that will kill us both.

I should be elated, but I only feel regret. I'm not in my right mind, and I know I should stay quiet, but I can't.

"Look, uh..." I realize I don't know what to call him. A blush burns my face.

"Call me Silan," he reclines and looks over at me with a raised brow, "Do not be ashamed. I didn't allow much time for introductions."

"Right, so Silan," I take a deep breath, "You know how your people and my people are kind of trying to kill each other right now? Well, there's this virus—"

His loud laugh cuts me off before I can finish. I frown and stare at him, waiting for him to explain.

His laughter finally quiets down, "I know. When will you humans realize that we will always be countless steps ahead? Your virus will do nothing."

My heart sinks, but I'm also relieved.

"Cheer up," he pulls me onto his chest, "I can cure you, too... You only need to cooperate. You've already done half the work."

***

With tears in my eyes, I take one last look at the duplicate of myself standing before me. She's like me in nearly every way – more so than a conventional child – only, she is better. She is part Silan. I will miss her even though she's existed in this universe only a month. We will always be linked and although she is me, she is also my daughter.

I'm not worried about her, I know she is strong and brave and capable just as I am. Growth and memory therapy sessions have prepared her to assume my life back on Earth, the humans that once knew me will be none the wiser. She will be fine.

Still, I am saddened and somewhat regretful of the choices I made at times. Other times, I am immeasurably pleased with myself, confident I made the right decision.

They were always going to win, anyway.

I am still putting the pieces together, but most of it fell into place shortly after Silan chose me. The Ioncinites – that's the real name for the ETs – have been observing Earth for thousands of years. They have watched us consume and destroy everything our species touches at an alarming rate.

Eventually, they decided to step in. The core plan was subtle, they would breed with the earthlings until the population with Ioncinite blood was at an influential level. Through their link to the Primary, they would manipulate the course of Earth's population to a less destructive existence.

Humans reacted to the arrival the way humans do – with violence. The Ioncinites had no choice but to fight back while the replicating took place. Their gestation and growth is rapid, and they have even more ways to speed it up. Thousands of captives have given birth to replicas of themselves, to be returned to Earth and assume the lives of their mothers, then creating more Ioncinite hybrids.

Originals like myself will travel with the Ioncinites to return to their home, where we're told we'll be welcomed.

I hug Maci2 one last time and wipe the tear from her cheek as she does the same for me. She waves once before climbing into the transport pod.

So that's that. My first and only child, gone in a month. At least I know she will accomplish great things. She is the Primary for the Ioncinite hybrids that are returning on earth. She will have the ability to control and shape their populace, as will her offspring.

This is why Silan's choice was so important, and why they remained fighting with Earth for so long; he needed to create a Primary, and he was unhappy with all the captives presented to him... until me. He said it was my bravery that impressed him.

Silan comes up from behind and pushes my hair off my neck, planting a kiss before whispering in my ear. "I know this is difficult. I would like to ease your pain and I can think of several activities that might accomplish that."

My body responds to his suggestion even though my heart is still heavy. I nod and he grips my hand, leading me back to his cabin. If there's anything that will cover up the pain, it's hours of fooling around with Silan. I let go of his hand and hang back a little just to watch his ass while he walks down the hall. That helps brighten me up a bit.

I'm optimistic. The duplicates will return to Earth and Maci2 will convince the humans that the leader was killed and that the remaining forces decided to retreat. I don't know what explanation the Ioncinites gave her to explain why the virus didn't kill her, but they seem convinced it will work. They're rarely wrong, if ever.

As for me, I'll be okay. Silan is equally as sexy as he is fascinating, and outside of the bedroom he treats me as an equal. Inside the bedroom... well, I'm treated kind of like a toy, but that's only because I enjoy it so much.

I stepped onto this ship convinced that I was a dead woman. I think it's fitting that I found a new life.

Facebook

https://www.facebook.com/LilaValeAuthor/?fref=ts

Goodreads –

https://www.goodreads.com/author/show/14952097.Lila_Vale

This book is a work of fiction. People, places, events, and situations are the product of the author's imagination. Any resemblances to actual persons, living or dead, or historical events, is purely coincidental.

THE SUCCUBUS'S SIN

SHORT STORY

BY: TAYLOR ROSE

Nadia

I walk down the busy city streets of Sin City, my heels clicking against the pavement with every step I take. Click. Click. Click. The streets are filled with people, pushing at each other to go in different directions. Tourists walk around with cameras, trying to capture each moment on film. While the citizens of the city do anything and everything to make a quick dollar. Mortals are so weak. So pathetic. So below me. Click. Click. Click.

Each person I pass on the street stops to stare at me, not that I blame them. I'm a prize. An anomaly. The wind picks up, and lifts the silver sequence dress I'm wearing and flashes my black lace thong. Well, everyone around me just got a free show. My ass cheeks were just put in the limelight from that god awful wind. Using my hands, I pull my dress back down, holding it tight to my mid thighs. It's already super short and skimpy. In my line of work, your body is what makes you money. I have to make sure I look drop dead gorgeous every night, or face the consequences. It distracts the guys, giving my boss an easier night of work.

After about a ten-minute walk, I finally start to hear the pumping bass of music. I can feel the energy change around me, wanting to be absorbed into my body.

"Not yet, be patient my precious Nadia," Lucifer's voice echoes through my mind, reminding me to focus on my job. I can always play later.

"Yes, oh great one. I'll eat later. I'm just so hungry... Can I at least have a snack before I complete my task?" I ask him pleadingly. I always work better on a full stomach, needing the energy to keep me focused.

"Always so difficult. Fine, you have ten minutes. Not one second more," he hisses at me, the anger in his tone causes me to flinch back.

"Not a second more," I promise him and hope to god that I won't be late. He seems more volatile than normal, and that says a lot, considering he's the angel of darkness.

I look around the street, trying to find a willing victim. Scanning the crowd, I find a lone man standing with his elbows crossed against his chest, leaning against an alley wall. Perfect. I start walking towards him, letting my guard down so that my energy can pull him towards me. As soon as my energy is released, his gaze meets mine. His eyes are smoldering with hunger, taking in every inch of my body. I continue walking to him, getting closer and closer with each passing second. I swing my hips with every step, letting my body do the hard work for me. My long black hair swings past my hips, glistening from the lights above.

The second I get within a couple of inches, I grab his head in my hands and crush my lips against his. I feel him moan against me, I've hit my mark. I slide my tongue into his mouth, letting him get a taste of my mouth and the addictive qualities I was blessed with. Without warning, his body slams into mine. His cock pressed tightly against his jeans, pushing into my stomach. Perfect.

I run my hand down his abdomen, feeling the muscles popping through the fabric of his shirt. As soon as I reach the waist of his pants, I scratch my nails against his V, leaving marks of my conquest in its wake. I push him further down the alley, where no prying eyes can witness our escapade. Once we get far enough, I drop to my knees in front of him. Using my teeth, I pop the button of his jeans and slide his zipper down. His cock is so hard, it springs forward, causing his boxers to make a tent. I kiss his head through the fabric barrier. I can already feel how damp the area is, just from our kiss. My hands pull down his boxers, leaving him completely vulnerable to me.

My tongue takes the lead, swirling around the head, coating my mouth with all of his juices. I feel his sharp intake of breath, giving me even more reason to continue. I take him in my mouth, my tongue working its way around his cock as my free hand pumps him, slowly at first, building up to his climax. His fingers thread through my hair, pushing my mouth further and further down, getting in as deep as he can. Wanting to get this over with, I use the one thing I know will get him to release. I run my tongue over a small bundle of nerves, right where the head meets the shaft, still pumping vigorously. Small strokes. I can feel him getting harder in my mouth, getting ready to burst in my mouth. He makes a groan that comes deep from within his body, loudly proclaiming he's about to blow. Within a second, I feel his hot liquid shoot into my mouth. With his orgasm comes his energy. It flows freely through my body, giving me the charge I needed for the rest of the night. I feel like the energizer bunny, my whole body buzzing to life in that very second.

I wipe my mouth, getting every drop off of me. Turning my body around, I start walking away, needing to make it to Lucifer in time. Punishment from him is never fun, it's excruciating. My heels click as I walk, well more of run away.

"Hey! Come back here!" blowjob guys yells at me. No thanks, you just gave me everything I needed. Thanks, dude.

I run towards the club, knowing I have exactly sixty seconds to make it to Lucifer. Luckily the bouncer knows me, so I don't have to wait in line. I run right past him, without even a greeting and rush straight into the huge club. The beat from the music, pulses through my body. Getting me even higher than I already am. Walking past the dance floor, I see bodies grinding to the music. Pulsing together, looking like a sea of hot and horny people trying to get a good lay. Even though it's dark in the club, they have flashing lights and lasers flying through the air, creating the perfect night club atmosphere. The bar is full of people, trying to inebriate themselves, to give them that little bit of liquid courage they need for their nights endeavors. As I pass, the bartender winks at me, knowing that later he will get his happy ever after. He's always the one

I go to when I need a jolt of energy. But not tonight, sorry buddy. I wink back, and blow him a kiss.

I shoot up the stairs, taking them two at a time. In high heels, that is not an easy feat. Finally, I make it to the top. I twist my head around, looking for the boss man. I see him standing in the waiting room and I break out in a sprint, getting to him just in time.

"Three, Two... Oh, look who finally decided to grace us with her presence," Lucifer sneers at me, his lips pushed into a flat line. He gives me a look, telling me how lucky I was to make it to him in time. Damn, that was a close one.

"I made it with exactly one second to spare," I tell him with a smile plastered on my face. Thank fuck. What crawled up his ass and died?

"You did, luck is on your side tonight, my dear," he says as he uses his hand to pull something out of his pocket. As soon as the item is revealed, I visibly flinch. It's a beautiful ruby necklace, in the shape of a heart. Does he want me to wear that tonight? I don't understand. "This is the necklace of the heart. It belonged to Lust, one of the seven deadly sins. You have heard of them, haven't you?"

I nod my head yes, because while before I thought this was some sort of torture device, I now realize it is indeed the opposite. The seven deadly sins have been around for as long as anyone can remember. It's said that they were the first offspring of Adam and Eve, until they branched off because they didn't like the rules. They were the first to turn to the dark side. Lust, was one of the seven deadly sins. She wore this necklace to lure in her victims, like a venus fly trap. It releases endorphins in the man you chose to take, making him completely willing. It's priceless.

"What… Why do you have that?" I ask him, wanting to know how he came about such a priceless artifact. And what he is doing with it now?

"I've had it for some time," he says as he places the necklace into my hand. As soon as the item makes contact with my skin, a burst of energy shoots through my body causing me to take a deep breath. "It's a gift. I want you to have it, Nadia. Use it in any way you deem necessary."

What. The. Fuck? Is this some kind of sick joke? Before I have time to ask him, he takes it back out of my hand. My hearts sinks in my chest, I knew this was too good to be true. He grabs me by my shoulder and spins my body around, so that my back is facing him. He runs his hands down my back, pushing my hair to the side of my head with his ice cold fingers. All of a sudden, I feel a shock wave of heat flood my body as the necklace is placed around my neck. I can feel the heat radiating off of the ruby, sinking into my skin. I hear a snap, and realize that he just clasped the necklace into place around my neck. Fucking shit. I guess he wasn't joking, this beauty is now mine.

I close my eyes, and wrap my hand around the ruby laying in the middle of my chest. It's the perfect length, hanging right in the middle of my cleavage.

"Use me wisely," rumbles through my mind. Damn, this necklace is even more powerful than I was originally led to believe.

"So, what is it that I have to do tonight?" I ask the angel of darkness with a breathless tone to my voice.

"The fight tonight is the most important one yet. I need you to catch the fighter's attention wearing the blue, get him to focus on you so that the other can win. This is serious, my dear. The other fighter has to win tonight. Your job, as always, is to be the distraction," he explains to me in a commanding tone. No wonder he gave me this necklace; he needs me to use it to enhance my own abilities. Piece of cake.

Together, we walk through the waiting room we were just in, and enter the fighting room through a wall of red velvet fabric, meant to act as a door. As soon as we step inside, second hand smoke fills my lungs, causing me to cough. It always takes a couple of minutes to get used to the difference in the air. People light up cigarettes and cigars while watching the fights. Most of the people in the audience have placed some kind of bet, so the nicotine helps them relax, I think. Mortals are a weird bunch. Finally, I've gotten used to the smoke lacing the air. Now that oxygen is flowing freely through my lungs, I glance around the huge room and notice some changes were made since that last time that I was here. There is a huge boxing ring in the middle of the room, surrounded by some sort of cage. They have never had a cage fight here before, my heart starts pounding, becoming giddy with anticipation. Dark red velvet curtains hang down from every entry or exit, creating a lustful feeling. Different types of weapons hang from the walls. Swords, daggers, lances, and many other items that I have never seen before. More and more people start filing into the room, running from dealer to dealer, placing bets for the fighters.

All of a sudden the lights are turned off, making the room pitch black. Cheers fly out of the mouths of all the viewers, echoing throughout the room. A spot light shines in the center of the ring, where a lone man wearing a white shirt and blue jeans is standing. He must be tonight's announcer. They find a new one every month, to keep up a new image.

"Welcome! Tonight is the night all of you have been waiting for... The cage fight of the century! On my right, we have Devon Johnson aka *The Hammer!*" he says while lifting his right arm up in the air. The crowd goes wild, obviously wanting *The Hammer* to be the victor. Of course, this is the guy in the blue that I need to distract. He's huge, at least almost seven feet tall with muscles cascading down his whole body. His triceps are bigger than my head, literally. Why is he the one I have to distract? It looks as if fighting is his life. I'll have to step up my game tonight. I start walking up closer to the cage, making my way to his opponent's side. Devon will get a better view of me if I'm in his sights.

"On my left, we have a new member of our fight club! Lane Wilder aka *The Grim Reaper!*" the announcer pronounces each syllable as though he's actually terrified of the guy. Come on, grow a pair, man. *The Grim Reaper,* while it is a scary name, does not do this man in front of me justice. He's even taller than *The Hammer* by at least six inches, and seems to have at least twenty-five pounds on him. He looks like the devil himself, and although he is scary, the only person who should be afraid is Devon. He is about to receive an ass whooping. If the guy looks like this, why on earth do I need to distract his opponent? He doesn't look like he's going to need any help winning this fight.

I make eye contact with *The Hammer,* giving him a coy smile while lifting my dress up a couple of inches, showing him the skin I'm hiding from everyone else. His eyes open so wide, they look like they are popping out of his skull. A small smile plays at his lips, and he licks them in anticipation of what I will do next. While his attention is focused on me, I run my hand down my stomach to the inside of my thigh, tickling the sensitive skin there. I stick one of my fingers under the lace of my panties, and start to rub small, slow circles around my clit. Drool starts pouring out of *The Hammer's* mouth. I stick my finger inside of myself, right as the bell rings for the fight to start. *The Hammer* was so busy watching my little show, he didn't even realize it was time to fight. *The Grim Reaper* walks right up to him and punches him in the face, hard. So hard, that you heard the crunch of his nose being slammed into his skull. Blood gushes from *The Hammer's* face, looking like flowing lava. He falls back, slamming down into the ground, head first. No movement. No breathing.

Nothing. You could hear a pin drop in the fighting stadium.

The announcer walks over, and checks *The Hammer's* pulse with his fingers. After about a minute, he stands up and walks right up to *The Grim Reaper* and grabs his hand. He pulls it over his head in the show of victory. The crowd goes wild, but not because they are happy. Almost everyone here bet against *The Grim Reaper*, and him winning just lost all of them a shit ton of money.

"The winner is *The Grim Reaper!* With the fastest time for a fight to end," the announcer bellows to the crowd of screaming fans. People start throwing drinks at the cage, pissed off about not getting the win they all wanted. Lucifer nods his head at me, thanking me for helping the other guys win. That was damn easy.

"Good job, my dear. Meet me in the back room for your reward," he says in my mind, his voice caressing it with each word he speaks. You have to listen when he uses it, it's one of his secret influences.

"Of course, I'll be there in just a minute," I tell him, wanting to get away from the crowd as fast as I can anyways.

I push through the crowd, wanting to get away from everyone. The energy they are leaking is putting me in a sour mood. I want to be happy, not feel like my whole world just got ripped from me. I walk through slowly, not wanting to cause any attention my way. The last thing I need is some guy trying to come on to me. I'm not in the fucking mood. All of a sudden, I feel someone grab my ass. Not just a normal graze, it feels as though this person is trying to rip it off of my body. I spin around, to get a look at the pervert who just touched me. Before I have a chance to say anything, the culprit is laying in a pool of his own blood, *The Grim Reaper* standing above him with a smile on his face.

"Take that, you piece of fucking shit," he spits at the guy on the ground. His voice is raspy and sounds like a fucking wet dream. He grabs my hand, and starts pulling me towards the back room. "Let's get out of here, baby."

"Let's," I tell him as he swivels through the rest of the crowd. After about a minute of maneuvering, we make it to the smallest red curtain in the room. He pulls me right through, almost making my arm pop out of its socket. The room we enter looks like a medieval torture chamber. Chains hang from the ceiling, a guillotine is against the far wall, torture devices hang from the walls, and there is a stretcher in the middle of the room.

"What are we doing in here?" I ask him, curious as to why he would bring me to a place like this. This is not the back room.

"I'm giving you my payment. Thank you for your help in distracting the numb skull I was forced to fight. You made my job a hell of a lot easier," he tells me as he pulls off his shirt, showing me his glorious chiseled abdomen. The sweat on his body glistens, making him shine. He pulls me to him, and captures my lips in a heart stopping kiss. It's not sweet, it calls deep down to my soul making me need him.

I try to do my normal routine and drop to my knees, but he picks me right back up, not having it. He grabs the front of my dress, ripping it in half, leaving me exposed to his eyes. It falls off of my body, landing in the floor with a thud. I'm not wearing a bra, so my breasts are free, bouncing from the ripples of my dress being removed. Hunger gleams in his irises, eating up all that my body has to offer.

He picks me up, kissing me while his hands roam my body. I'm so distracted that I don't even realize what he's doing. Before I have time to get away, he has me strapped to the stretching table. My hands and feet bound. I look up at him, shock clear in my eyes. I have never had someone else dominate me before. I'm always the one in control, it's embedded in my nature. His face carries a smug grin, while his hands work the button of his jeans, popping them open. One of his hands runs down my body, leaving scratch marks, my signature move, while his other hand pulls down his zipper. He pulls his pants and boxers down in one slick motion, and tears my panties off. I'm so wet, my lady juices drip onto the table I'm currently laying on. Fuck, I never knew being dominated could get me so horny.

"Don't speak!" he commands me, and even though I try to say something, nothing comes out. Not even a squeak. What. The. Fuck? I nod my head in understanding, even though I understand absolutely nothing in this moment.

Lane walks over to the wall, and grabs a studded flogger. He swings it around, giving it a couple of test slaps against the air. He walks straight up to me and starts kissing my inner thigh, licking and biting at the same time. I feel my juices leaking down my leg, wanting to be tasted. He licks it up, and growls. Actually growls.

"You taste like ambrosia," he growls each word at me, still licking all of it up into his mouth. He takes his cock in his hand, and rubs it against my entrance. Teasing me. Finally he sticks the head in, only a little and I internally whimper, wanting more. Wanting all of him. I push my hips up, trying to get more. He uses the flogger and hits the inside of my thigh. FUCK. That fucking hurt.

"Bad kitten. I'm in control here," he says as he places a kiss on my forehead. Dickhead. He's a fucking dickhead. I hate him.

All of a sudden, I'm laying on my stomach, hands and feet still bound. How and the hell did that just happen? He's a warlock. He has to fucking be. He pushes my feet closer to my hands, so that I'm now on my knees. Using the flogger, he hits my ass. Hard. So hard, I can feel blood dripping down my back. Those spikes hurt like a bitch.

In one motion, his cock is inside of me. Pumping in and out of me at an inhuman speed. He uses the flogger while simultaneously fucking me. His free hand is playing with my clit, moving around it in fast circles. Building me up to my peak, and then stopping. He sets the flogger down, and starts spanking me instead.

"You feel so good kitten, I've wanted to fuck you since I saw you standing on my side of the ring," he explains breathlessly.

He grabs my ass with his nails, leaving red marks down the whole thing. He picks up speed, slamming into me so hard I'm surprised I'm still in one piece. He pulls out of me, and I feel a hot liquid stream down my back. Fucking shit, he just came. What the fuck about me, asshole?

He lays down, face staring up at me. The look on my face must be awful, because he starts laughing at me. He sticks his head up to me, and uses his tongue to circle my slit now, instead of his fingers. One of his hands is clawed into my hip bone, while the other pumps into me. His teeth graze my clit, and tremors rake my body. I can feel my energy flow from my body into his. Motherfucker. He's a fucking incubus. And he just stole some of my energy. He laughs because he realizes I just figured everything out, and his breath starts a series of aftershocks, causing my body to convulse again. Fuck.

"Fuck you Lucifer, an incubus. Are you fucking kidding me?!" I scream at him through our mental connection. I'm fucking livid. Even if he did just give me the best orgasm I've ever had. I just broke the law.

"You have to find me first, my little succubus. Happy hunting," he chuckles, knowing there's nothing I can do about this now.

My life is so fucked. Now, I'm a fugitive. What am I going to do?

Other books by Taylor Rose

Hanson Hell Series:

Queen of the Gods Book #1– RELEASE DAY May 1, 2016

The Ocean's Pull Book #2– TBD

More to come! This whole series is already planned out. At least 8 books in total.

Queen of the Gods Description:

When life gives you lemons, you're supposed to make lemonade… right? Arissa Steel always took everything life threw at her. Being abandoned by her mother. Having the same weird dream every night. The love of her life being just a "friend". Until one day, life threw her what she thought was a fantasy. The Greek Gods and Goddesses are real, and they are hanging around. She has a big part to play in their future. Who would have thought?

Hale Hanson has always been the star, outshining everyone around him. Never knowing who your real friends are is awful. Leave it to Arissa to break the mold, to tell him how it really is. She has never cared about his status or how he can help her move up the social ladder. All she cares about is him. They formed a bond so special, it was unbreakable. Or, so he hoped. Hale finds himself thrown into a life he never imagined possible. Will Ari still stick by his side? Or will she leave him alone to deal with her own problems?

What happens when life throws you something that is so out of this world that you can't tell fact from fantasy? Does love really conquer all? Or does everything crumble around them when the unthinkable happens?

Welcome to Hanson Hell! Once they suck you in, they don't let you go. Become a God or Goddess in your own right, and embrace your destiny!

Small Excerpt:

Hale

I follow Ari as she walks down the stairs and can't stop staring at her ass and the way it swings while she walks. I'm so distracted by her body that I almost miss the guys in the kitchen. Almost. I decide to go in and check to make sure everything is okay, but as I walk into the gigantic kitchen that my house holds, I hear a few male voices arguing. It's a good thing I decided to check on them, we don't need WW3 happening the first day Ari comes back. What on earth do my idiot cousins have to be fighting about right now? I walk closer so that I can catch the conversation they are having.

"What do you mean you're not cooking anything for dinner?" Zane gripes. Oh no, if any of them are hungry, that needs to change now. They all act like drama queens when they need to eat. Nineteen year old men who start whining about needing food is just sad, and trust me when I say, you don't want to be around them when they get that way. If they could eat me, they would start a bonfire and roast me on a stick. No joke, one time they actually tried. Fucking barbarians.

"I didn't realize I was your personal chef, Zane. You're a grown ass man, I shouldn't have to cook for you every single time your stomach grumbles," Denny replies sarcastically, while taking a kitchen knife from the counter. He starts twirling it through his fingers, and flicks it at Zane. The kitchen knife flies through the air making a whistling noise, because it's moving so fast. Zane ducks out of the way just in time, and the knife get stuck in the wall instead of somewhere inside Zane. I told you, fucking barbarians.

Before anything else happens, everyone else in the house comes rushing into the kitchen to see what all of the ruckus was about. Ari leads the way and walks straight up to Denny and smacks him upside the head. Ha! She just shoved him back in his place. But who am I kidding, she puts all of us in our places.

"What the hell is going on in here?" she screeches, her voice an octave higher than normal. She must have forgotten that everyone here acts like a child.

"Zane was hungry, and Denny didn't want to cook. Denny threw the knife at Zane, which you all heard, and then came running in here," I start explaining to her. She shakes her head as if she can't believe

Denver would throw a knife at someone. Ari, you know them better than that, sweetheart. Come on.

"Denny threw a knife at Zane?" she asks, her voice dripping venom. She's glaring at both of them, and if she was Medusa, they would both be solid stone right now.

"Hmm, how about we all go out to dinner instead?" I ask nonchalantly, hoping and praying everyone agrees.

I already ate, Hale, I don't want to go," she says turning to stare daggers at me. What did I do? I'm trying to fix this situation.

"We can go to your favorite place Ari, you can get that chocolate cake you love so much," I say, bribing her to come with us. I haven't seen her in almost a year, she can't leave yet.

Everyone else looks at each other, and I can see that they all want to go. Silently, they all turn to face her, and pout their lips. Eyes on the ground, giving her their best puppy dog pouts. She can pretend all she wants that it doesn't work on her, but we all know better. A minute into the pouting session she stomps her foot on the ground and growls at us.

"Fine, but I want two pieces," she states, making everyone hoot and holler. Yes. We got her.

Before she has a chance to change her mind, we all hop into our cars and step on the gas. Time to go eat.

Arissa

We walk into "Darcy's Bakery" and see that a new hostess has been hired. She didn't work here the last time I was home, and none of the guys seem to recognize her, either. She grabs our menus and seats us at a table in the center of the restaurant. We all take our seats, and open our menus, even though everyone already knows what they are going to get. We always get the same things when we come here, never changing our minds. You think after looking at the menu for ten minutes, you would come up with something else to try. Nope.

I look around the table to see each of their menus folded shut on the table. They must be starving, because they didn't even look at them for five minutes this time. Of course they are hungry, Denny threw a knife at Zane for god's sake. After a couple of minutes of waiting, our server comes over to grab our drink order. All of my boys order their drinks and dinner at the same time, not wanting to wait longer for their food than necessary.

Before our drinks have even arrived, I hear a screech and turn around to see what lunatic started yelling in the middle of a crowded restaurant. My eyes bug out of my head, when a tall brunette walks right up to me and pulls me up from my chair into a long hug.

"Felicia? What are you doing here?" I ask her while still being squeezed in her arms.

"I live in the next town over, I didn't think I would see you until our break is over," she exclaims with a huge smile on her face.

"I didn't think I would see you either, I had no idea you lived so close to me," I say, not wanting to be rude. She's really the only friend I have at APA, but I really wanted time with my boys.

"I was just stopping in to bring dinner home to my mom," she says, flipping her hair over her shoulder. It's then that she notices who I'm with, and her eyes bug out of her head at the same time her mouth drops open. Before I even have a chance to explain, she leans in close to me and whispers, "Who on earth are those hunks?" all while wiggling her eyebrows at me. This is exactly why I never mention them to my friends.

I turn around and most of the guys are staring at me, with blank looks on their faces. Except for Zane. He can't seem to keep his eyes off of Felicia. He keeps looking her up and down, taking in every single detail of her body. Who would have thought? Zane has never taken an interest in a women, so much so that I honestly wasn't even sure if he was attracted to them. Seeing him drink her in, makes me realize he just needed to find the right one.

I look back over to Felicia and notice that she can't stop staring at Zane. She even licks her bottom lip and tips her head down. As if she can sense me watching her, she turns to me and a blush sweeps over her whole body, making her look like a giant tomato. She shakes her head yes at something, even though no one said anything, and pulls up a chair right next to Zane himself. What the hell just happened?

"Felicia, these are my best friends from back home. This is Hale, Cameron, Tyler, Brock, Denver, and..." I say, but before I have time to introduce her to Zane, she speaks for herself and says "Zane," while looking deeply into his eyes. How and the hell did she know his name when they haven't even said a word to each other? Freaky.

It's at that moment that our food arrives at the table, and all the guys dive right in. Scarfing and munching as much food in their mouths that they can eat. Except Zane. He takes his time, eats his food slowly. Which is really fucking weird because he was the one bitching about being hungry in the first place. Do none of them realize how weird this is? No, just me? Okay, maybe I'm going crazy.

I take a bite of my cake, and all other thoughts leave my mind. God, it's so good! Gooey and rich. I take another bite and wonder why I argued about coming here in the first place.

FEEL FREE TO STALK ME ☺

Facebook Page:
https://www.facebook.com/taylorroseauthor/?ref=aymt_homepage_panel

Street Team:
https://www.facebook.com/groups/114297799238019 9/

Goodreads Page:
https://www.goodreads.com/author/show/15110353.Taylor_Rose

Amazon Author Page coming soon!

Thank you to each and every person who took the time to read this book and my short story! Readers are the most important thing to an author, we love all of you so much! Happy reading! <3

Love,

Taylor

This book is a work of fiction. The names, characters, places, and incidents are products of the writer's imagination or have been used fictitiously and are not to be conceived as real. Any resemblance to persons, living or dead, actual events, locales, or organizations is entirely coincidental. The story in this book is the property of the author, in all media both physical and digital.

Pepper's Play Pen

By

Mia Sparks

Leo

Everything was the same-old, same-old. Loud music and drunk people, the men looking for girls to fuck and the girls wiggling their asses at men to get their attention. After five years of basically living in this club, nothing really interested me. That was, until I spotted this dark-haired beauty a while ago. Unlike her friends she had the curves that men love. Men like me. I don't know how long I'd had my eye on her, but I was going to make my move. But why was I feeling... nervous?

Fuck! It wasn't as if I lacked female companionship. But this girl? There was something about her... she wasn't like the rest of those bitches. She was different, and tonight she was going to be mine.

As I watched, her friend suddenly started to scan the dance floor like she was looking for something. A few seconds later she raised her arm in my direction as if she was pointing at me. Then the object of my fantasies slowly stood up and turned my way. I had five seconds of the most intense eye contact with her before she sat down again.

I crooked my finger at one of the servers. "Hey, Lizzie, what are the guests at table 23 having?"

Lizzie looked at her notepad. "Hmm, martinis."

"Order one and a Sex on The Beach," I told her. She nodded and while she was waiting for the drinks, I grabbed two napkins and wrote my name on one and my number on the other.

"Give the martini to the blonde and this napkin to the dark-haired girl with the Sex."

Lizzie smirked and walked off with her delivery and I headed toward to DJ.

***

Rae

Things happen for reason, at least that's what I kept telling myself as I looked at Vicky. She and my other friend Teena, have known each other since preschool. I loved them like sisters, but sometimes I wished they would just leave me alone.

These two are the sexiest bitches on earth with very outgoing personalities. It was a wonder how we got along so well. Well, it's not that I didn't know how to have fun; I did have my own fantasies. I liked to party and with few drinks in me I could even pull off, somewhat, acting like a sexy bitch like they did. But normally, I was pretty shy, not an outgoing person at all. Was this one of the reasons God put us together as friends? Maybe He meant for us to be a partnership, for them to drag me out of my shell and help me to face my weakness? If so, it was taking a hell of a long time.

I snorted softly at my own inner joke and raised my martini to my lips for sip.

"So, are you going to try it?" Vicky's voice pulled me out of my daydreaming. Over the past couple of months, since I broke up with my last boyfriend Ron, these two girls have been trying so hard to get me laid. What was it Teena said? Oh, yeah, 'a *good fuck will help you with everything, it's like magic. Trust me, Rae, it's good for your soul.'*

But I didn't know if I wanted to try this shit again. What experience I did have was with a few of my exes. They'd never made me feel any of the stuff that my friends were always raving about. Sometimes, I wondered if they made up their stories based on their fantasies.

Vicky's lucky; she had a body to show off and it looked as if every man in here was desperate to have a chance with her. All she had to do was flip her long, wavy blonde hair and smile a little, while wiggling her slender hips. The pout she sent their way probably didn't hurt either.

I'd tried to emulate that look in my mirror at home, where no one could see me making a fool of myself. And, I didn't look sexy at all, like they did.

I looked at Teena out on the dance floor! Her shiny auburn hair was cut into a jaw length bob and gleamed under the hot, multi-colored, flashing strobe lights. Her short, slim body was perfectly proportioned and all the guys loved her bossy tendencies. Like now.

She'd just grabbed the guy she wanted by his collar and he was dancing with her. Later, he'd let her have her wicked way with him. In the end, he'd come out very happy and wanting more. Then, of course, Teena would tell him to fuck off.

I sighed and settled back against the cream leather couch. It was dark and secluded in this little corner of the club and just a tiny bit quieter too, so we didn't have to yell to hear each other speak.

"Hey..." Vicky leaned toward me and whined, "come...on!"

"I'm not like you, Vicky, I don't have the confidence to just... DO IT!" I flung my hand towards the dance floor; Teena caught the movement and waved. "Unlike you and Teena, I am just a big-assed boring girl with poopy brown eyes." I grumbled.

"Oh, stop it! You have the ass of men's wet dreams and your eyes are not a poopy color but a very sexy brown! When was the last time you got laid? Wait! Oh god, you aren't still hung up over that asshole, Ron, are you?"

"No!" I hissed, feeling my cheeks flush as I looked around us to make sure no one heard. The asshole boyfriend Vicky was talking about was totally out of my mind, ever since I caught him with some girl in his bed.

Vicky took a long sip of her drink through her straw. "Good. I'm glad to hear it. So you're horny and need to find a guy to fuck."

I gaped at her, shocked by her crass words even if they were true. She glanced at me without the least little bit of shame.

"No need to feel embarrassed. We all feel like that sometimes, but most of us get out there and do something about it." She stood and scanned the mass of gyrating bodies.

With a little shake of my head, I was about to lift my drink for a sip, when I got a prickly feeling on back of my neck.

"Ohhh... Houston we have a perfect target for you at five o'clock," Vicky said giddily. She lifted her hand and pointed surreptitiously to a place that was out of my line of sight. Standing, I stared out over those bobbing heads, following the line of her finger and suddenly my eyes landed on a stranger's face in the crowd. He was at the end of the bar and seemed to be hiding until his eyes latched onto mine.

He was too far away to make out much more than the fact that his hair was the color of antique brass and his dark eyes shone with an intensity I'd never felt before.

With a little gasp, I set my hand over my suddenly pounding heart and turned quickly back toward to our table. I focused on my drink like it was the most interesting thing in the world, desperately hoping Vicky didn't catch my reaction. She didn't need any more encouragement.

"Let's make this happen!" Vicky grabbed my arm and tried to pull me up. I jerked free of her grasp and lifted my martini to my lips, drinking it all in one gulp then shook my head madly from side to side. So much for hoping she didn't notice.

"Come on, Rae! Let's go dance in front of him and show him how sexy you are!" When I didn't move or reply to her, she continued. "Before he leaves? Or worse--someone else sees him and snatches him out from under your nose! I know you like the look of him. I can tell!" She stamped her foot at me and pouted seductively. I glared back at her and continued shaking my head.

"No, no, no, Vicky." I felt like stamping my foot right back at her. She put her hands on her hips and looked at me.

"Hey, bitches," Teena appeared and sung in a happy voice. "Are you guys going to come and par-tay!" She looked between us, still dancing to the music pumping out of the sound system and singing along. "Pop, pop. Pop that thing!" Her hips did a little circle then swiveled from side to side. She giggled and shimmied her head, then she frowned and tipped her head to the side.

"Hey, what's up?" she asked as her eyes switched between us. "What's going on?"

I shook my head at her. "Nothing."

"Nope, not one thing. Rae's just being her usual scaredy-cat self and refusing to dance for a guy."

I glared back at her but she just raised her brow and I couldn't deny her assumptions. "Oh, shut up."

Her smug look made me roll my eyes and sigh.

"Umm, excuse me?" A voice piped up behind us. "I have a drinks order here."

I peeked over Vicky's shoulder and saw a server with a small circular tray in her hand that had two drinks on it. One was obviously a martini, but the other came in a tall glass and comprised of a dark red liquid that blended into orange and had a slice of orange and cherry on the side. It looked delicious.

"Did you order these?" I asked Teena with a smile on my lips.

"Hell, no. I only do the receiving, not the other way around. Yeah, even for you, my best bitches," she said and cocked her hip to the side in sexy pose.

The server shook her head and replied. "Oh no, they're a gift."

Teena frowned at her and said. "But, there are only two drinks on that tray."

The server looked at her and shrugged. "Sorry, it was just those two that were ordered."

"Oh, but there are three of us!" Teena spun around, flapping her hands angrily at no one in particular.

I felt a frown pulling my eyes together. "A... gift? From whom? And really, should we take drinks from strangers?"

The server looked at me and placed a gentle hand on my wrist. "Oh, I understand your concerns but these came straight from the bar. And are from that gentleman over there." She pointed behind her at the end of the bar and my eyes met *his* again.

"It comes with this." She looked pointedly at a square red napkin. "Which I have to give to you and no one else." She shared a conspiratorially smile with me.

"Sex on the Beach for you." She passed the colored drink to me, along with the napkin. The glass had a smaller round drink mat beneath it, to soak up the condensation beading on the outside.

"And this martini is for you." She gave Vicky the martini then walked away. I flicked my gaze to the red napkin.

Why do I need this?

Did I have something on my face? Could he see it from way over there?

And he wanted me to wipe it off with this? Vicky noticed my confusion and sighed loudly before tapping my hand.

"Read it." She started jumping up and down as I played with the red paper self-consciously. "Come, on, what does it say? Read that damned thing. READ IT!"

"No, don't," Teena shouted and reached for it. "Fuck him, he didn't get me a drink. What kind of douchebag does that? He has to have known I was with you guys. Really! Look, we are like a sexy matching set. Like Charlie's Angels!"

Vicky slapped her hand away. "Geez, Teena! You were out on the dance floor and you just got back, the guy's not a mind reader." She spun on her heel and fixed her eyes on my hand. "Read it!"

Huffing in fake irritation, I said. "Okay, okay!" Then, I just gazed at it.

"RAE!"

I jumped at Vicky's sharp yell. "Fine!" Flicking the napkin open, I just stared down at what I found. A single word. "Leo?" Puzzled, I give the napkin to Vicky with a shrug. Vicky grinned delightedly as she read it and passed it to Teena. Who looked at it for a brief second, then blew her nose on it before throwing it on the floor.

"I still don't like the fucker who didn't get me a drink!" Teena sniped in annoyance and gave two middle fingers to the napkin that she'd just tossed.

And then, a deep voice rumbled behind us. "May this fucker at least borrow some of your friend's time?"

We all jumped with shrieks of fright at the same time and then my eyes landed on *him.* The guy that I'd seen, the one that looked at me. He smiled at me, then slid his eyes to Teena.

"And here is your drink, m'lady." He held a martini glass out to Teena and received a happy grin in return as she grabbed the stem. She sauntered away and sat down with a pleased smile.

"Would you like to dance?"

I jerked my gaze to the guy's face and pointed at myself. "M-me?" Oh, for Christ's sake, could I act any more stupid, right now?

He laughed lightly. "Yes, you."

I flicked my eyes to my friends, suddenly unsure but they just grinned back at me like crazy dumb butts.

Teena made a moue face. "He can dance with you Rae; he got me a drink."

"So what do you say, Rae?"

A shiver ran down my back at the sound of my name on his lips. He. Picked. Me! Over my two sexy girlfriends!

"Leo." He stuck out his hand and without thinking, I placed mine in his warm one, then almost jerked it back as a spark flew between our palms. It raced up my arm and spread outwards making my whole body tingle. I blushed, looking at Vicky for advice but she just broke into a huge grin.

"Go," she said softly before pushing at my shoulders. Teena nodded in agreement, sipping her martini like some Grand Dame from a historical tale. Then they both gave me a double thumbs up.

Turning to our drinks, I grabbed mine and downed the whole glass before slamming it back on its napkin with false bravado.

"Okay, why not," I said as excitement blossomed in my belly.

I let Leo lead me down the steps to the dance floor, then laughed nervously and moved away from him. Much as I wanted to be in his arms now, this wasn't the right music for that kind of dancing.

Not that I was the greatest at this. The girls had tried so hard over the years to show me sexy dances, but I'd never seen the appeal before, nor had the motivation. I snorted quietly, because the song blasting out of the sound system was called exactly that. I'd seen Kelly Rowland's videos a million times courtesy of my friends, and I'd never felt the inclination to emulate her moves before. But as I watched the man in front of me in open mouthed admiration as he got his groove on, I did. Oh, god, did I!

Closing my eyes, I visualized Ms. Rowland and tried my best to strut my stuff the way she did. My hips swayed, my hands swished, and when I opened my eyes I steeled myself to graze my fingertips over his crotch. He grinned fiendishly and grabbed my waist, turning me so that my back was to his front. Then he held me close to him as we finished the song.

My heart was pounding out of my chest but not just from exertion. I was exhilarated from his touch and the feel of his hard body against mine. I wanted more, much more. He leaned close to my ear and whispered.

"You're so sexy."

I giggled and spun around so I could talk to him face to face. "You're not so bad yourself. In fact, you're awesome," I shouted back, then standing on my tip toes, I pressed my mouth to his ear. "I've never wanted to dance like this before. But seeing you dance the way you do? I guess it made my inhibitions disappear." The admission made me blush. Even with the bravery from the alcohol I'd consumed, I could still feel heat on my cheeks and dropped my eyes, embarrassed to have said something so honest.

"Hey." He slid two fingers beneath my chin and tipped it back up, just as the music changed to a romantic love song. I gazed up at him through half-closed eyes, ready to snap them shut if he made fun of me. He didn't, but he did make me feel better.

"Don't ever feel embarrassed for telling the truth. I like it, I kinda have a thing about it actually."

"Huh, what kind of thing?" I wondered as his arms surrounded me and I rested my head on his shoulder.

"I hate lies, can't stand them." His mouth tightened as he spoke and I stroked my hand over his lips.

"I never lie," I whispered back. His smile made his eyes crinkle with pleasure and that tightness on his lips eased as he pressed them to my fingers. My heart was pounding so fast it nearly drowned out the sound of an Ed Sheeran song. I closed my eyes and let myself drift with the music as we swayed together. God, he smelled good. His hand moved to cup my face, and I lifted my head to stare into his eyes. Heat filled my face as he returned my gaze. His eyes were this dark blue, almost like gray flecked with gold, so mesmerizing and intense.

"God, you're so beautiful, I wanted to dance with you the second I saw you," he murmured in my ear.

"Is that why you sent the drinks, to woo me?" I giggled.

He paused for a second, then nodded, pulling me closer then jutted his chin towards the D.Js glass enclosure. "And now, I've got you in my arms."

"In your loving arms," I joked lightly, even though my heart was beating a mile a minute at the intense look on his face.

"I don't think I can let you go." His eyes darkened as his head came closer. My heart tripped. His lips were soft and gentle as they made contact with mine. Then, he slid his tongue along the seam of my mouth and I moaned. He groaned back and nipped at my lip. I gasped as his tongue slipped inside and tangled with mine. His hands slid to my ass and tightened.

God! My exes never made me feel this excited.

"I want you." His admission surprised me. Pushing back, I gazed at him, shocked by how ardent and hopeful his eyes looked. I wasn't imagining things, he really was interested with me.

I glanced up at the raised floor to where our table was, looking for my friends for eye advice, but they weren't there. I was on my own. Did I want to do this? Hell yes! But I didn't want to look too eager, so I said first thing popped into my mind to buy some time.

"Leo, I need to use the restroom..."

He smirked as he ran his gaze over my face. "Come, I'll walk you there."

The restrooms were at the back of the club, down a short hallway but when we arrived, there was a sign on the women's saying the attendant was busy cleaning inside. Damn! So much for buying some time. I threw up my hands in disgust and turned away, but Leo grabbed my wrist and pulled me towards the men's instead.

"Ah, I don't need to go that badly." I hissed.

His eyes landed on my face and suddenly his mouth was hovering over mine. "I know somewhere else you can use."

"Oh?" My heart thumped wildly, as he took my hand and pulled me away from the door. Instead of going toward the exit, Leo continued further along the hallway to a set of stairs. I gazed about worriedly. Did he know of another restroom upstairs? The girls and I had been coming here for a few weeks and I'd never heard anyone mention it.

"LEO!" I hissed his name, but he ignored me and moved faster. "Leo, I don't think we're allowed up here. Isn't this private property? We could get into trouble."

***

Leo

Rae pulled back on my hand, digging her heels in, which dragged me to a halt and I turned to look down at her. She was on the step below me and goddamn, I could see right down her cleavage. Her full breasts were pretty much on display from this angle and I wanted to cup them in my hands, to squeeze them together and rub my face in them. She tipped her head up and her eyes rolled over me. She looked impressed with what she saw and that made me smile.

"It's okay, I know the owner," I replied, then moved down two steps so that we were almost eyelevel and crushed her mouth to mine. She moaned loudly but I didn't care if anyone heard us. What were they going to do? Inform security? Not likely. Rae's tongue touched my bottom lip hesitantly but when I opened my mouth she slid it inside. I groaned at how good she tasted, as her tongue twined with mine.

She pulled back slowly and I wondered if I should let her go, because I had the feeling she wasn't used to behaving like this. She wasn't like other girls, who gave themselves to complete strangers. But even though we'd just met, it didn't feel like we were strangers.

Then Rae wrapped her arms around my neck and pressed her body closer to mine, making me forget all about letting her go. All my blood rushed south leaving me feeling light-headed, so I lay my head on her chest for a long couple of seconds.

"Leo?" Rae's voice held a hint of worry when I didn't immediately stand upright. "Are you alright?"

"Mmm," I gave in to temptation and buried my face in those luscious globes of flesh. She trembled and stood on her tip-toes to rub her sex against my hard-on. It felt so damned good, but it was nowhere near what I wanted. "Fuck, Rae. Come on, let's get upstairs."

I practically dragged her the rest of the way in my rush to get her into my office.

Pulling the key out, I unlocked the door and pushed it open and ushered her inside.

I sighed heavily when the door shut behind us.

"Leo, how did you get the key to this place?" Rae asked.

I debated telling her, but decided now wasn't the time for that explanation. I didn't want to scare her off, and it might if she knew who I really was.

"I told you, I know the owner," I replied evasively as I stroked her cheek. It was enough to distract her from asking more. "Bathroom's this way." I led her towards the door on the left-hand side of the room. The one on the right was a small bedroom. I spent a lot of nights in there.

Her eyes inspected the room as she followed me and her whistle of appreciation made me smile. "You like it?"

"It's gorgeous, so different from most offices. They're utilitarian. This? It's like..."

"A home away from home?" I suggested.

She looked at the dark red, deep cushioned couch set along one wall. The oak bookcase filled not just with folders for work but normal books as well, to the long oak and walnut desk facing the tall windows to my right. Dark burgundy drapes hung from each of window adding to the homey feel. But it was the handmade rug on the floor that really set the place off. Sunrise yellow, ochre and a pale blue made up the pattern, it was a soothing mix of colors and one of my favorite things in here.

Right now, the couch was the main attraction and I led Rae over to it, then stopped before we sat down. "Ah, bathroom?"

She blushed and ducked her head. "No, not really... well, not for the reason you're thinking!"

I smiled at her, knowing full well what she'd wanted to do in there. "You can go freshen up, if you want." I walked her over to the door that hid the bathroom.

"I'll mix us a drink if you like?" She looked at the door, then to the wet bar I'd walked to. "What would you like? Martini? Sex on the Beach? Me?"

Blushing, she darted into the bathroom while I fixed a dirty martini for both of us and waited for her to come back out. When she emerged, her hair was smoothed down over her shoulders, the deep brown so dark, it was almost black. Her almond shaped eyes, gazed up at me, as she joined me at the bar and accepted her drink.

"Cheers," I clinked my glass to hers and she took a tentative sip, then looked impressed.

"This is really good," she said taking a bigger gulp.

"Hey, easy, you don't have to be nervous. I'm not going to do anything you don't want me to."

She looked at me sideways and bit her lip. "No?" She walked away slowly and I followed, frowning in confusion, thinking she'd heard me wrong. "I mean, I won't hurt you." I added for conformation.

She nodded absently and when she reached my desk, she ran her hand along the edge. "I have a fantasy." She twisted her head and looked at me over her shoulder then licked her lips.

"What kind of fantasy?" I asked quickly.

"Ah, hmm, the usual?" She laughed self-consciously and sank her teeth into her bottom lip; it trembled with nerves.

"Tell me," I urged. She looked at me for a moment, then turned to lean against the edge of the desk.

"Well, I'd be your P.A or... something." She launched into the details of an infatuation with her imaginary boss. I listened attentively, smiling as the scenario got hotter and moved closer when she reached the part where he stripped her.

"Do you want me to undress you and take you over this desk?"

Her lips parted as she nodded her head silently.

Smirking, I added, "If we were a proper working couple, you'd say, Yes, sir."

Eyes wide, she gulped and whispered. "Yes. Sir."

God, that did something to me. Taking both our drinks, I placed them on the floor and reached for her dress. My hands slid over her shoulders to the zipper at her back. I eased it down, keeping my eyes on her intently. She shivered, pulling her hands free as I pushed it to her waist. Sliding my hands around her hips, I drew her closer so she was standing again and the dress fell to her feet.

"Rae." Her name left my lips on a whisper of breath. She was wearing simple white lace lingerie, nothing overtly sexual but against her golden skin it took my breath away. "You're gorgeous. I fucking want you." My hand caressed her breast making her nipple peak and she arched her back.

"That feels good," she moaned.

My lips glided up her neck to her ear. "It'll feel better naked."

Tracing the contours of her spine with my fingers, I reached her bra and unfastened it, and her full breasts spilled free. "Holy fuck, Rae. They're perfect." I muttered in amazement.

She blushed again as my hands slipped to her waist and tugged her lace panties to the floor. She stepped out of them and the dress, leaving her in nothing but hold-up stockings and heels. My cock strained to get free from my pants and she shuddered from the hungry look I raked over her.

***

Rae

Breathing heavily, Leo cupped my face and spoke hoarsely. "On the desk or over it?"

I shivered from the gravelly tone of his voice. "You decide, Sir." I whispered, playing the game.

His eyes darkened as he muttered thickly. "Bend over. Now!"

Moving quickly, I did as I was told. Leo brushed his fingers over my pussy.

"You're wet, Rae." I couldn't see him but I could hear the smile in his voice. "That turns me on, knowing you're ready for me."

He pressed against my back, the buttons of his shirt hard on my skin as his hands move upwards. They drummed on my stomach, sending sparks of electricity to my extremities. Breathing deeply, I sucked air back into my lungs. His hands skimmed over my breasts as he pulled me upright. His touch was electrifying, making my nipples so hard they ached.

"Ooh." The softest of moans escaped my lips as his mouth opened over my shoulder and he licked the sensitive skin there. He nipped at my ear as his hand circled around my neck and jaw. I gasped as heat rushed to my belly. Fuck the fantasies! This was much more exciting! Twisting in his arms, I met him face to face and he crashed his lips over mine. I clung to him as his tongue twined with mine and he groaned into my mouth.

His hand swept to my ass and he hissed when I nipped his bottom lip. I lifted my eyes to his as he stroked his hands back up to my shoulders. I trailed my fingers down his white shirt, unbuttoning it as I went, then pressed my palms to his hot skin. His muscles rippled beneath my fingertips as I grazed them over his washboard abs then tugged at his belt.

I kissed my way down his chest and belly until I reached his navel. His happy trail led my mouth from there, to the waistband of his pants, which sat just above his lean hips. Running my tongue over my lips, I looked up at him and saw his gray eyes darken, turning nearly black as the pupils dilated.

Heart thumping with excitement, I ripped the belt free, opening the button and zipper. My eyes focused on his groin as I tugged the pants and boxers down to his knees.

His thick cock was hard and sprung upward the second it was released from his underwear. Dropping to my haunches on the floor, I squeezed the base of his shaft as I covered it gently with my mouth. He groaned loudly, encouraging me as I moved to the head of his cock.

Sucking the entire swollen head into my mouth caused him to jerk and thrust between my lips. His thighs shook as my free hand slid down my belly and circled over my engorged clit. Leo watched avidly as I began rubbing it to ease some of the tension building in my core.

"Shit, Rae, do you have any idea what you're doing to me right now?" His cock slipped free from my mouth as he straightened up.

I shook my head, no, but smiled at the obvious fib. Tangling his fingers in my hair, he guided my head back to his cock and with one thrust, he was deep inside. He hit the back of my throat, making me gag until I swallowed, taking it all. My hands curved around the backs of his thighs, pulling him towards my mouth as I opened my jaws wider.

"Fu-uck!" His gasp of pleasure sent reciprocal waves washing over me. I grabbed his balls with my other hand and squeezed them, maybe a bit too hard, because he hissed and pulled them free from my clenched fingers.

"I need those," he mock growled, pulling me up and placing my ass on the desk as his mouth crushed my lips beneath his. Drawing back, he bent down to fish his wallet out of his pants and removed a condom. I watched him roll it over his huge cock and my core clenched with need.

He moved closer, the tip of his hard shaft brushing my wet entrance. His hands sinking into my ass as he pulled me to the edge of the desk and thrust inside.

"God!" My eyes fluttered closed on how indescribably good he made me feel. "Leo, fuck me," I demanded, clenching his hard length within me. He did it hard and fast, so hard I was ready to come almost instantly. When he pulled out I whimpered in protest but he just smirked devilishly and turned me around before placing me belly first against the desk, spreading my legs. His cock slid between my ass cheeks and into my hot, aching core. He plunged in and out. Harder. Faster. Deeper. Pounding my ass cheek with his hips. Until he sent me over the moon.

"Jesus, fucking Christ," he hollered as he emptied himself, then breathing heavily he collapsed on top of me.

Leo gently pushed off me and helped me to stand up. My legs were a bit wobbly. I'd never, ever had such hot sex. I slumped into his arms and mumbled something to that effect. He chuckled and started to lean down to kiss me when a loud knock startled us. I yelped and crossed my arms over my chest and groin.

"Hold on!" Leo shouted out. He picked up my lingerie and gave them to me, before pulling up his pants and boxers to cover his condom encased cock. Then he helped me into my dress. He zipped me up and paused with his hands on my shoulders. He leaned over and kissed my neck as his right hand slipped between my boobs.

The knock came again.

"JUST FUCKING WAIT THERE!" He roared furiously.

I spun to face him. "We better go," I whispered. "I told you we'd get into trouble."

"We won't, don't worry. I'll take care of it." He kissed me softly. "But yeah, you better go," he added reluctantly. I pouted a tiny bit, then hurried to open the door and found a huge, burly guy standing there. I squeaked with fright as his eyes landed on me. I waved and ran out, hoping Leo could really take care of himself.

Hurrying down the stairs, I put my hand on my chest to calm down my pounding heart and felt something between my cleavage. I fished it out and saw it was another napkin. When I unfolded it to look at it, I saw his number. Ha! He put his phone number in my boobs while he was helping me get dressed! That had to be mean something!

This was so exciting, so much more fun than I'd ever imagined.

When I got back to the table the girls pounced on me. "What? What are you doing here?" Vicky shrieked, staring at me.

"Yeah, one minute you're dancing with Mr. Hotness and then you vanished, so we thought you took our advice and left with him for the night." Teena complained and shook her head. "What happened, where is he anyway?"

I gazed at both of them and felt my cheeks heating. "Nothing, he... ah, had to talk to someone and I didn't want to interrupt."

They both looked at me with suspicious eyes. "Are you fucking serious? He left you like that? That's just fucked up." Teena sneered in disgust.

I tried to keep my face as straight as possible and squeezed the napkin in my hand. Everything would be fine. I knew I would see Leo again, because after all...

I had his number.

Follow me –

Goodreads –

https://www.goodreads.com/author/show/14739481.Mia_Sparks?from_search=true&search_version=service

Facebook –

https://www.facebook.com/profile.php?id=100010951561538&fref=ts

This book is a work of fiction. People, places, events, and situations are the product of the author's imagination. Any resemblances to actual persons, living or dead, or historical events, is purely coincidental.

Welcome To The Dark Side

By

Erin Trejo

Stepping off the train at three in the morning should be eerie but not for me. The sound of the train screeching away as I stand on the platform, only seems to arouse something inside of me.

I've always been a loner and the odd girl out. I didn't care though. I liked to be feared. I liked being the freak that no one took a chance to talk to. It made me feel inferior to others.

I glance around the platform looking for that shadow that always seems to be here when I am, but I don't see it tonight. Strange how you grow accustomed to something that you never saw in the light. I know it's a man, a well-built man just by the way his shadow dances across the concrete.

Walking toward the stairs, I wonder where he is. I don't care to know who he is, that just doesn't come into play with the things that are running rampant in my mind right now. Thoughts of my hands wandering over every inch of his solid body has me licking my lips. I've never been the type to take no for an answer, and I won't take it from him either the next time I see him.

Something about the darkness that seems to radiate from him sets my nerves on fire. I want to take him like no other woman has before. My lips around his cock as he fists my hair in his strong grip.

"Christ Natalie! Get yourself together." Walking down the stairs and toward the road, the people of the city come into view. Why that platform is always so desolate is beyond me. It's been that way for the past year though. Since my accident nothing seems the same.

I was walking home from work one night when a man lashed out at me. I never saw him coming. Thinking I was going to die, I tried to remain calm but the blade cut deeply. I remember trying to scream, but words never formed on my lips. I laid there in a pool of my own blood for a long time. Visions of my boyfriend Josh swarmed my mind. I loved him with all I had in me. I remember asking to die. Asking someone, anyone to take the pain away.

When I woke up, the world seemed different. People I once knew were gone, all my friends vanished. This new world is cold but I love it.

"Cindy! Why are you out tonight?" Spotting that little blonde bimbo walking toward me I figure I need to speak.

"Tony sent me out for the night. How was work honey?" I hate when she calls me honey. Honey is for the sweet girls, I'm far from that.

"Tony is an asshole. Work is what it is. How long are you out here for?" Making my way past her, I hope she speaks quickly.

"At least another few hours." Thank God for that little miracle. That girl is one whinny little thing.

Stepping up to the door to the makeshift apartment I share with my friend Denise, a calmness engulfs me.

A smile tugs across my face. I know that feeling. That feeling means that Dean is here.

Dean is my on and off boyfriend. It's been hard for me to settle on just one guy. There are so many to choose from.

Walking up the stairs the aroma of Chinese food hits me. Denise is a magnificent chef! She works at a local restaurant making all sorts of things. I always know when she's home since the house smells divine.

"Denise, it smells amazing in here." Stopping dead in my tracks at the sight before me, I suck in a breath.

Denise's head snaps up just as Dean's cock slips free from her lips. Her head tilts slightly as she glances over at me.

"I didn't know you'd be home so early." From this position Denise looks so different. Her eyes; the sparkle that's in them, is nothing I've ever seen on her before. It entrances me.

"Nat, are you OK baby?" Dean's voice pulls my attention in his direction. The smile on his lips should infuriate me but it doesn't. Something dark and sexual tugs at my insides.

"Was I not invited to the party?" Dropping my purse to the floor, I slip out of my heels as I make my way over toward the two of them. Dean has always dreamt of this. A threesome with the two of us, but the look on Denise's face tells me she never expected it. I can't say that I blame her, I never thought I would want it with her. Granted I have thought about it with Dean, Denise just never seemed the type.

"Kiss me." Climbing onto the bed, Dean smiles as he speaks. Leaning in, I do as I'm told and kiss him fiercely. His lips are so soft against mine.

Feeling hands on my back, I jerk slightly before relaxing into Denise's touch. For being the freak, I never thought I would like another girl having her hands on me but Denise is proving me wrong.

Her hands gently glide over the small of my back while Dean smothers my lips with his. I never knew having two people touching me at once could be so erotic.

"I want to be inside of you. Fucking you hard but Denise wanted to play too." When Dean pulls back I want to lose my mind but the words he's saying has my pussy throbbing with need.

When I feel Denise shoving my skirt up my thighs, Dean's lips move to my neck. How can I even think when I feel like I'm floating?

"Get up here. On my face. Now." Dean growls as I rip my shirt over my head. *Who knew I could move so quickly?* Yanking my panties down as I go, I straddle his face. The moans and groans that escape him are feral. I can tell he wants this as much as I do.

"I'm going to eat every last piece of you. You can suck my cock while I work her over." Glancing over at Denise, she licks her lips. Damn the heat in this room has kicked up a notch.

Dean's hands yank my pussy into his mouth. His tongue strokes between my wetness, sending pleasure through me. I love the feelings Dean sets off inside of me.

Riding his face, his hands land on my hips pulling me in closer to him. Denise is straddled in front of me and her pussy is dripping wet.

As much as I'd like to enjoy the ride I'm taking, I can't stop thinking about touching her. Reaching forward, I slide my fingers under her ass and toward the front. Denise's body lifts slightly giving me access to that little clit of hers. Damn, just feeling how wet she is turns me on even more.

"Goddamn!" I can't stop the words that fall from my lips. I never felt another woman so wet for what I'm about to give her. This is new and I want it so much more of it.

Sliding my fingers inside of her, she clenches around them. I suck in a breath at this new feeling. It's amazing that a woman's body can feel this way. Of course I've played with myself multiple times but this, this is something off the charts.

"Fuck her Nat. Do it." Dean's tongue leaves me bare and wanting more. I don't need to tell him either, he knows. His mouth slams into me as Denise arches her back. With her ass up and pussy staring me in the face, I slide my fingers in and out of her. I don't miss the whines or groans that she tries to hide from me either. She is fucking enjoying this as much as I am.

Reaching up with my other hand, I find her clit. Who better to know what a woman wants than another woman? At least that's the way I'm seeing it right now. Her body astounds me as if the female body was new to me.

I can feel myself closer to climax as Dean increases his suction. The man is a god with his mouth. The harder he sucks, the faster I slide my fingers in and out of Denise. The way her body is locking down around me, she's as close as I am.

"Shit! Denise!" Screaming her name as I finger her harder, I explode. I lose all control as my body shakes. Dean's hands grip me roughly and I know he's done but when I feel the juices flowing over my fingers, I want to cum again.

Denise swallows as her body jerks around me. The three of us cumming in unison is beyond my wildest dreams.

Moving to lay next to Dean, Denise does the same.

"Are you happy, Pet?" Dean rubs his hand up and down my arm as I sigh. I don't know if happy could describe what I feel in this moment.

"Ecstatic would be more like it. I haven't felt so alive in a long time." Dean chuckles slightly before I hear Denise giggling too. They must not have expected that from me.

"Oh, Pet. You have pleased me tonight. I never saw that coming out in you. Did you like to feel Denise?" Never being the shy type before, I won't start now.

"I did like feeling her. It makes me feel so unrestrained and powerful." Growls rip from his throat before he turns his head to capture my lips. Soft, sweet pecks adorn me before he pulls back looking me in the eyes.

"You are ready now. I can't wait to see how this plays out for you. You have been amazing to me, Pet." Confusion is all that occurs to me. What does he mean by that? Is he leaving me? What am I ready for?

Before I can speak, Denise props herself up next to him with a smile plastered across her face. It melts me inside to know that I made her feel the way she does.

"You are amazing Nat. I have wanted you for so long. I couldn't stand it any longer." Watching her lick her lips, I want to taste her. I want to make her cum all over again.

"In time you will have her again." Jerking my gaze back to Dean, he smiles. I don't understand any of what he's saying. Sitting up, I look down at him.

"What do you mean? Are you leaving me?" His chuckle changes slightly. It grows deeper, darker.

"You were never mine to keep. Perhaps one day we will find ourselves meeting again. Tomorrow you will meet the King." Shaking my head, I don't know what the hell he's talking about. None of this makes sense. I wonder if he's on drugs?

"Dean I don't get it. Who the hell is the King?" Dean sits up next to me before gripping my face in his hands. The look in his eyes is so soft and full of concern.

"You will understand tomorrow. Don't worry over this tonight. Tonight was for us to enjoy each other. Let's not ruin that." He presses his lips to mine and all sanity is gone. It drifts from my body like a breath.

Pulling me down with him, I close my eyes and drift away.

Sleeping has never come easily to me. It was always an assemblage of darkness and fire. I don't mind either, so sleep should be easy for me but it isn't. There always feels like there is something else out in that darkness. Something that is silently calling to me. It wants me to come to it but I have no idea how.

Waking up alone surprised me. I never thought Dean or Denise would be gone before me.

Stretching I stand and head toward the bathroom before climbing into the shower. As much as I'd like to keep last night with me forever, I know it's time to face the day ahead.

I quickly change and head out the door ready for the day today. I work as a secretary for a sleazy lawyer. He doesn't pay worth a shit and he is the biggest slime ball you'd ever meet but it is a job. After the accident, no one wanted to hire me so I took what I could get.

The air is humid today as I walk toward the train. I don't own a car and never really cared to either. The train suits me just fine.

Walking up the stairs, I notice the little old man that always sits on the bench at the top of the steps. Every morning he smiles up at me and says that the day is getting closer. He must be senile.

"Ah lovely. Today is the day. Can you feel it?" Just like every other day I smile politely at him before I respond.

"I sure can. The air is awfully heavy today." Smiling as if I have a damn clue what he's talking about, he nods as I walk past. Some people just overlook the elderly. They hold a past in them that intrigues me, but this guy, he's a complete nut job.

The train ride to work isn't any different than any other day. It's dark in the 6th car which is the way I like it. Maybe I'm a vampire. That would explain my lack of enjoyment of being in the sunlight. I giggle to myself slightly before I get to work for the day.

"Mr. Adams office, how can I help you?" Roaring noises shoot through the receiver. Here we go with the strange prank calls. I've been getting them a lot lately. Mr. Asshat must have pissed someone off.

I hang the phone up as Mr. Adams walks over to my desk. With his wrinkled shirt and toupee, you would look at him and think he was the homeless one. He looks nothing like a lawyer.

"Natalie. Are you getting those strange calls again?" With a smile on his face, I nod.

"Yeah. First one of the day. I think you should be more careful of who you make mad." Setting my gaze on his, he laughs.

"I don't think that was my doing. Could you be a doll and get me some coffee?" Turning around he walks away. Rolling my eyes, I stand and make my way to the break room. Well, if that's what you want to call it. It looks like an old bathroom if you ask me.

Pouring his coffee, a strange feeling overtakes me. Shivers roll through my body as the hairs on the back of my neck stand. It's not a horrendous feeling. It's calming, soothing.

Shaking it off, I walk down to Mr. Adams office setting his coffee on the desk in front of him.

"It's getting dark out Nat. I hear we are going to get some bad storms coming in. Why don't you take the rest of the day off?" Glaring at him, I don't know what's wrong with him. He never gives me a day off.

"I'm fine with working through it, Mr. Adams." He places his hands on his desk as he stands and smiles, shaking his head.

"No. I must insist that you take off. I don't want you caught out in those storms. I'm closing up early today anyway." Shrugging my shoulders, I don't want to argue with the boss.

"I'll see you tomorrow then." With a quick nod, I turn and head back out front.

Pulling my cell phone out of my purse, I dial Dean but get no answer. Trying Denise, it's the same.

"Thanks a lot, guys. Leave me alone the whole damn day," mumbling to myself as I head out the front door in the direction of the train. I've never had to catch one this early, so I'm not sure of the times.

Making my way up the stairs, it is suddenly quiet. Eerily quiet.

Looking around, there is no one else on the platform but him. My eyes instantly find him in the shadows.

My heels click on the pavement as I make my way towards him. With every intention to take him as I have planned out in my mind, I lick my lips.

"Early day?" His deep, raspy voice floods me with heat.

"I heard there were some bad storms coming." Stopping a few feet in front of him, I still can't make out his face. He's hidden by the shadows.

"That's what I heard as well. How was your night Natalie?" My heart kicks up a beat when he says my name. It isn't from fear either, although I don't know how he knows my name, it's sexy coming from his lips.

"It was unreal." Chuckling the man steps forward. I can see him. All of him. He's gorgeous. His tanned skin begs to be kissed. His dark eyes pull at something inside of me.

"Unreal is one way to describe it I suppose." Shaking my head slightly, does he know? Does he know what I did with Dean and Denise?

"Do you ever wonder why you never fit in? Why you never found the old friends you had?" Something comes over me, and I want to tell him everything. I don't understand this feeling, but I want to give him every part of me.

"I thought they left. They moved on after my accident." His eyes sparkle as he moves closer to me. My breathing has quickened and my body is on fire. I want this man. I feel like I've known him forever.

"Do you want to kiss me Natalie?" Nodding my head, I don't think words will form. He takes a step closer to me before his arms wrap around me. Something so familiar flows through me. It's almost like I felt when Josh would hold me.

Looking up into his eyes, he parts his lips slightly as I lean in, brushing mine over his. Heat floods me as I deepen the kiss. His arms tighten around me until I feel like I can't breathe.

My hands roam over his chest before I get to what I really want. His groans are swallowed up as I take them with my mouth. He tastes so good.

Sliding his pants down his legs, I back him against the wall behind him. He doesn't fight me, which I'm thankful for. He actually wants me; I can feel it.

"You watch me." It's a statement not a question. I know he watches me.

Gripping his cock in my hand, I slide it up and down.

"I've always watched you." He feels amazing in my hand but I want more. I want him to tell me why he watches me, what he wants, but this overwhelming need for him takes precedent.

"Why?" His eyes lock with mine as my body comes to life. Fire ignites in my veins.

"You are meant to be mine, Natalie. I wanted to make sure you could handle your role." Dropping down in front of him, I take him into my mouth. His hand grips my hair as I suck. Bobbing my head, he forces himself into me further. After a few strokes, he pulls back.

"Stand up." Quickly doing so, I can see the approval in his gaze. He likes it when I follow directions.

"I am going to fuck you hard and fast. The first time will be quick but after that, I will make you cum a million times, painfully slow." His words breathe new life into me. I want him to fuck me. I want him to make me cum.

Grabbing my hips, he lifts me before spinning around and pinning me to the wall. His cock is mere inches from where I want him, no, where I need him.

"I will give you what you want, but you must understand that you belong to me." The way he speaks sends my body into an inferno. The heat sizzles through me.

"I belong to you." The words leave my mouth just as he plunges inside of me. The pleasure and pain hits me quickly. I never felt anything like this before.

He fills me so completely. He feels like my other half.

Thrust after thrust he slams into me with such force. The feelings that soar through me are unexplainable.

"Are you ready?" Breathlessly, I nod my head as the orgasm threatens to consume me.

One last rough thrust and my body explodes. My eyes roll back as his seed hits me deeply.

As I try to come down from the high, my vision blurs. Visions of me lying on the ground in a pool of my own blood surface. I can see it as clear as day.

A man leans down near me with a slight smile on his face.

"I love you Natalie. I would have waited for eternity for you. I will make them pay for what they did to you, but I can't be angry that I will have you sooner than we thought. Rest now, Pet." The man. It's him. It's Josh. How can that be? Josh wasn't there when that happened to me.

"It's OK Natalie." Shaking my head, the visions clear and reality is back. The man is still holding me, but no longer inside of me.

"Who are you?" His smile brightens as he sets me on my feet.

"I am your knight. I am all that you have ever wanted. All you need. I have waited so long to make you my queen. Even when you were alive, I waited. I knew it was you. I always knew." His smile stays in place as I look at him. I know him. I can feel it.

"You were Josh. You were the one I loved. The one I wanted. How can that be?" He drops his head before looking back up at me.

"Do you remember when you were lying there dying? You said, "Please take me. Take the pain away." I did just that. I took the pain away." Still confused, I stare at him. Something about him tugs at me. It wants me, and I want it.

"I remember but." Shaking my head once again his hand comes to rest on my cheek.

"I am him. I am Josh. I am Dean. I am yours. Don't you understand that you didn't fit in for a reason. You were meant to be mine. Do you remember the saying that you heard once about the devil?" His grin is something I want to hold onto forever. It's beautiful.

"The devil always takes what is rightfully his." The words tumble out before I can register them. That's who he is. That's who I am. I belong to him. Just like I always knew, I didn't fit or belong anywhere else.

The realization hits me as a grin spreads across my face.

"Welcome to the dark side, my Queen."

Follow me –

Goodreads –

https://www.goodreads.com/book/show/26569468-reckless?from_new_nav=true&ac=1&from_search=true

Facebook –

https://www.facebook.com/indieauthorerintrejo/?fref=ts

This book is a work of fiction. People, places, events, and situations are the product of the author's imagination. Any resemblances to actual persons, living or dead, or historical events, is purely coincidental.

Dangerous Desire

Samantha Harrington

Chapter one

What can I say about lust? It's the epitome of desire, when you can't keep your hands off each other, no holds barred, pure attraction…. That's what I felt the first time I saw him.

That moment when your eyes meet for the first time. The smile that graces your face when you see that the affection is returned. The butterflies, the faster beating heart, the quicker breathing. All of those things I felt the first time I saw him. Jason…

The atmosphere of the bar was busy, but not the kind of busy where you can't move between your chair and the bar, but enough to give you the buzz of conversation as it filters through the air.

I take note as he moves effortlessly behind the bar, serving the patrons as they request drinks. Watching his hands as they hold the glass, tilting it at the perfect angle to pour the beer. It's tantalizing to watch, makes me wonder what else his can hands can do.

I try to distract myself, immersing myself in conversation with my friends, but my eyes keep meeting his. That colour send shivers down my spine: grey with a mix of light brown, a contrast I get lost in. His hair is a mousy colour, long enough to grip hold of, and to weave your fingers through as you kiss. His tall six-foot-two-inch frame towers above me, his lean body hidden by the black shirt that clings to his arms, hiding the sexy I was sure was underneath. The hair is a lighter shade on his full beard—not the harsh type that would scratch your skin as it caressed its way down your body. No, this is the sort that would heighten the pleasure, with each pass.

I wander over to the bar with my best friend. The other barman seems chatty enough as he takes mine and Alane's order: Smirnoff Ice for me and Budweiser for her. Josh, the other bar man, chats to us for a little while he cleans up the bar as the last of the crowd starts finishing drinks and saying goodnight. He seems nice and funny, keeping us giggling as we drink.

The night passes slowly and the tension mounts between us. I wander outside to have a cigarette and see him leaning against the wall, no doubt having a break. We have met a couple of times this evening while I've been smoking, exchanging polite pleasantries about everyday crap. But I'm itching to get my hands on him, to glide them down his chest, to see what lies beneath.

I wander around the bar, finding what could only be classified as a quiet little corner, a few tables and chairs and a couch make up the little room. It's not open and I feel odd about snooping around, but my curious nature gets the better of me.

I see him stacking chairs against the other wall of the little room, his body lifting the stacks of chairs as he proceeds to tidy them away. There is no one in here but me and him. It's then that the energy in the room heats up rapidly.

He smiles at me again and it's that sort of smile you know you can't walk away from. I step a little closer to him, looking up into his mesmerising eyes, my fingers itching to move closer to him. So I take the leap, my hand gripping his black tie, pulling him closer to me. His hands grip the side of my face, bringing his head down to mine as we kiss for the first time.

I open immediately for him when I fee, his tongue against my lips, teasing and tasting all at the same time. My hands drop from his tie and I weave them into his hair, pushing myself closer to him. We kiss for what seems like an age, but in reality it's only minutes.

Pulling me towards the wall and pressing me against it, his hands finding my waist, his lips devour my mouth again; it's addictive. His taste, his touch, I want more. No, I need more.

"Come home with me?" his accent ripples across my skin, heating the fire further.

"Yes." I whisper. Because right in this moment it's what I want, what I need. He kisses me one last time before he heads back to the bar, probably getting ready to close for the night.

I head back a couple of minutes behind him, my fingers lingering against my lips, tracing the seams where his lips had been against mine.

I spy Alane at the bar talking to Josh. The room is now empty except for us, and the guys are closing everything down.

"Hey Natalie, where did you go?" Alana asks me, slurring her words a little as she tries to compose herself against the bar.

"Went to the little girl's room, after I had a smoke," I tell her hoping, she can't see the blush that's creeping up my neck. I glance across to the bar and see the little smirk on Jason's face.

"Here! I got us another drink, before the called for last orders, so drink up and we can grab a cab home together," she tells me. Shit. How can I get out of this as I have no doubt I'm going home with Jason?

"I'm not heading that way, Alana." I try to communicate with my vague answer, telling her really what's happening. I see by the nod that she gets it and has my back.

I step closer to her and take my drink off the bar, pretty much downing it in one gulp, wanting to get out of here as quick as I can.

I head outside with Alane and make sure she gets in the taxi ok, not wanting anything to happen to her because I want to get laid. That would make me the worst best friend and Alane is my best friend. She has been in my life only a short time but it feels longer, like a missing piece had been found, and I couldn't imagine my life without her in it.

It would feel like a colourless rainbow.

"You going to be okay, Nat?" She asks me, concern evident in her voice.

"I'm going to be just fine Alane; I will text you as soon as I get home." I say to her. She is only looking out for me as she knows this isn't me, it's not something I do; meet a guy in a bar and go back to his place so that I can get fucked.

I don't know what it is with Jason, he just feels different, like I can trust him not to hurt me. Well, only in the way that I want him to since its been so long. I have a feeling that I won't remember what to do, but based on the way he kisses, I have no doubt that he will guide me and bring me back to the land of the living.

I watch as the cab departs and I turn to see him standing out front waiting for me.

"You ready?" he says to me.

Hell yes, I am. The only way to answer is to show him, so I lean up and give him another kiss. As he pulls away he just nods as he leads the way.

Chapter Two

I don't really pay much attention to his place as he leads me towards the bedroom. The double bed is pretty much all I see. As soon as the door closes behind me we come together, tongues colliding. His hands are on my face again as he leads me towards the side of the bed, never breaking the kiss for the slightest second. His beard feels heavenly against my face as he owns my mouth and I try to nip at his bottom lip, loving the feel of him, not ready for him to pull away. His hands drop to my top, lifting it above my head. My hands go to his belt buckle, undoing it so I can finally see what he's hiding. His shirt is next, leaving me breathless at the sight of him, slim and lean. But you can still see the power he wields, the tattoo on his chest a single piece that stands out and fits him perfectly.

After pulling clothes off I finally get to see him, in all his glory, and I'm not disappointed. Fuck me! I love what I see, and I can't wait to taste it. I wrap my hand around his cock, gently teasing at first, not wanting to rush, wanting to savour the moment. This one crazy moment.

The kissing and teasing continues until I fall back onto the bed. Pristine white sheets surround me as he leans over my body, my legs instantly falling further apart. The anticipation of feeling him inside me is a heady mix of lust and passion, one I'm soaking up every ounce of. I look down and see him guiding his cock towards me. I'm wet and ready for everything he has to give me and my nipples tighten with anticipation. His hand is wrapped around his cock, the head teasing me; he pushes inside and I'm done.

His thrusts are fucking torture, each one hits the spot, making me climb higher, but not enough to push me over the edge. I can't seem to get enough of the way he kisses me; it's like being branded, owned, cherished, but most of all, fucking wanted. My legs go on to his shoulders, making the pressure more intense. I feel the head of his cock, buried to the hilt, as his thrusts become harder and deeper. I climb, wanting to fall off the cliff, craving that release.

Our position changes, with him rolling me on top. His mouth claims mine again, his tongue taking what it wants and, at that moment, what he wants is me. His cock pushes inside again, deeper this time; we find a rhythm that is electric. I feel every inch of him filling me up. Not wanting it to be over, but wanting to feel release at the same time and knowing that I caused that sparked that passion that's in his eyes. Knowing that his cock is hard for me, feeling how hard it is just for me, I continue to kiss him as he thrusts faster and deeper.

I feel the tightening in my belly, that tell-tale sign that I'm going to climax, and when I do, it's bliss. Fucking euphoric. He pushes in deeper a few more times and follows me over the edge, his release coating my insides. I collapse on top of him, my breathing a little heavy. He pulls out and pulls me into his side. My hand is tracing around his chest, knowing that in a moment I need to get dressed and wait for reality to catch up.

Getting dressed, I head home, knowing that I won't sleep as the excitement is still fresh in my mind. It's like it's on a loop playing over and over again, making me relive every exhilarating moment.

I text Alane and let her know I'm home okay. As soon as she reads the text my phone starts to ring, and I know it's her. She will be wanting to check and make sure; then she will want all the juicy details. That's what best mates do; they share everything.

"Hey Alane, it's me and I'm home ok, nothing wrong to report," I say in a dreamy voice.

"Well now that we have that sorted, are you going to tell me all about it? You know I can only live vicariously through you, so come on spill." Her excitement is evident in her voice as she talks to me.

"It was amazing, Alane. How can I describe it for you? It's impossible because you can't describe perfection, but I will say this: It was hot, sexy, and left me wanting more." I don't really want to tell her all the ins and outs because I don't want anyone to shatter the illusion.

"Did you get his number? Are you going to see him again?" Her questions make me pause for a second. Shit, I didn't get his number.

"No I didn't get his number, but I will go back to the bar tomorrow and give him mine. That way it's up to him," I tell her. I really hope that he wants my number and that I wasn't just a meaningless fuck.

I say goodnight to Alane, have a quick shower and fall into bed not even bothering to put my PJ's on.

I toss and turn, getting all hot and bothered through the night, chasing another release. My hand wanders down my body, caressing everywhere his hands or lips trailed over me. My hand finds my center wet and waiting. I slip a single finger inside, relishing the images in my head of Jason doing this to me. I work my hand faster until I feel my orgasm right on the brink. I think about his cock, working its way inside, and it's enough to drive me over the edge.

I finally fall asleep, only to be woken by the alarm going off on table beside me. Time to get up and start the day. I get ready for work, putting my hair up in a messy ponytail, just throwing it up and getting my uniform on. I apply a little make-up to complete the look.

I only have to work the tills for a couple of hours today, filling in for a young woman who has a dental appointment or something, the manager said. It's been a while since I've been on the tills. Normally I'm in the back helping unload the pallets that come off the lorry, getting ready to stack them on the shelfs. That's the thing about working at a supermarket; you get to know your job quickly, as it never really changes.

The day passes in a blur, the endless beep of each item that I scan, the nameless faces as they pay for their goods, the screaming children asking for more toys or chocolate. That's why shops tend to put sweets at the tills. It's done on purpose so that the mums have to buy it when their children are screaming the place down for it.

I clock out and make my way home, throwing a pair of jeans on, a blue cami top, black Toms, and my outfit is complete; I'm ready to go. I had texted

Alane at lunch to see if she fancied coming to the bar again with me tonight. Of course she said yes; she wouldn't want to miss out on catching all the juicy details.

I hope Jason is working tonight I never really thought to ask as I was leaving his place, but we will go on the off chance that he is. I'm just going to have one drink and slip him my number. The next move is up to him. I'm just hoping he makes the next move.

`Chapter Three

The bar is heaving tonight. There must be some sort of party going on, so Alane and I find a table in the far corner. I place my bag on the table, pulling out my purse so I can make my way to the bar. I haven't seen if Jason is working yet because I can't see through the throng of people.

My smile breaks as soon as I get to the bar. Standing on the other side is Jason, looking as sexy as ever. He smiles that secret, sexy grin and I know it's only for me; the one that kind of says, "oh you know where this is going."

"What can I get you?" he asks me. And as soon as I hear his voice it's like a spark ignites and I realise I'm not leaving here without him.

"Smirnoff Ice for me and—" he cuts me off before I can finish.

"Budweiser for your friend," he says. Is it bad that I'm excited that he remembers what I ordered most of last night?

"Thanks," I say. As he turns to go get our drinks, I can't help but watch his ass as he bends to get them from the fridge. He pops the caps on both drinks and places them on the bar in front of me. I supposes it's now or never, so I open my purse and pull out the card with my number on it. I give it to him along with the money for the drinks.

A little smile graces my lips as I notice he puts the card into his pocket, and proceeds to take payment and bring me my change. He hands it over with a little wink, as I grab the drinks and make my way back over to where Alane is sitting.

"Well, did you see him?" she asks me in a higher tone than her normal one.

I just nod as I take my seat, not sure if I'm able to form words without sounding like some giddy teenager. I look over to Alane, who is staring at me with rapt attention, waiting for me to say something; anything, I suppose. I blurt out the first thing that comes to my mind. "I think you will be going home without me again," I say to her.

"I kind of already figured that out as soon as I noticed he was working," she says to me.

I can't ask for a better best friend. She is always there for me, no matter what.

"I gave him my number, and he put it in his pocket, so that's good, right?" I ask her, needing the verification from someone else that this isn't all in my head.

"Well, that's a turn for the books. So you don't want this to be just a weekend deal then?" Her question startles me. I hadn't even really thought about it.

Do I want this to be something more? Do I want to see him for more than a weekend? When my heart skips a beat, I know the answer....

"Yes, I do." I whisper to Alane. And I realize it's true. I want to see where this will go, if the passion stays or if we ride the course until it fizzles out.

As the night passes, the drinks are flowing nicely. When I feel vibrations in my back pocket, I pull my phone out and look down to see I have a text.

Unknown: *You look sexy, meet me in the same room as last night in 5 mins x*

I look up and notice he's watching me from behind the bar. I smile back as I hit reply.

Natalie: *Can't wait x*

It's all that's needed. I don't need to write an essay as a reply, just straight to the point. My body burns for him and I can't wait to get my hands on him again.

I save his number in my phone and look up at Alane, who is watching us both with a grin. Necking my drink, I stand and tell Alane I need the little girls room. She just laughs at me and waves me away, knowing that I'm going to have a stolen moment with Jason.

I walk into the little room where we shared our first explosive kiss last night. I turn around and see him come in behind me, flipping the catch on the door so that we won't be disturbed.

Walking closer I reach up and wrap my hands in his hair, pulling him closer to me.

It's that first spark of pleasure as his lips meet mine; I could kiss him all day and be happy.

He leads me towards the little couch, tugging me down on top of him. I'm sat astride his lean frame, grinding against him as we continue to kiss each other. His lips find my neck and kiss the tender skin. The fire is in full force by the time we are practically naked. I don't really care as long as I feel him deep inside of me soon. Can you go crazy from lust? Right now I think you can, but I'm heading into this with my eyes wide open, wanting it.

I stand up and place my knees on the couch, holding the back for support. He's standing behind me now, teasing me with his cock, and I love the anticipation of what he is about to do. He has me wetter than I can remember. I think it's because I know how good it was from last night and I'm just craving it again.

"Jason… Please, I need to feel you fuck me," I plead. I don't care what I sound like, begging for his cock like this.

He slides inside in one thrust, impaling me on his impressive cock, his hands gripping my hips, as he begins to thrust, deeper with every stroke. And I'm falling; the pleasure is too much. The orgasm hits me by surprise, so he pulls out and sits down pulling me on top of him. He's quickly thrusting back inside. I try to set a pace, but it's hard on the little bucket couch. He picks me up while still buried inside of me, moving me against the wall, each push and pull making me climb quickly again. This feeling is one I don't ever want to lose, to be so perfectly full that it borders on pain. Yet it's the kind of pain you don't want to live without. It's a pain you crave.

He drops me to my feet and I sit on the couch, watching as he palms his cock, watching each stroke with rapt attention, the head teasing my lips and begging for me to have a taste. I don't hesitate to wrap my lips around his cock, feeling the silkiness of his head gliding past my lips, tasting the pre-cum that coats his cock as he gets closer to his release. I push my mouth lower enjoying the feel of him hitting the back of my throat. It's then I realize I want to feel all of him. I watch as he works himself faster, his grip tightening around his cock, pumping it just millimetres from my lips. I watch as the tip swells, placing my mouth around him again, waiting to taste everything he has to give me. I feel the first warm spurt hit the back of my throat and I love it. He keeps working his cock until he is spent and I swallow every drop, feeling that sense of satisfaction that I made him cum in my mouth.

I stand up, he wraps his arms around me and we just stand there together for a minute. Then I feel a little kiss against my forehead.

Getting dressed, we head back out of the little room and towards the bar. I see Abby at the table where I left her. Sitting back down I see she's gotten another round in, so I quickly take a sip and try to keep the smile from my face.

We head home a little while later. I'm lucky that Alane only lives down the road, so we share a taxi and say goodbye as I head up the street to my place.

Stepping inside, I make my way into my room, stripping down to my black thong. I hit the bed and fall asleep in minutes, fully sated.

Chapter Four

When I wake I see a text on my phone saying that last night was amazing. I feel a sense of elation that he has acknowledged that it was more than a weekend fling.

I run a bath, soaking in the warm water, enjoying the way it feels as it glides across my body. I wash and grab the towel from the rail, stepping out of the bath. I wrap the towel around my body and start getting myself ready for work.

We chat via text throughout the day, just really talking nonsense, but it's the sort of nonsense you talk about just so you can keep talking to each other. Every time I check my phone my hearts flutters when I see the little icon showing me a text from Jason.

Works drags by and I know it's because I really want to see him. We have not arranged to see each other yet, we are just talking getting to know each other through words instead of just bodies. Don't get me wrong, our bodies have great chemistry with the way we seem to fit perfectly, but that's lust. You can't sustain a life built on nothing but passion. You need to get to know the person who sets your world on fire.

I want to get to know Jason; his likes, his dislikes, what makes him the man I have seen glimpses of.

Later that night I'm sitting on my couch, Kindle in hand, reading some smutty romance with a glass of wine at my side. The story goes on about love at first sight and all that.

But that's not real; it's a myth. To have anything in this life you have to want it and work hard to get it.

Nothing happens without effort, or without bumps along the way, but one day if you stay true to yourself and be who you are, you will be happy.

My phone pings again and I look down, expecting it to be another text about little nothings, but what I see makes me smile.

Jason: *I want to take you out on a date and give you the night of your life. x*

His words are just what I needed to hear to reaffirm what I thought, that this isn't just some quick fuck but maybe, just maybe, the start of a journey.

I hit reply.

Natalie: *I would love nothing more. x*

The End

My links. Feel free to stalk I love it...

Facebook:
https://www.facebook.com/SEHarringtonAuthor
Twitter: #Author_S_E
Goodreads:
https://www.goodreads.com/.../show/7793436.Samantha_Harrington
Website: www.samanthaharringtonauthor.com
Amazon:
http://www.amazon.co.uk/.../e/B015RG9O.../ref=sr_ntt_srch_lnk_1...

My Books

The Volkov Mafia Series

Obsession

Faith I had it all, friends, designer everything and money. With my degree in the bag it was my time to shine, a new beginning just for me. To live my life my way and not to conform to anyone else's plan. One day changed all of that and everything I knew was taken away from me. When It happens, that one catastrophic event, the person I was before was ripped away from me in the blink of an eye. How could I deal with the pain of betrayal? Will I ever be able to deal with what happened? To find my inner strength to get me through or will the person I once was cease to exist? After everything that happened and everything I learn, can I ever go back to who I was before? Who can you trust, when you lose

yourself?
Warning: This book contains mature themes and language. This book may contain triggers for some readers.

Intended for readers 18+ only this is a dark erotic romance
Buy Link: mybook.to/Obsession

Unexpected Christmas

Faith

We have been to hell and back. As we wait for the impending arrival of our baby, and getting to spend our first Christmas together. Will it all go to plan? Or will fate have other ideas.

Damien

The past Six Months have been bliss. Watching Faith bloom every day, knowing that she is carrying my child. Doesn't get better than this. She is strong. She is mine.

I fly back out to Russia, end up stuck here longer than I expect, will I make it back in time for Christmas, or will I miss more than just that?

Join Faith and Damien as the celebrate the holidays, will it turn out how they hope? Join them in this little holiday treat...

Mature readers only 18+ due to graphic and sexy scenes

Buy Link: mybook.to/UnexpectedChristmas

Fractured

Malcolm

She destroyed me, she fractured my heart too many times. I still need her, I still want her, now all I have to do is go get her. Show her I'm the only man she needs.

Camilla

I'm lost, I'm broken, I'm ruined.
Through the torment and the suffering, he brought me back from the brink, then I took our son and ran from the only man who ever loved me.

I can't be in his world, I'm not strong enough to fight for him, the only man I will ever love.

Can Cami and Malc overcome everything that has happened, to get their happy ever after, or is the past and present to much to fight against.

getbook.at/Fractured

Ecta: The Divide

****Trigger warning. 18+ readers only as contains scenes of a sexual nature, violence and strong language.**** For centuries, the people of Skywaard have been content in their industrial civilization in the clouds, isolated and separated from the primitive people of Ariviil with their strange potions and magic. They have been sequestered for too long, however, and resources are running low. The only way the people of the skies will survive is if they find a way to work with those who walk the lands. That is where Sebastian comes in. Up until now, he has lived a charmed life of debauchery, growing up in a noble ward left him wanting for nothing. Still, he finds the life of sex, drugs, booze, and women can leave a man feeling rather... empty. Driven by a longing for purpose, he abandons the comforts of Skywaard and departs for Ariviil. He wants adventure, and he finds it. In walks the intoxicating little package that is Loriella. She's an outcast, ostracized for possessing a gift that the people of Ariviil fear. People always fear what they do not understand, even in a city built on magic. She accepted this fate a long time ago resigning herself to a life of isolation and loneliness... until she meets Sebastian. They say you crave what you need, and she needs him with every ounce of her being. Will he turn her away when he learns of her gift, just as her own people have done? As the entwined souls from incompatible worlds try to negotiate a treaty between their people and navigate a romance doomed for disaster, they uncover an even darker reality brewing on the horizon that no one saw coming. Will they be able to make peace among the chaos, or will it all end in war?

Buy Link:

US: http://tinyurl.com/hkcq9yx

UK: http://tinyurl.com/zwyo9gh

Club Secrets & Whispers

This is a FREE short introduction into a brand new series coming Late 2016

Have you ever wondered what goes on behind closed doors?

Well now you don't have to.
Follow the journeys of the members of club Secrets & Whispers.
See how they really feel about their clients, and who they enjoy most.

These little shorts will leave you wanting more, needing more. craving more.

Are you willing to go behind closed doors?

18+ due to adult content, scenes of a sexual nature, may cause triggers

Buy Link:

Mybook.to/SecretsAndWhispers

Sign up for my Newsletter

http://eepurl.com/bUWn7D

For Charlie...My Sister....Love you to the moon and back....

Virginia.... You girl, are amazing...Thank you... For everything...

House of the Rising Sun

By

LJ SeXton

New Orleans was a city of many nicknames: The Big Easy, The Crescent City and The Birthplace of Jazz just to name a few. It's also the city of many myths and folk tales of zombies, vampires, voodoo and haunted hotels. *Some myths truer than others.* But it's a beautiful city with its old plantation homes, The Cathedral, and it's above ground cemeteries. The French Quarter at night is where I like to be. People walking from bar to bar, restaurant to restaurant, dancing in the streets. That's my time to hunt. I don't hunt for sport or trophies, I hunt for nourishment and sexual pleasure. But not always pleasure for myself, pleasure for him, Master. I prey on an unsuspecting naïve young woman to bring back to him. They either become a feeder, a giver of pleasure or a slave. But they all end up in the same place...The House of the Rising Sun. Just like the song, no one can pinpoint when it originated, or who originated it.

There are always assumptions about what it actually is, a house of ill-repute, a bondage club, and the greatest assumption is a place where the undead do unholy, unspeakable things. Well each assumption holds a note of truth.

It's Mardi Gras, so many people are crowding the streets. I can smell the naiveté and debauchery in the air. Each human has their own unique scent to them, some sweet, some floral and some sour. I walk through the throngs of drunken college students and tourists. Young men watching scantily clad young women show their tits for strings of plastic beads and young couples ducking down alley ways to get in a quick fuck. I'm looking for the bar that is the loudest and with most people. That way if the person of my choosing becomes a missing person it's harder to get an eye witness with so many people around. I find the one I usually frequent around the busy season; it's on Bourbon Street, a very popular section. I walk into Lafitte's Blacksmith Shop Bar, named after Jean Lafitte -- privateer, entrepreneur, sailor, diplomat, spy, hero of the Battle of New Orleans. Lafitte led a colorful and mysterious life in the New World. Much like everything in this city, he also has myths, such as birth place and his age.

The bar is packed wall to wall people. Their scents are all blending together, but there's one scent that stands alone. I follow it through the crowds of bar patrons until it is so strong I finally see who it belongs too. When I see the petite, blonde and busty young woman whose scent has drawn me to her, she is sitting at the bar with two friends. I walk up, stand at the bar beside her and order a shot of Absinthe. One of the young ladies with the busty blond looks at me and smiles, batting her eyelashes in an attempt to flirt. I raise my shot glass and give her a wink as I let the green liquid slide down my throat. Now the other one joins her as they both watch me slowly lick the stray liquid off my lips. Finally, my prey turns in her seat. She beautiful and her face is filled with innocence.

"Whatcha drinking?" her sweet little voice asks me. As I stare at her I cannot find my voice to answer her. Her friends stand there giggling. "Hey, you okay?" She places her hand on my arm, bringing me out of my trance.

"Oh sorry, yes I'm fine," I say as I look at the bar tender and order a round of Absinthe. "Please ladies, drink on me. Should we toast to a night filled with beauties such as yourselves?" I hold up my shot glass and so do her friends. "Wait. What is this?" my blonde friend asks as she examines the liquid in the tiny glass.

"Some call it The little green fairy, but you may know it as Absinthe." She sniffs the liquid then shrugs her shoulders as we all down the liquor. "Oh how very rude of me not to introduce myself. I am Nikolaz Beaumont." I put my hand to my chest and bow to the ladies.

"Well, Nicolazkolaz, I am Trinity, this is Shelly and this is Jackie." She points to her friends as she makes the introduction. The one she called Shelly has long brown hair with hazel eyes. She is very pretty. Jackie has a pixie cut with dyed black hair. She is also very pretty. They would both be a favorite of Master's. But Trinity, she is exquisite, her blonde hair falling to just below her shoulder blades, her blue eyes dancing when she smiles. To be so petite she has a tight little body and I would like to tie her to my bench and show her how a man such as myself can make her little twat wet with not even a touch.

As the night goes on we drink and talk. I watch each one to see how inebriated they are. Since I am not truly alive I don't get inebriated; I drink absinthe for the taste. Trinity has slowed down on her liquor intake as her friends continue to slam whiskey shooters.

"So would you ladies like to join me and some friends at my home for a little fun?" I'm looking at only Trinity when I ask. The other girls are all but begging Trinity to not end the night.

"How far is your house from here?" She asked with a raised eyebrow but a hint of fear in her voice.

"We can take a taxi there. It's about fifteen-minute drive."

"Well we have a car. I can drive since I haven't drunk any alcohol in hours, but we can't stay very long. We are taking a tour in the morning of the cemeteries." She grabs her car keys as we make our way out of the bar. We walk down Bourbon St until she hit the key fob and the little hybrid lights come on.

Once we get to the tiny car Shelly and Jackie get in to the back seat so my tall slender legs can have a little extra room. Once we are almost out of the French Quarter I direct Trinity on where to go. We get to the dark dirt road and travel up it a little way until we see the old plantation house sitting alone with dim lights shining through the windows and a sign with a sun rising over a beautiful river. As we pull up the young ladies are enchanted and a little excited, which is a good thing. Their naiveté is what he lives for; easier to break their will. Once we are out of the car Trinity is apprehensive to enter. "Mon ami, what is bothering you about entering my home?" I ask as the other two step on to the porch.

"Is this The House of the Rising Sun?" My little petite poppet knows of the rumors that are spoken about the house.

"Yes, Trinity, it is." I grasp her by the shoulders gently to show her no harm will come to her. "I've heard stories about this place. None of them good, I might add." She stands there staring over my head at the lit up sign.

"You have nothing to fear here. I will make sure no harm comes to any of you. Nothing happens here unless you allow it."

She continues to stare at the house a few more minute then we begin our ascent up the stairs.

Once we enter it's a calm atmosphere. There's a little bar set up in the room just off to the right of the foyer. A few people are having drinks as low music plays in the background. There are men in suits, a few girls dressed in beautiful gowns giving the men they're full attention as they stroke their cocks in a not-so-discreet manner. I find an empty booth in the back corner of the room and I escort the young ladies our seats.

"Would you ladies like a drink?" Shelly and Jackie ask for a beer but Trinity asks for a glass of soda. I leave them to whisper as I go to fetch out beverages. When I return, he is at the table with them, his eyes all but tearing the clothes off Trinity.

"Hello, Father. Ladies, I see you met my father. Masters Beaumont this is Trinity, Jackie and Shelly."

He bows his head at each young lady as I take the seat that is empty next to Trinity as he has squeezed in the opposite seat with the others.

"Ladies, your beers. Trinity, your soda--I hope Coke Cola is fine."

She takes a sip and nods.

"Son, where did you find such beautiful ladies?" My father asks as he stretches one of his long arm behind Jackie and Shelly.

"They were at my favorite little watering hole, Lafitte's."

He lets out a deep laugh. "I should have known," he says as he grabs his drink glass and takes a sip. "So ladies where are you from?"

"We're from Michigan, here for Mardi Gras." Jackie answers after a long drink of her beer.

"Oh, are you enjoying our fair city?" He asks while looking directly at Trinity.

"It's very beautiful. The old homes, the swamps. I love that it's steeped in history, also the myths and scary stories." She says as she giggles.

"Ah, yes, the scary stories. There are so many scary stories of ghosts, hoodoo and vampires." He says with narrowed eyes. "Can I show you ladies around my lovely home?"

Trinity shakes her head no but the other two agree to go with my father.

After they have followed him out, Trinity and I sit there quietly. Until the song "House of the Rising Sun" begins playing and she starts to laugh. "Kinda Ironic, isn't it?" Her laughter continues and it sounds as beautiful as she is.

"Can I take you upstairs to show you something?"

Her laughter ends abruptly as she thinks over her answer. "Sure but then I need to find my drunken friends so we can head back to our hotel."

I stand and extend my hand to her. She places her dainty little hand in mine and we make our way back to the foyer to the steps. As we make our up, a few of the working girls and their johns are coming down. As each descends the stairs they greet me. I look back and my guest is not at all amused by the half-dressed ladies. I pull her to stand next to me. "My father's, umm...employees." I whisper in her ear. I see the goose bumps form on her skin as I lightly run my tongue along the ridge of her ear. We continue up the stairs to the second floor, I lead her through the big wooden doors that hide my bedroom behind them. I walk to the set of French doors that lead to the balcony. I open them and beckon her to follow me out.

She steps out the doors and her eyes are wide as she takes in the view. "Oh, god, it's beautiful." She moves closer to the railing.

"You can see the lights from the city." I stand next to her and take in the sight that brings me calm when the storm that is my father is raging.

"I love to sit out here some nights for hours. It's serene," I say as I move over until I can feel her skin against mine.

"How long have you lived here, Nikolaz?" She never looks away from the scenery as she asks. "A long time mon ami, a very long time." She steps away from the railing, turns to go back into my bedroom. "Nikolaz, how old are you?" she asks as she walks up the books on the very large wall just left of the French doors.

"I am thirty years old." She runs her fingers over the very old furniture that furnished the room. "This is not the room of a thirty-year-old man. This is the room of a man that has lived a very long life." She stops at my king sized four-poster bed with the thick black curtains that shroud me from the light.

"I'm just a man who has a fascination for antiques." I walk up until I am standing in front of her. We stand in silence looking into each other's eyes.

"Your eyes are so dark. They're black in color, I've never seen any others like it."

I wrap my arm around her waist drawing her closer to me. "I'm told they're my father's, very unique indeed." I lower my head until our lips are close enough that her scent is controlling my body. I lift her chin slightly and gently place mine to hers. Her lips are soft, plump and feel so good against mine. I hear a moan release from them as my tongue gently enters her mouth. Our tongues find each other and dance a tango as she presses her body to mine. I know she can feel my hardened cock on her stomach. She gasps, then steps away.

"Nikolaz, will you show me the rest of the house?" she asks as she backs away from me far enough that I feel the loss of her warmth.

"Mon ami, there only few rooms I can show you that wouldn't send you yelling into the night." I step towards her and she steps back. I stop before I scare her off, before I've had a taste.

"Show me, Nikolaz. I want to see what you believe to be so bad that I would run away."

I walk to her, taking her hand once more. Without a word I take her down the hall to another set of wooden door but these are locked. As I reach in my pocket to retrieve the key, I glance over to see Trinity standing there in anticipation, like a child on Christmas morning. I unlock the door and turn to her. "Remember you were warned." I take her hand as we enter my play room. I shut the door and turn on the dim light. She stands in the center and looks all around her. She stops when she sees the huge wooden cross with cuffs for one's wrists and ankles. I have whips, floggers, belts and various tools to inflict pain and pleasure. She directs her attention back to the cross. She walks over to it and steps on the platform at which it is attached.

"Isn't this called St. Andrews cross?" she asks as her hand lightly grazes over the smooth wood. "Yes that is what it is referred to."

She picks up one of the wrist cuffs examining it. "Have you cuffed many women to this cross, Nicolaz?"

I walk up next to her taking the cuff from her hand. "Mon ami, yes I have, but only willing participants." I say as she moves around the cross.

"What do you to them once you have them on it?" She looks to the wall of whips and floggers. "Well that depends. Someone new to the cross I would start out with something soft like a feather. I would run it over the most sensitive part of them. Then if they need more maybe a crop. I would spank their ass and some like their like pussies spanked too." I get close to her ear as I say the last part.

She is flushed, her skin is goose bumped and I can hear her heart beating fast.

"Mon ami, would you like to be cuffed to this cross?" I hold one of the ankle cuffs in my hand as I look at her biting her bottom lip, standing there trying to hold her thighs tightly together to relieve the ache her wet little twat is feeling from just the thought of being spanked, and nodding her head yes.

Once I have her naked and cuffed to the cross, I ask her what it is she would like from me. She looks to the wall of crops in front of her and without a word I know she is a girl who likes to be spanked. I go over trying to decide which to use.

"The middle one," she says.

Oh, the wide one. I believe I have somewhat of an expert on my hands. "Trinity, what would you like me to do? Spank your round perfect ass or slap that bald little twat?" She is trying to close her legs because the ache is back and it's so much worse.

"First I want to see you, naked."

I look at her with raised eyebrows. "Is that what you want? To see my large, hard cock?"

She is trembling with desire as I slowly remove my clothing. Her eyes are heavy with desire; I can see her licking her lips like a woman who has seen her first drink of water in days. I can smell her arousal and it's making me crazy. I kick my abandoned clothes to the other side of the room as me and my crop make our way to her. I step behind and run the crop up and down her ass cheeks. Then I lightly smack her ass, and her breathing speeds up.

"Again!" she yells, and I of course oblige her.

"Harder Nikolaz!" she yells in a much thicker voice. It's the voice of lust. I spank her harder, as requested. Then I move around, slap her cunt hard and she moans loudly, so I smack it again and again until I can see she has orgasmed. I set the crop down. I cup her wet little cunt rubbing my finger through her wetness until I find the sweet right little hole.

"Oh Trinity, so wet. So tight." I take my index and middle finger and enter her, slowly moving in and out. When I look up at her, she has her eyes closed and her moans begin to get louder. When I feel her walls beginning to close in on my finger I remove them and replace them with my mouth. I cover her whole pussy making sure my tongue touches every part of it. I feel her hips grinding against me but she can't move the way she needs to because of the cuffs. I release her ankles and spread her legs. "Fuck, I have never seen a prettier cunt before." I again begin an assault on her clit with my tongue. She is writhing and trying to pull me close to her with her legs but she is not strong enough. I can feel myself getting aroused; I also feel my fangs descending.

I do not want her to be my feeder and I do not want to make her on of his whores; I want to make her mine. I look up at her and she is so engrossed in her pleasure. I look at her inner thigh and see the vein I need. If I bite her, she will be mine. I softly bite at the flesh before I clamp down. She does not scream, or try to move away; she is moaning as I suck her blood just enough to not turn her but to make her only desire me. Once I have taken my fill I slam my cock into her hard. As soon as I do her walls start pulsating and she is praising her god.

"Oh god, yes, yes!" she cries as I keep slamming into her soft, wet twat.

"More, Nikolaz, more!"

I pick up my pace and my sweet release is coming. As I grind my hips into her making my cock go deeper, I feel her shake and her pussy clamps down on me as I feel my orgasm come like water from a fire hose.

Once she has caught her breath, I release from the cross and carry her to the couch. "You are mine now, Mon Ami," I say as I kiss the top of her head.

"Forever and always," she says as she drifts off to sleep.

Follow me –

Goodreads –

https://www.goodreads.com/author/show/13609001.L_J_Sexton?from_search=true&search_version=service

Facebook –

https://www.facebook.com/Author-LJ-SeXton-734537879993958/?fref=ts

INFERNO

By

Kat Mizera

Dante

Dante Lamonte was the kind of man who was rarely alone. Whether he was on the baseball field, in a night club or hanging out with friends, he was always surrounded by people and they always wanted something. Tonight, however, he was actually by himself. Sitting at the bar in one of the most exclusive sex clubs in the world, he wasn't even thinking about sex. He just wanted to get away from a life where being a professional baseball player seemed to dwarf everything. He didn't have a lot of friends and kept it that way on purpose. Usually, that's exactly what he wanted. But not tonight.

Tonight he was fucking lonely, and he wasn't the kind of guy who got lonely. He'd created a persona that portrayed him as an asshole specifically to keep people away. He did this to protect himself from people who wanted something from him, so he had no business wanting to change anything or feeling sorry for himself. He probably just needed to get laid, but although he was at a sex club, he wasn't interested in this lifestyle. A man with a dominant personality already, he didn't feel the need to bend some poor woman over a table, strap down her hands and legs and fuck her until she succumbed to his will. Women did that for him anyway.

The bartender put another drink in front of him and Dante nodded.

"Lady over there looks as miserable as you do," the bartender said in a conversational tone. He held up his hand when Dante started to protest. "I'm not trying to find you a sub—she's a first-timer. Heard she works for some pro sports team and got herself on the guest list but I don't think this is her scene. She looks overwhelmed and you look like you need to talk. Maybe you two would enjoy each other's company." Without another word, he ambled off and Dante couldn't resist turning to look at the woman in question.

For a moment, he wasn't sure who the bartender was talking about. Then he saw her, a curvy brunette in a short, sleeveless dress and high black pumps. Her dark hair was long and thick, falling down her back in soft waves. Her thighs were a little rounder than he normally liked, but her calves were toned and sexy beneath them. When she turned, he was drawn to her mouth; full and round and covered in red lipstick. He immediately pictured it wrapped around his cock and he felt himself start to stiffen.

Turning away, he took a long drink and tried to keep himself from looking at her; he came here specifically to *get away* from clingy women. When she got up and moved towards the restrooms, he followed the sway of her round little ass until it disappeared behind closed doors.

"I'm telling you," the bartender appeared out of nowhere. "She's ripe for the taking."

"I don't need to take anyone," Dante murmured.

"Ah, but I think you do, my friend." He continued down the bar.

When she came out she was making her way back to her seat at the bar when her eyes locked with Dante's. She blinked and seemed to just take him in. Dante was a little mesmerized too, staring into big, long-lashed eyes that he couldn't discern the color of at this distance. He gave her a little nod and she quickly looked away, hurrying back to her seat and lifting her drink. He chuckled to himself, realizing they both seemed nervous. Maybe she *was* the kind of girl he could spend a few hours with tonight. Maybe the damn bartender was right?

Before he changed his mind, he picked up his drink and made his way down to her, sinking into the empty bar stool next to her.

"Hi." He met her curious gaze with a casual smile.

"Hi." Her fingers closed around her drink in a death grip.

"I'm guessing by the look in your eyes you don't come here often?"

She shook her head. "Never. I'm in town on business and I got a guest pass through a friend. It's…" She hesitated.

"Overwhelming?"

She nodded. "I don't think this is my thing."

"It's not my cup of tea either, but the only time people leave me alone is when I'm in a place like this."

"I thought that was you." Her eyes met his and he realized they were green or blue or some other exotic color that didn't match her dark hair and olive skin.

"Then you know my name. What's yours?"

"Becca. Rebecca Hernandez."

"Very nice to meet you, Becca." He extended his hand and smiled as she shook it.

"So if you're only here to hide, what's the lure?"

"I'm out, having a drink, lots of beautiful women to look at..." He shrugged. "Not everything is about sex."

She smiled for the first time and he thought she was beautiful. "Personally, I don't have time for sex."

He raised his eyebrows. "That's a damn shame, Becca. A body like yours is made for sex."

She flushed, her cheeks turning pink. "I'm a chubby Latino girl with fat thighs and a big butt. In my circles, I'm invisible."

"Then you're running in the wrong circles, *querida*." The Spanish word for "*sweetheart*" made her flush again.

"You're Cuban, right?" She tilted her head.

"Half; my father was French. Why?"

"You're Hispanic—you probably understand women with big asses but I'm sure the women you sleep with don't look like me."

"No." He shook his head. "But they should."

Her lips parted slightly, and once again he had a vision of that mouth on his body; anywhere on his body.

"You're beautiful, Becca." He reached out and touched her cheek.

"But you don't want to sleep with me." The look on her face was so defiant he couldn't help but smile.

"I didn't come here to get laid," was all he said.

"Point taken." She turned away but he caught her chin with his fingers, forcing her to look back.

"I would reconsider for you."

Becca

Becca wasn't the kind of girl who came to places like this. She'd only had a handful of sexual partners and those experiences had been extremely forgettable. She didn't have a boyfriend and rarely dated. Her focus had always been on school and later her career. She was 28 years old and didn't have a clue how to talk to, much less flirt with, a man like Dante Lamonte.

She knew who he was, of course; everyone did. Known for his antics both on and off the baseball field, he was notorious for womanizing, partying and making a nuisance of himself. He was also the sexiest guy she'd ever been this close to. Sitting beside him, she was close enough to look into his eyes, and they were mesmerizing. They were the color of melted caramel and she'd never seen lashes on a man that curled the way his did. His lips were full and perfectly shaped, set above a square jaw that oozed masculinity. His nose was long and straight—no doubt from the French side of the family—and his thick dark hair was cropped close to his head.

Masculine didn't even begin to cover his body. Probably six foot one to her five foot five, he had a runner's body with broad shoulders, a flat stomach and lean hips. His thighs looked magnificent in tight black jeans, and she found herself wishing she could slip her hand inside his shirt to feel his skin.

"See something you like?" he asked with a soft chuckle, startling her.

"No! Yes. I mean, of course, you're very good-looking." She sighed and drained her drink. "I should go. I'm not very good at—"

"Are you not interested in the club or not interested in me?" He didn't seem to be mocking her as he waited for her answer.

"You don't understand." She stared at some imaginary point of interest on the other side of the room wondering how much to tell him. It wasn't like she'd ever see him again, right? "I've never had a pleasurable sexual experience; it's always awkward and uncomfortable. I feel chubby instead of sexy. I can't have an orgasm. I can't relax. I came here tonight because I thought maybe a stranger, someone who works here, one of the doms or whatever they're called, could help me figure out what I'm doing wrong, but now that I'm here..."

His warm hand covered hers. "What are you afraid of?"

She looked sad. "I, I don't...know."

"Tell me."

"I just got promoted to my dream job," she admitted. "I'm the new head of Media Relations for the NHL expansion team in Las Vegas. If the team found out, I could lose my job!" She started to get up.

"Becca, wait." He reached for her. "I understand. Really."

"No, you don't. When you do things that are inappropriate, you get a slap on the wrist and maybe your team fines you, but they can't afford to lose you. I'm just a publicist, and this is my first big-time job in the sports world. If I fuck this up, I will never work in sports again."

"No one will find out," he said quietly. "Confidentiality is strictly enforced here."

"It's not that simple." She shook her head. "My mom counts on me too—if I lose my job we don't eat. I've had to help take care of us since I was 14. I finished college and got a good job, but I still have thousands in student loans. I pay the mortgage, my car, groceries—almost everything. My mom is a maid, so her money doesn't go very far. I'm the breadwinner in the family so my whole life revolves around my career. I can't afford—"

"Sometimes, *querida*, you have to trust. That's why you came here, isn't it? To test your resolve and see if you can find someone who makes you feel good?" His eyes burned into hers with so much passion she could barely think.

"I don't know," she said with a tiny whisper.

"I do. And I promise no one will ever find out anything that happens here tonight."

She wanted desperately to believe him, but she was nervous. If anyone ever did find out she'd been here, it could destroy everything she'd worked for. Even though she was an adult and it was legal to be here, this could be professional suicide. Or just incredibly humiliating.

"Do you think what they do here can help me?" She looked at him imploringly.

"Maybe." His eyes were inscrutable.

Dante

He had no idea why he wanted her so badly, but he did. The idea of the sweet, insecure woman beside him going to one of these hard-core doms made him uncomfortable. He knew what went on in these places and he didn't believe a stranger could give her what she needed. She definitely needed someone to take control; there was no doubt about that, but she required someone who wouldn't just take control of her body. She needed to trust someone enough to explore the passion within without making her feel used; a sweet girl like Becca needed tenderness to go along with the physical aspects of good sex.

When her nervous, shaking fingers closed around his he knew he would never let one of the professionals at this club touch her; if anyone was going to do this, it would be him. Whether it was here at the club or back in her hotel room, she was going to be his. He couldn't resist the idea of taking the shy little beauty and showing her what she'd been missing. There was something beguiling about her, and for the first time in a long time he was enchanted by a woman.

With their hands linked as though they were on a regular date, he felt something stir in his gut. The chaos in his life prohibited him from dating someone like her and he didn't want to admit how much he liked it. Warning bells were going off in his head, reminding him that he already had a woman in his life that was turning it upside down; the last thing he needed was a virginal little temptress with haunting eyes and a luscious body to complicate it further.

He'd almost convinced himself to walk away before he did something he regretted when he felt her lean towards him.

"What is it?" he asked softly, pushing her hair behind her ear.

"I don't, I wouldn't, I don't think I'd like to do anything in front of others." She lowered her gaze.

"That's probably not for you at this stage," he agreed.

"I've heard stories about people having hot wax put on their genitals—does that turn you on?" she demanded, wrinkling her pert little nose. "I mean, would you...?"

"Not a chance in hell!" he laughed. "The warmest thing I like on my cock is a woman's mouth." He saw her flush, but instead of shrinking away, she seemed to catch her breath.

He bent his head and found her lips. She hesitated, so he waited, letting her open her mouth when she was ready. He lazily tangled his tongue with hers, drinking in her sweetness and kissing the spots that made her shiver.

"Dante, what... what are we doing?"

"Kissing?" He ran his knuckles across her cheek.

"I don't think I can do this—being here makes me afraid."

"Do I make you afraid?"

"No."

"This isn't my world," he admitted quietly. "The only reason I came here is because it's really the only place no one bothers me. I've dabbled in some of the dominant and submissive games, but it's not how I like to make love." His lips were warm on her neck as he continued to whisper. "But you, *querida*, I can feel how much you need something new—if you can trust me, maybe I can help you find what you're looking for."

"Why?" she asked, her pale eyes blinking in the semi-darkness.

"Because I think you're beautiful. In another time and place, I would wine you and dine you and make love to you in a candlelit room. My life, unfortunately, does not allow for relationships like that. Instead, I can only give you tonight—anything you want or need. No strings, no questions asked, and my word of honor that no one ever finds out we were here."

For long moments she said nothing, her icy fingers still gripping his as she contemplated what to do. Finally, she slid off the stool and rested her head against his chest, her face buried in the softness of his shirt.

"I don't want to be hit. I don't want anyone to gag me or burn my privates! I just want to have an orgasm. Is that too much to ask?" He could tell she was trying to keep tears from slipping from her eyes but he felt them betraying her.

He reached out to brush them from her cheeks. "I can't imagine the types of selfish bastards you've been with that didn't take your pleasure into consideration, but if you wanted to try again, with me, I could make that happen."

"Here?" Her voice was barely a whisper.

"I think here, away from everything that you know, would be more comfortable." He softly stroked her hair.

"But you said you don't like..." Her voice faded in confusion.

"Are you asking me to play the part of a dom tonight so that you can submit to me? Is that what you want? Someone to take over and make you surrender?" He fisted her hair, just enough to force her to look up at him.

Her eyes were big and round and anxious, but she managed a tiny nod.

His lips touched hers, gently, like a whisper against her mouth. "Then that's what we'll do. There'll have to be different rules for you, though. There's not enough time to teach you what all of this means."

"What do I do?"

He linked his fingers though hers again. "Trust me."

Becca

Becca was afraid she might throw up as they left the manager's office. He'd had them both sign something saying they were consenting to whatever it is they were going to do but she wasn't paying attention anymore. Mostly, she'd just stood there and let Dante handle it. Somewhere in the back of her mind she was aware she didn't know what she was doing here or why she was going to let an infamous baseball player teach her about orgasms, but for some reason she trusted him. More than that, she *wanted* him.

"Are you sure about this?" Dante put an arm around her shoulders as they made their way into an elevator that led to the private rooms on the second floor.

"Yes." Her mouth felt dry as she nodded.

"Then from now on you don't tell me no."

She frowned. "What if I don't like it?"

"You have to trust me. I know your boundaries; I know what you want." He paused as they stepped off the elevator. "You know your safe word?"

"Red." She looked up at him solemnly.

"Once you say it, it's all over, so think carefully before you use it. I will help you with this, but you gotta commit to the experience." His eyes were intense as he stared down at her.

"I will."

"You can't say no." His deep voice was raspy now, his accent slightly more discernable. "You let me do what I want, when I want, how I want. *Me entiendes*?" *Do you understand me?*

"Yes."

"I don't care if you call me Sir or Master or any of that bullshit, but if you don't do what I say, I'll punish you like they do. The whole idea is for you to... submit." Dante's eyes were gentle but serious. "If you're not willing to try, then there's no point." She could see his jaw working but his fingers were light on her face. "Tonight is all about finding out what makes you hold back."

He opened the door and let her walk in before him. The room was spartan but clean and pleasantly cool. There was an extra-large bed in the middle of the room, a night stand with a lamp, and a door she assumed led to a bathroom. She hesitated as she looked around, unsure what to do.

"Come." He led her to the bed. She shivered slightly when he pulled her towards him and kissed her with slow, delicious precision. He nibbled her lower lip before thrusting his tongue against hers. This time she met his kiss with interest, her fingers clutching his biceps. She'd never been kissed like this and it was better than anything she'd ever imagined.

"Take off your clothes."

When she didn't move right away, his voice got harder. "*Now*. If I have to do it for you, you're gonna get a spanking."

Her mouth fell open. "You said you wouldn't hit me!"

He scowled. "I said I wouldn't find a riding crop or paddle and blister your ass—but a few swats with my palm will teach you to obey. I know your limits and you said you trust me—this is the last time I explain myself."

The thought of him spanking her made her legs quiver and she quickly slid the dress down, revealing a lacy black strapless bra and matching thong. She tried to suck in her stomach but knew it wouldn't matter; her stomach wasn't big but it would never be flat. She was built like all the women in her family and they all had thicker waists.

Dante was watching her with a slight curve to his lips. "You're lovely, *querida*. I know you're thinking, you're fat, but you're not. I love your curvy body. I want to bury my face in your breasts for a coupla days..." His grin was impish this time.

Dante

This was going to be harder than he thought. She was absolutely bewitching; completely unaware of how sexy she was, her innocence tugged at his heart in ways no woman ever had before. Her little hiccup of pleasure as they'd kissed almost derailed him from his mission, but he managed to pull away and put on his most serious face when he told her to take off her clothes. She didn't want to, it was written all over her face, but luckily she acquiesced.

Laying her on the bed, he wished romance would work, but he knew better. No, she needed to be fucked. *Hard*. However, if she was as inexperienced as he thought, she wasn't ready for a cock like his. He needed to arouse her first, and get her wet enough to take him. Lubricant was probably a must no matter what, and he made sure it was within his reach. Then he slid down between her legs and parted her thighs. Her pussy was beautiful, pink, delicately formed and practically virginal. But as he'd suspected, she wasn't even the least bit wet, and that would be a problem.

He lowered his head and planted a soft kiss on her clit, making her gasp, before sliding his tongue down to her core. He flicked gently, grasping her hips in his hands and moving her against him. She sighed, an almost imperceptible sound of pleasure, and he flattened his tongue against her. She moved a little, her body reacting to his touch even though he sensed her mind was trying to pull back. He flicked and licked, unable to remember the last time he'd enjoyed a woman this much, but she was so tightly coiled he could sense that her brief moment of pleasure was already starting to recede.

Dante knew the moment she began to drift away from him. She'd been starting to relax and then her whole body tensed. Looking up, he saw her fists clenched at her sides and her eyes squeezed shut. He sighed with disappointment; he was going to have to move into the role he'd been hoping to avoid; regular sex just wasn't going to work with her.

Pulling away, he spoke her name sharply, making her jump. "Why are you fighting me?" he demanded, his eyes narrowed.

She swallowed. "I, I didn't mean to."

He sat up. "You know what this means, yes?"

Her eyes were wide and uncertain as she shook her head.

"I have to punish you."

"Dante—"

"You *do not* have permission to talk." He slid off the bed and went to the night stand. Everything he needed was there and he wondered how she would react; hopefully, she would have the orgasm of her life by the time he was done.

"I—"

"One more word, unless it's your safe word, and I put you over my knee." He met her eyes and she instantly closed her mouth. Moving back to the bed, he put the items he'd collected off to the side and reached out his hand. "Give me your wrists."

She hesitated, undoubtedly sensing he was going to restrain her.

"Disobey me once more and I will take you out to the bar, strap you down on it, and allow everyone in the club to take a turn trying to make you come. Either we do it here in private or I let others do it out there." He had to bite his lip to keep from chuckling when she instantly held out her wrists. He captured them and attached them to the Velcro strap that dangled from the head of the bed. Pulling the rope taught, he let out a breath at the vision she made with her large, round breasts now jutting up from her chest. He reached out and took one fat nipple between his fingers and gently rubbed, increasing pressure until she moaned.

"That's a good girl," he murmured, leaning over and finding her lips. He kissed her tenderly, wanting to put her at ease. She would resist when he bound her legs, so he slowed down, letting her adjust to his tongue in her mouth and his hands on her breasts.

Sliding his hand down her smooth skin, he caressed her stomach, making little circles with his fingers. She was soft and warm, and though tonight was about her, he couldn't resist burying his face between her breasts and using his hands to bring them together. They were large, probably double D's, with round, raspberry-colored areola and fat nipples that came alive under his lips. He lightly used his teeth as he suckled one and she gasped but didn't move away. A smile played on his mouth, noting that she liked it a little rough, even though she didn't understand that yet.

He slid one hand between her legs and chuckled when she tried to squeeze them shut.

"Open for me, baby girl. I've already been in there."

She slowly spread her legs and he used one finger to slide up her slit, delighted to find her growing aroused. *Finally*. He moved his fingers between her silky folds and she tensed. Moving quickly, so she didn't have time to worry, he pulled the restraints from the side of the bed and wrapped the first around her thigh, just above the knee. She made a noise of surprise but he'd moved on to her other leg before she could say anything, and then adjusted the ropes so that her legs were wide open and pulled back towards her shoulders leaving her pussy tilted up, completely exposed and open for him.

"Dante!" Her breath came in short gasps and he held up a finger.

"Not a word!" He gave her a no-nonsense look and she closed her mouth. "You're still fighting me, *querida*. So now your pussy, your ass, your breasts, they're all mine for the taking."

"But..." The gleam in his eyes made her stop talking.

He knew she was on the edge, unsure whether to use her safe word or let him keep going or burst into tears, so he put his hands on her face and kissed her. His tongue toyed with hers as he whispered to her in Spanish, telling her she was beautiful and that he was so proud she put her trust in him.

He moved away, reaching down to slide off his boxers. He saw her eyes widen as she got her first look at his fully erect cock. Lots of women reacted that way; many had never seen a pierced penis and he waited, holding it in his hand so she could get a better look.

"You like it?" he asked casually.

"Will that hurt when it's inside me?" She seemed more curious than afraid and he shook his head.

"No one has ever complained, but if it does, you'll tell me, okay?"

"Okay." Her voice was a whisper as she watched him roll the condom on.

He reached for a small package and ripped it open.

"What's that?"

"*No more talking*—I let you ask a question because I know you've never seen a piercing like mine, but no more." He paused, watching anxiety move across her pretty features. "I think you need a blindfold."

"No! I don't!" Her eyes widened again, but he simply pulled the silky scarf from the drawer and tied it around her eyes.

"Dante!" Her cry of distress actually made his chest tighten because he didn't want her to be afraid of him, but this was for her own good. She couldn't continue to go through life unable to enjoy sex or have an orgasm, and this seemed to be the only way to break through the mental barriers she'd put up.

"Easy, baby girl. I'm right here." He stroked her cheek with his fingers. "I won't leave you alone while you're tied up, and you always have your safe word if it's too much. But I really, really don't want you to use it. I don't know if I'll ever recover if you deprive me of the honor of watching you come for the first time."

"O-okay." She was shaking, her entire body quivering against the restraints and Dante moved between her legs, holding himself up on his forearms as he looked at her sweet face. She needed him to do this. In a perfect world, he would date this gorgeous creature and bring her the kind of pleasure she deserved. Instead, tonight he would dominate her body in order to release the demons in her heart, before going home to face demons of his own.

Becca

She'd never been as terrified as she was right now, but she forced herself to breathe through the fear. She could do this. Dante freakin' Lamonte had offered to not only have sex with her, but to show her how to enjoy sex. She'd never been able to do that, so being spread out in front of him like this was as exhilarating as it was embarrassing. Her heart was racing and she had to remind herself that all she had to do was use the safe word and she would be free.

With the blindfold on, she didn't know what he was doing but she could hear him rustling some paper and then his fingers were moving between her legs. He was putting lubricant on her and for a moment she was confused; then she remembered how big his cock was and the metal studs that protruded from it. His fingers moved to her buttocks and he spread them slowly. She yelped when he rubbed lube into her asshole and cried out when he slid something hard up and into her rectum.

"Dante!"

"One word and I take you out to the bar." His voice was hard and she whimpered. "Does it hurt, *querida*?"

She tried to focus on the unfamiliar feeling in her ass. "N-no." She couldn't keep her voice from quavering.

"This will feel good, I promise."

As he spoke the plug in her ass started to gently vibrate and she groaned.

"Easy, little one." He stroked her calf, his warm fingers bringing her heartbeat back to normal. "I promise this will feel very, very good."

She tried to nod, but couldn't seem to move. Her body was tingling and when Dante's lips pressed against her clit she couldn't stop the moan that escaped. His tongue circled it in soft, teasing flicks that made her arch against him. A finger slid inside her and she felt him moving in tandem with the vibrations in her ass. A strange yearning settled over her and she panicked, moving her head from side to side.

"Dante, no! Please—"

She felt a sharp slap on her ass and he growled. "You. Do. Not. Say. No."

The vibrations in her ass stopped and suddenly she didn't hear or feel anything. A different kind of panic washed over her this time. Had he given up on her? Was he leaving? She almost called out but then the vibrations started again, harder this time, and she felt him move the thing in her ass, pushing it further inside her. Something else touched her now, different vibrations, right on her clit. Her breath was coming in gasps, a combination of fear and pleasure weaving through her chest as she bucked against the restraints. Part of her wanted to run, but a bigger part of her really wanted to stay.

"Sweet little one." His breath was warm against her mouth, his hard body now pressed on top of hers. His hands were on her thighs, stroking and calming her, and without warning he sheathed himself inside her with one hard thrust that made her cry out. She'd never had a man his size and the pressure that mingled with the vibrations in her ass and on her clit made her tense, as if she needed more. He was rough, intense as he started to fuck her. She unconsciously jerked as her pussy stretched to accommodate his girth; he filled her to the point it bordered on pain, but each stroke brought her closer to something her body wanted. She didn't know what to do, unsure what would give her the release she desperately needed. When he pulled out a moment later, the emptiness between her legs was unbearable; she realized in that moment she was his. He was in charge, he could make her do whatever he wanted and the only relief would be to give in.

"Please," she begged. "Dante!"

He pressed himself between her slick folds, slow and smooth, until his cock disappeared into her, and watched her start to come undone.

"Dante..." Her voice was a breathy whisper as he began to plunge in and out again, his cock hitting every erroneous zone she had. He was relentless, moving harder and faster, his balls slapping against her, the vibrations in her ass intensifying. She moaned, her chest rising and falling as urgency started to build deep in her belly.

"That's it, little one." He curled his tongue around hers just as the first tremors of an orgasm made her pussy flutter and grip him tighter.

"Please!" she begged again, her hips snapping against his, the sensations overwhelming as her slickness allowed him to move effortlessly now. "Dante! Don't stop!"

He released her arms from the restraints and she instantly wrapped them around his neck, pulling his mouth back to hers. He yanked the blindfold off just as her orgasm exploded around them both. Her scream shattered the silence, her body convulsing as if it had a mind of its own. Watching him watch her was the sexiest thing she'd ever seen and he was losing control too. Their eyes locked as he slammed into her, ejaculating so hard he moved both their bodies as the cum rocketing out of him made him jerk.

He freed her legs and for a long time neither of them moved, their eyes still locked in a gaze so intense it felt impossible to look away, hearts and bodies shuddering in the aftermath of something that couldn't be put into words. His face had turned soft and loving, one hand slipping down to remove the two vibrators. He tossed them aside before running his fingers down her cheek. His lips grazed hers tenderly, causing tears to fill her eyes.

"I'm sorry," she whispered.

"For what?" He licked an errant tear. "Wasn't this what you wanted?"

She nodded miserably.

"Then why are you crying?"

"I feel ridiculous now."

"No. God, no." He rolled to the side, pulling her close. "I loved this—watching you come was the most sensual thing I've ever seen. I wish…" He broke off, shaking his head.

"I gave you everything I had tonight—you can give me honesty."

"You must read the tabloids—you know the cluster-fuck that is my life. I can't bring you into that hell, no matter how much I want you. Except here." He brought her hand to his chest. "You will always be right here."

She watched his handsome face, trying to memorize it. He'd given her something she'd thought she would never have; it should have been enough and she silently scolded herself for wanting more, for wanting *him*.

"I know you don't understand," he whispered, fingers in her hair. "But I have no choice, *querida*."

"Do you love her?"

Maybe she understood better than he thought.

He scoffed. "I'm not capable of love, little one."

She pressed her forehead to his. "I do understand. But you should understand that you are definitely capable of love, because tonight that's what you showed me."

He hated what he had to do. "Forgive me for leaving you, *querida*."

"I already have."

DID YOU ENJOY DANTE AND BECCA'S STORY?

LOOK FOR THEIR FULL-LENGTH NOVEL COMING LATE IN 2016!

GO TO www.katmizera.com or www.facebook.com/authorkatmizera

for updates on "Dante's Inferno" and other stories by Kat Mizera.

Apple Bite

By A.R. Von

The air has left my lungs; he's captured my eyes with his own. I'm trapped and I *don't* want to leave…

~*~*~

I knew exactly how I would confront him since the open house a couple of weeks ago. He's the first guy to ever make my heart stumble on its beat just from a glance and I'm twenty-three fucking years old! One would think I would've experienced something like this at least a couple of times by now.
When I found out he wasn't an attending student, but a teacher….I began to panic. I needed to think about how I could make it happen, how I could possibly make him mine without causing trouble for either of us. I *have* to have him, even if it's just for a few hours.

~*~*~

Finally walking into his classroom, I realize it's been too long since I drooled at the sight of his tall, lean, commanding male form. Two weeks is a *very long* time for a horny chick. He doesn't look much older than me, maybe twenty-five—give or take a year or two. His eyes are the brightest crystal blue, so clear one would swear you could see straight into his soul. I've seen those sin-filled eyes look both warm and cold today, as he talks to his aide—teacher's assistant or whatever they call them in college classes.

I'm assuming the hazel-eyed hot guy who's standing alongside my hot professor is about my age. This puts me in a bit of a predicament. My planned line of attack was for only him, not him plus one. I have to rethink my approach, maybe. There's no way I'm turning back now, regardless. I've never had two men before, but I *am* definitely open minded to the possibilities…

The icy cold look the professor carries is a constant and shows all others around him he means business. Fuck me; it's such a turn on!

The warmth I see from him just so happens to be only when he looks at me—at least that's what I think I see. Even though it's only been twice that I've appreciated his gaze on me, lingering on my body with a hunger I felt to the tips of my toes. Twice now, I've felt my knees weaken and my mouth run dry from just his gaze alone. He has me anyway he wants me—at least he will. All I have to do is let him know I'm his, see if he'll have me and find out the deal with Assistant Hot Stuff.

Now see why I'm currently here, in this very classroom, a class I honestly don't belong in—with the reddest apple I've ever seen sitting in my sweaty palm. I'm all ready to give it to him—the apple, I mean—for the moment, and introduce myself, but am regretting not having a second apple on hand. I rub the apple against my breast until it gleams a bit more. Looking into it, I see my reflection distorted, yet visible on its surface. This apple is going to be my hook—the *thing* that's going to bring this masculine treasure into my life and between my thighs just as I've envisioned he would be from day one! I'm a woman obsessed, determined and hungry.

I'm now seeing Professor Johnathan Sweetwater and his assistant Marcus Talent–two delicious men standing in the front of the class. Mmm, his name alone does things to me that have never been done before—both of their names affect me. It makes me wonder if the professor's taste is sweet as I imagine it would be, possibly as sweet as the ripe apple warming in my sweaty hands as I stare openly at him. As for Mr. Talent, I can't help but to wonder *what* his talents are—that's if he has any. Which I bet he does...in spades.

I imagine myself on my knees, in front of him—the professor. His slacks parted, his stiff cock pointed at my lips, begging silently for me to suck it, lick it, devour it whole until it fills me with its essence. It'll demand for me to dominate it as only a wanton woman can with her lips wrapped around it. My pussy moistens just from the thought alone, even more so when I mentally place Mr. Talent behind me—his fingers deeply embedded in my moist hot heat.

Well damn! I have to stop this train of thought or I'll embarrass myself by dripping—visibly—down my

thighs and all over the seat before I even get to talk to him and hand him my...gift.
The seats are an uncomfortable auditorium style wood, very old and worn. The possibility of a splinter is *very* high for me. I take a seat anyway. It's not as if I really have a choice if I want to get what I crave. I make sure the seat I choose is a bit close to the front of the room, but not too close. I want to be in his line of vision, so I can umm, flirt lightly—and tempt him, them—with all I have to offer. Okay, at least some of it. I also want to be sure I'll be able to see him the entire duration of the class. Get my fill before the great finish, so to speak. I'm confident this will be a sure thing. Very much so!
My hair is currently wrapped up in a tight bun, purposely done, to keep my neck exposed. I've always been told I have a sexy neck, so why not add it to my ammunition of seduction? Then again, I've also been told my hair is sexy. When loose, its chocolate waves flow down to just below the top of my ass. I hope to one day, stand before sexy Sweetwater in nothing but my hair flowing over my breasts, teasing my erect nipples with its airy strands while he—Johnathan—feasts on me with only

his eyes. That's just for starters. A warm-up if you might. From there, he'll move on with his hands. Then graduate to his lips, tongue and teeth. The thought causes me to shiver.

I'm not sure what he's into, if he has any fetishes or women types. I want to at least open up a few options I believe many men find tantalizing to explore further, so I can attract him into my enticing web of seduction. I place my hand over my mouth to smother my chuckle. I don't want to bring attention from anyone else in this room but *him*, only him. Okay, and Mr. Talent too. I don't mind if his eyes linger on me as well.

Adjusting myself more comfortably while making sure my eyes remain on my fine ass target, I place the apple on my lap. Making sure it sits in this area and when he looks my way, I can bring his attention to it right between my thighs. The part of me that craves for him to fill it, to touch, pleasure and pound as only a fervid man ravaging a woman's sex could do. I've pictured it so many times over, since the first day I saw him, and hope it's truly how he is as a lover. I would love to still feel him for days after we've fucked. Yes, most definitely.

I can't keep still; my thighs clench and I find myself moistening more and more from his smooth commanding voice. It's such a sexy voice that's bringing more erotic pictures into my mind than I can currently deal with. I don't even have any damn napkins or tissues in my bag. I have to stop thinking, for now.

The class flies by rather quickly and the students are leaving to go wherever it is they need to be. Both Professor Sweetwater and Mr. Talent are standing by the whiteboard.

I know now is the best chance to make my move. So I sit here blatantly staring at them both while they continue to glance at me with—what I believe to be—a hunger that's only present when a man wants a woman badly.

Moving my legs as sensually as I can muster while glancing at first the Professor and then Mr. Talent from under my lashes, I finally bring *his* attention to the apple I brought for him.

The professor takes a tentative step forward, moving towards me while glancing around the room and speaking softly to Mr. Talent.

I can't help but look around as well. There's one more student walking out, then it'll be just me alone with him and Mr. Talent.

The professor is coming closer and closer.

As he does, my heart speeds up to a frantic beat—a beat that only turns me on more due to its ferocity.

He's now only a few feet away from me where he pauses while still glancing at the apple. "Is that for me, Miss...?"

I smile and lift the apple from my lap to hand it over to him. "Yes...Sir. I brought it for your enjoyment. It's only a small treat for the hot professor to indulge in."

He smiles as he bends forward and takes the apple from me, "Ah, so I'm 'the hot professor', am I? What's your name, sweetheart?"

I need to stand, so I shift forward in my seat. I want to be closer to him, smell him, and taste him. I'll answer his question first, then I'll try to make some bold moves—Well, bolder moves. I answer him, but not with my real name, of course, "M-my name is Julia. Julia Strokes, Sir."

He smiles brightly at me.

His smile just pulls me in even deeper into needing him.

"Nice to meet you Julia. Is there anything else you have for me today?"

Here comes the bolder, naughtier me. "Yes, but you'll need to lock the door in order for me to give it to you, Sir. And you might also want to have your assistant leave the room..."

He looks back as if he forgot about his assistant also being in the room. He smiles and gestures for the other man to come to us.

Mr. Talent is so tall, his legs so long, that he reaches us in only a few steps. Stopping right beside the professor.

They look at one another as if silently communicating. Whatever it was that passed between them seemed to be agreed as they both faced me with sexy upturned lips. "I'm intrigued, Julia. As is Marcus. He will be staying in the room with us. That's unless you have any objections to having him here?" They both look at me awaiting my answer.

Is it greedy of me to want them both? To experience something that may never happen again in my lifetime. Nah, I decide it's an opportunity presenting itself to me for the sole purpose of me going for it.

"I'm fine with him staying," I speak softly, a touch of fear creeping up on me. Why, I have no fucking clue.

He nods his head and claps Marcus on the shoulder. "Good, very good. Go over to my desk and wait for me there—both of you. I'll be only a moment."

I—we—both do as he asks. I glance over at Marcus and ask him what's on my mind, "What should I call you? Mr. Talent? Marcus? Sir...?"

He smirks and moves closer to my side. "Marcus is fine. I love the way my name sounds coming from those full lips of yours. Please feel free to say it...often."

I gulp down my rising ardor and turn to watch as the Professor walks over and locks the classroom door. The loud 'click' reverberates through the room like a gunshot. I can't help but jump a little from the loudness of it which—in turn causes Marcus to chuckle. Both things just added more to my anticipation. The fact that I'm actually going to get *exactly*—no make that even *more* than what I crave—and the fact that it's going to happen in just moments causes my pussy to flutter in utter happiness. I'm hoping the next time it spasms it'll be with one of these fine men's tongue, fingers or cock deep within me.

His footsteps now echo in the nearly empty classroom. His eyes are a constant—from me to Marcus and back again, as he steadily approaches. The moment he gets within touching distance he pulls my top apart—no hesitation—buttons pinging everywhere.

I can't stop the gasp passing my lips. That was *very* unexpected, but I like it, a lot. It's even hotter than anything my imagination played out. Actually, none of the scenarios came close to this and he didn't even do much yet.

He glances down at my breasts held snug in my electric blue lace bra then raises his hands and—none so gently—scrapes his fingernails against each already hardened peak.

The combination of pain and pleasure that flows through me is incredible—different. I've never felt tingles on my nipples before—fuck—it's as if these perky babies are connected to my clit. The circular motion he's continuing to make is bringing me so damn close to orgasm, it's disconcerting.

He stops and just stares at me, my shirt open, my face flushed and my breathing erratic. He motions Marcus to come closer to us—to me.

Marcus does so in less than a heartbeat.

"Do you want to taste Miss Strokes, Marcus?"

"I'd love to, Johnathan." Marcus leans down and nibbles at my neck for mere seconds. Before I can react or speak, he takes my mouth like a man possessed. Sucking my tongue and lips, owning my mouth as it's never been owned before and it's hotter than fuck. Before I'm ready for him to stop, he does. Stepping back and waiting.

For what, I'm not sure. Staring at the crotch of his slacks—looking at both of their crotches, I see each has a predominant bulge that's begging me to touch them. The professor's cock looks huge and I've only seen it pushing against the fabric. Marcus' doesn't look any smaller; actually, it looks as if it might be wider than the professor's cock. My hands gravitate towards it as if in silent command. I brazenly rub my hand along its length, humming in satisfaction at its size.

I'm now boxed in between the two men. Removing one hand from Marcus, I slowly move it over to touch the professor. My, oh my! The professor *is* well endowed indeed. I'm going to enjoy the fuck out of this!

The professor tugs me from Marcus' warmth, pulling me close for his turn at kissing me.

Fuck, can he kiss too! He's taking me like a man *totally* overcome with desire. Only allowing me to rub him for a few seconds, stopping my enjoyment by placing his hand upon mine *and*—sadly so—halting our ferocious kiss. "Not so fast, Miss Strokes. First, I need you to turn around, lean over my desk facing the board and spread your legs as wide as you can while remaining comfortable." He pauses while waiting for me to obey his request—which has been only a handful of seconds. I guess I'm not quick enough for him. He quickly growls out to me, "Do it, *now*!"

I don't question anything, I just move. My body wants whatever he's—they're—willing to give me. Gentle, rough, fast, slow—anywhere and everywhere. I'm theirs for the taking. I stand there, my breasts hanging halfway out of my bra while awkwardly bent over his desk waiting for what's to come. All is silent except for a brief whisper from their low conversation and the blood thrumming loudly in my ears.

His movement is given away by the breeze against my moist upper thighs. Then a soft, tentative touch which I can tell is from Marcus, not the professor.

"Why, Miss Strokes..." The professor pauses.

I can't resist but to turn my head slightly to see what is happening behind me. What I see causes me to turn back around and bang my head—a little too painfully—on the desk. Fuck! Johnathan sucked my wetness off of Marcus' fingers. Than they kissed as if it's something they've always done, a regular occurrence. I can't help but briefly wonder if it is something they do on the norm.

The professor pulls me from my thoughts with his powerful voice, "You're all wet and ready for us. Aren't you Miss Strokes? I could just shove my cock in you with one thrust and I'll not meet a bit of resistance, only your warm welcome heat and wetness. Am I correct?"

I don't answer him. I know he's not really asking the question, he's just stating the obvious.

He has now lifted my skirt, revealing my ass for his and Marcus' eyes to take in. He begins gently stroking the creases below each cheek, humming as if he approves. Then he shocks me by tearing off my matching lace thong in one pull, tossing it on the desk right in front of me where I can see it.

They're so wet I swear they'd dry to the damn desk if we left them there long enough. Not going to happen. I'll make sure to grab them up real quick once I get what I want *and* give him what they want as well, of course. I'm not *that* greedy.

His hands journey up to my hip, lifting me so he can get to where he wants to be—my center. He bypasses my clit and glides against my dripping wet lips—teasing me at my opening, only allowing the very tip of one finger to enter me over and over again.

Is there such a thing as blue ovaries? You know, how men say they get blue balls, I wonder if it's actually possible for woman to—Grrr. I decide to get a bit bolder and push myself against his fingers so more of them will slip in—deeper and right where I need them to be. I'm sorely disappointed as he pulls away.

"Ah, now, now Miss Strokes. I'm a firm believer of punishment to those that misbehave and don't do as they're told. Unless you want me to spank your sexy milky ass red, *do not* do that again." He turns to Marcus. "Marcus, move to the front of her. Remove your cock from its confines and allow it to hover in front of her—far enough away, so she can't reach…just enough so she can see what she's missing for being naughty."

Spanked? What am I a kid? Fuck that. I begin to push up on my elbows but a firm hand lands on my lower back stopping my movements. Marcus is now in front of me, his cock so temptingly close to my lips. I can't help but to lean a bit closer to him. Then he and the professor immediately pull away from me.

I instantly miss their body's warmth against mine.

"Please Professor. I need—"

"I warned you, Miss Strokes. A fair warning, I might add. Now you face the consequences of your actions and will count for me while you enjoy the view of what you can't have. Consider the lovely view a bonus, a present if you wish..."

"Wha—?"

THWACK!

Holy fuck, he's serious and it stings!

Nothing happens and no one says anything for I don't know how long. Now I think I fucked something up.

I'm brought to the realization by Professor Sweetwater, "Miss Strokes. If you don't count, I will just start from one over and over again until you do. Right now, I'll be kind and only lay ten spanks on that pretty arse of yours. That should allow it to turn a nice shade for me to enjoy. Now count. Start at one, now!"

Thwack!

"One..."

Smack!

"Two..."

Whap!

"Three..."

I begin to feel a warm heat on my ass that's beginning to bloom into something else.

Something...naughty and I'm enjoying it just as much as my teasing—and glistening view.
Now that he's reached the end of my punishment, I actually want more. But this time I want to lick Marcus' highly aroused cock while the professor spanks me. Hmm, maybe if I do something else wrong, it'll happen? Nah, I'm not going to mess around anymore. I need someone inside of me soon and I don't want to take the chance of fucking it all up for myself.
"Very good, Miss Strokes. Now turn around and kneel at my feet. I'll be giving you your very own special treat for taking your punishment as well as you did. Marcus, come stand beside me, so you can treat her as well."
I quickly move to kneel, the cool air feeling amazing on my warmed ass. I kneel and nothing else, waiting for further instructions. I want what he's about to give me—what they're both about to give me. I don't need any more punishment, not at the moment anyway.
"Release me, Miss Strokes. Open my slacks take my cock out and taste it. There's one rule you must follow, no using your hands while you taste, only

your succulent lips and velvety tongue until I state otherwise. You start with me, and then you can taste Marcus. You wait for my say so before removing your mouth from my cock, do you understand?"

I nod my head and move to release his cock, so I can taste him. I pull his pants—along with his boxer briefs—down to his ankles, swiftly moving forward to take a tentative lick of the reddened head of his cock. It's already weeping for me and I'm happy to suckle each and every drop from him.

He's holding onto my bun, controlling my mouth's movements along his length. I'm not there for very long before he pulls me away with a string of curses.

"Now to Marcus."

I turn my body the small amount it takes to reach Marcus' cock and do to him what I've just done to the professor, having to loosen my jaw further, so I can accommodate his girth.

Marcus doesn't grab my hair as the professor did, no. He has both of his hands lightly resting on the sides of my face.

This allows me total control of *my treat* and fuck, do I love it. I breathe deep then take him deeper which causes him to groan and step away from me. A loud pop from my suction sounds then I find myself being lifted up.

"Bend back over that desk Miss Strokes," the professor tells me while donning a condom. "You'll take me in that juicy pussy of yours while you milk Marcus' cock dry with that lovely mouth of yours."

Yeah, I love the sound of that. I move faster than I thought I could. Once I'm in position, neither male wastes any time entering me. The professor makes good on his earlier threat and enters my pussy in one hard thrust.

Fuck, does it hurt so good! He stays completely still once his groin is flush with my ass. I feel a light touch under my chin and he raises it just enough so Marcus' cock reaches my mouth. Once my mouth is surrounding his dick, the professor begins to thrust. Starting off slowly, then going faster and faster. Harder and harder as if he can't control himself—doesn't want to control himself.

My orgasm is about to reach its peak. I feel Marcus' cock grow even harder between my lips. My channel tightens around the professor's cock on its own rhythm, trying to milk it for all its worth. Once I hum on Marcus' cock it seems to trigger a chain reaction.

I'm coming, my mouth is being flooded with cum and the professor is cursing up a blue streak as he climaxes too.

Fuck was that fantastic! I could go for more of this—anytime...

None of us moves for a short while, each of us trying to gain our bearings.

I break the silence with one simple word, "Wow."

Both the professor and Marcus chuckle lightly, agreeing with my one word description. Then each of us gets ourselves together. Myself, not even close to as well as the men. My top is almost button less. I have no panties and my hair came loose from its bun...at least that's a quick and easy fix for me.

Thinking quickly, I tie my shirt in the front. Revealing my abdomen—which is something I don't normally feel comfortable doing. Then I go to grab my useless, discarded panties.

Marcus snatches them away from my fingers. "Mine," he states, close to how a petulant child would.

I just shrug my shoulders unable to say anything. Only smile. At least they won't be left in the classroom or anything. I grab to rest of my things, picking up the apple that has managed to sit right on the corner of the desk and take a bite of it then hand it to the professor. "Thank you, Sir." I turn after placing the apple in his hands and give Marcus a very thorough apple flavored kiss, then walk out of the classroom without looking back.

There's nothing left to say. We all got what we wanted.

Oh, how great it is to have a husband that's a college professor and a lover that is always down to play with us. We get to play the most amazing erotic games all the time with none the wiser...

A.R. Von

A.R. was born and raised in Bronx, NY and is the oldest daughter of two girls. She holds an Associate's Degree in Computer Science and Information Technology, which was only briefly used. She's a mother of two entertaining teen boys (as well as a lovely fawn Chihuahua, whom she considers her furry daughter.)

She's also a wife to a delightfully handsome and amazingly funny man-beast. She loves anything dragon and fantasy related. In her free time, she enjoys exercising, writing, listening to music, hiking, cooking, dancing and reading. She also loves a great adventure in and out of a book!

She writes to free her mind of its constant wondering and clutter. She thrives on the fact she can share some of it with readers that have the same passion for a great story.

She loves to hear from her reader's and chat away, so feel free to reach out to her any time.

A.R.'s website: http://ar-von.com/

A.R.'s fb page: https://www.facebook.com/ARVon2

Twitter: https://twitter.com/ARVonDreamZ

WINGS of CHANGE

By

Cee Cee Houston

The night air was cold and crisp, the stars sharp bright dots scattered across the width of the heavens above me. Normally, I would say sky, but when I gazed upwards at that amazing vista of dead suns the word just came to me.

"It's so still and quiet," I whispered to myself and it was now that I had finally left the trees behind.

I heard the sound of frozen twigs snapping under the heels of my boots as I slipped slightly on the icy ground. I lowered onto my hands and knees, feeling my backpack snagging on the dead branches. I ducked my head into the gap in the hedge that I remembered from my childhood adventures here with my eccentric grandmother and her crazy tales of seeing ghosts from the past!

I pushed and wiggled in the tight space. No one had come through here in a long time. Gran had been bedridden for the last two years, and even before that, I had been at college in New York. I'd been caught up in having a normal life at last and had almost forgotten my gran's tales.

***

But then she had passed away last week and now it was just me, as my parents had died when I was a baby. Gran had raised me, and every summer we had come here to this tiny isle of Braenghar. It was barely more than the stone circle and my gran's holiday cottage. We had a boat to take us to the mainland where she lived throughout the rest of the year. Well, apart from one night late in December. Then she would leave me in the care of a neighbor. She'd always been full of life when she came home the next afternoon, but there was a lingering sadness in her eyes, which got deeper with each year.

***

After the service, an older man walked up to me. "Hello, you must be Keita Soifra?" He waited a moment for me to acknowledge him and frowned when I didn't answer. "Gunna's granddaughter?"

I tipped my head up to look into his face, which was protected from the icy rain by a wide brimmed Derby bowler hat. His eyes were strong and wise, not at all old looking, unlike his body. "Um, my name is Kay," I replied. "I've never heard that other name before."

He nodded like he understood. "Well, it's your given name." He held out a gnarled hand which had a cream colored envelope in its grasp.

"This is from your grandmother," he said softly. "There not much point in holding a reading as you are her sole heir and beneficiary."

I took the envelope and gazed down at it, then frowned as I recognized my gran's handwriting but not the name scrawled in her familiar calligraphy.

I shook my head, feeling dazed and light-headed. "I-I don't understand," I said to the man in a faint voice. He grasped my wrist in a shockingly tight fist.

"You will… later. Just follow the instructions inside… to the letter!" He doffed his hat and hurried away from me, disappearing into the large crowd of mourners milling about outside the crematorium.

I had read the letter that night and then sat and stared at it for hours. I couldn't believe what my grandmother had written. It was crazy, fantastical, like one of the stories she told me when I was a child.

'You are fated, child. You always have been, from the moment of conception until this very day. I raised you to believe the unbelievable, the extraordinary but being away from me for so long, I fear you have changed. You must remember the old days, the old places. Time is of the essence now.

Go to our circle on the island. Take my ashes, scatter them on the altar. You must do this, and

before mid-night one week after my death. There you will see him. Bond with him, and you will be free. Refuse? Child, do not refuse. This is what you were born to do. Save yourself... and him.'

What did she mean? Okay, I got the gist of it. She wanted her ashes scattered at mid-night on the 22nd of December, but the rest? I shook my head in total befuddlement.

***

I sighed in relief as I burst through to the other side of the hedges and gazed into the wide open circle of land in front of me. The tall, imposing stones jutting from the pristine snow covering the ground were like vast sentinels from another time and place.

"Remember the old days?" I said thoughtfully, reciting gran's message. "Remember the old places!"

My words seemed to hang in the air or maybe it was just the steam from my breath. I sucked in another mouthful of chilled air then watched as it re-emerged in a warm opaque cloud. I wondered what had possessed me to come here in the dead of winter

This was certainly an old place, it had been here for millennia, but what old days did she mean? The ones when she came here with me or something else?

Was this where she went when she left me all those times as a child.

I sighed sadly. "Oh, gran, why did you have to die? I miss you so much."

An owl hooted in the distance and I twisted towards the sound, then ducked and threw up my arm as something small and gray flapped above my head. A bat! I blinked and watched it swoop above the circle of stones. I stared at it and felt a shiver run down my spine and then flapped my hands as the bat came at me again. Oh god, what if it was an escaped test animal and had rabies or something similar.

"Get away, shoo, get!" I waved my arms at it wildly which did nothing to deter it.

Woot ta-whooo!

The owl sounded again, closer this time and the bat seemed to slow in its evil dance. It turned towards the sound and even though it was blind, its eyes shone in the light from the full moon. A high pitched shriek issued from above me and then a bundle of light and dark fell on the bat. I jumped and almost started running as combatants dropped from the air right towards the middle of the stone circle. Then just at the last second, the bat shot upward and flew away.

The altar that gran referred to in her letter was just a raised area in the center of the circle and that's where the owl landed. I eased from the entangling bushes and shuffled nearer to see if there was anything I could do to save it. The owl lay unmoving on the large rectangular stone. Had the bat actually managed to kill it or was it just stunned into unconsciousness from the fall?

I crept closer to the biggest of the standing stones then knelt on the ground and shrugged off my backpack. The cold snow seeped into my jeans covered knees while I kept watch. Just as I had decided that it must have died, the owl's wings flapped slightly. Then its head lifted and I swear it looked in my direction and I felt heat wash over me. That was strange enough, but as I crouched there the bird scrabbled to its feet and—changed!

Fright and a weird compulsion had me holding onto the edge of the cold stone as I clambered to my feet. My heart thudded in my chest as I prepared myself to run! From what? I didn't know and I wasn't sure I wanted to find out. Only I didn't move... I couldn't. It was as if my feet were frozen to the ground and I stared in utter fascination at what was happening out on that snowy ground.

The owl's body shimmered and grew right in front of me, making me gasp with surprise as the feathers disappeared and were replaced by... skin?

Human skin and hair... and other parts.

Suddenly it wasn't an owl anymore but a man. A tall, pale skinned man with tri-colored hair, or that's how it seemed. He was standing with his back to me but I could tell from the shape of his musculature that he was male. He was long limbed with bulging biceps, broad shoulders that tapered to a narrow waist, and a *very* tight ass. My fingers itched to run over the smooth planes of that ass.

His thighs were long and sleek, as were his calves. His feet were buried beneath the deep snow and I suddenly wondered if he was cold. God, he had to be, I knew I was and I was fully clothed.

Then, he turned gracefully towards me and I saw his face. I swallowed thickly at the stunning picture of pure manliness. His chiseled jaw jutted toward me almost as if he knew I was there watching him. But now that he was facing me, I saw his eyes were closed so he couldn't have known. Thick brown lashes that I would have given my right arm to have swept across his wide cheekbones.

My eyes wandered over his wide, firm mouth and sharp, hooked nose. He wore his long, odd-colored hair swept back from his high forehead and the edges of it just brushed his massive shoulders.

When his eyes opened, I felt my mouth part in a huge 'O' of surprise. I had never seen eyes that color on a human before. They glowed a shimmering topaz and burned directly at me. I stared in fascination for several breathless seconds before I managed to tear my gaze free. I raked my eyes over his huge pecs and rock hard abdomen. He had smooth, hair-free skin, each dip and curve of his impressive eight-pack gleamed in the moonlight.

My gaze traveled downward to the biggest cock in the world. I gasped as it twitched to life, swelling thicker and impossibly longer as he started to walk towards me with his hand out.

"Oh, shit!" I squeaked and turned to run, slipping and sliding on the slick uneven ground.

There was a flurry of muffled movement behind me and then the ground was coming up to meet me. As I was falling, two strong arms wrapped around my upper body tackling me to the ground. I tried to bring my hands up to protect my face, but it was impossible as they were trapped too. I closed my eyes as I shrieked with anger and fright at being hurt.

I braced for the impact of cold snow and rough ground, but only felt a jolt that jarred my teeth and made my jaw snap shut. Then the coppery taste of blood filled my mouth and I realized I must have bitten my tongue. After a few seconds, I cracked open one eye to have a look around. I saw only the black as velvet sky and blindingly bright stars above me.

The man must have twisted at the last second and taken the full force of us landing together. As I took a mental inventory of any aches and pains, I slowly became aware of the man's body beneath me. It was big and hard but amazingly warm too. How could he be warm when it was freezing out here?

I tensed as I readied myself to push out of his grasp but he was incredibly strong. His arms still held me prisoner. I wiggled in an effort to get him to let me go, rubbing my ass unwittingly over that huge cock I had seen.

I heard a low groan close to my ear, then felt something hard poke against my ass through my jeans and panties. Oh my god! Did he still have an erection? In these temperatures? Even though he was naked and lying on his back on the icy ground!

Why? What the heck could have gotten him so aroused?

I jerked in surprise as his arms loosened around my waist and then his hands slid up my belly to cup my breasts through my jacket. He squeezed them so hard, that even through multiple layers of clothing, I felt my nipples bead in response as if he were touching them directly. I threw my hand over my mouth to cover my shock as a whimper of need escaped from between my parted lips. This couldn't be happening. No way was I getting turned on by some weird animal/man cross-over.

I had to be imagining this! Now, that my hands were free, I rubbed my head feeling for the bump I felt sure had to be there. This couldn't really be happening, I must have fallen and hit my head and I was lying in the snowy field, hallucinating! It was the only explanation for this that I could come up with, except when my hand brushed the back of my scalp, I bumped his chin and knew I wasn't dreaming after all.

I started to wriggle and twist in earnest, finally succeeding in breaking free. For all the good it did me.

I scrambled to my feet and darted away. I'd barely taken two steps before he had me in his grasp again with my back pinned to his chest. I tried to elbow his side or step on his foot, but he somehow managed to evade each attack.

"Kieta Siofra, do not struggle."

I spun in his arms and lifted my gaze to his face. "That's not the name I go by, geez I only found out about it two days ago. I'm called Kay, not Kieta Soifra, and how do know that name anyway?" I asked with an amazed disbelief.

"Because I was there when you were born. I named you!" He said with dark seriousness.

I pushed backward out of his arms. "You... named... me?" I stammered back, as I stumbled on the slippery ground and fell on my ass. "I don't understand how you could have done that... I-I m-mean you're not e-even hu-human, are you?"

He smirked then broke into a hearty laugh, making me frown and scuttle away from him still on my backside. "I'm just as human as you are." He reached down and offered his hand to help me up, I stared at it, then reluctantly slapped mine into his much bigger palm.

"Huh? How can you be human? You were just flying a few minutes ago..." I shouted my startled question at him as he pulled me from the snowy grass. "You... you were, you are... an owl!"

He pulled me closer and squashed me against his chest. "I'm what's called a shifter."

"Uh, I-I... see," I said even though I didn't, not in the least. "I need to get out of here." I muttered and pushed uselessly against his chest.

"But, you haven't completed your task, Keita..."

I glowered at his use of my fancy name to which he nodded reluctantly. "Fine... Kay," he murmured into my ear. "Nor have I." He added cryptically.

"Task, what task? What the hell are you talking about?" My hands balled into fists as I stared into his brilliant eyes. They held a hardness and determination in their amber depths that scared and thrilled me in equal measures.

"The bonding! Gunna explained in the letter, did she not? He knew my gran's name? Oh, hell, that freaked me out and gave me a huge burst of adrenaline. Whatever he was, he couldn't possibly know the things he did. I wanted to get away from him and everything his world held. Raising my hands, I swiped them to each side of my body and broke his hold again. This time, I didn't stumble. I ran as if my life depended upon it. Maybe it did!

My head was halfway into the gap in the hedge when he caught me and dragged me back out, kicking and screaming. The sounds of my voice pierced the stillness of the night but I knew no one would hear me.

Oh, God! No one would know if he murdered me right here, right now. A panicked giggle escaped my mouth as I fought to get away. He pinned me beneath him, his weight still as heavy but now it was hot too.

"Let me go, please, just let me go. I swear I won't tell anyone." I twisted my head over my shoulder and glared at him. "It's not like they'd believe me anyway. They'd be more likely to lock me up and put me in a straight-jacket."

He grunted, whether in agreement or not, I don't know, but he rolled me over so that I was gazing up at him and still trapped beneath his hard body.

"Hey, get off me!" I squealed and sucked in a huge breath, ready to scream. That never happened because his scent invaded my nostrils and I was suddenly surrounded by the smell of trees and earth, summer sun and fresh air. My hands slid up his chest and onto his shoulders gripping them and digging my nails into the muscles as I shivered with longing.

I sucked in air and more of his enticing smell and something else, a deep, musky scent that drew me to him. Warmth rushed over my body as he stared down at me. Hs eyes gleamed with a hunger that made my heart start to race. His face came closer and closer until his lips hovered just above mine. I squirmed as heat filled my face and my breath came in short pants.

"You're so beautiful," he murmured and brought his hand to my face. His fingers traced over my eyelids and cheekbone then cupped my jaw. "I always knew you would be, but you are so much more than I could ever have imagined."

I felt my forehead crease into a frown as I gaped into his amber eyes. What did he mean? *'He always knew I would be?'* I opened my mouth to ask but he pressed his thumb to my mouth dragging it slowly along my bottom lip. Then his mouth crashed down, kissing me ferociously. He claimed my lips as his own while his tongue slid inside and twined with my mine.

Pleasure rolled over me, filling my body with a lightness I hadn't ever felt before and my questions were forgotten.

I threaded my fingers into the thick, silky hair at the nape of his neck, the long strands covering the back of my hands. He groaned into my mouth and I felt his cock move.

Want filled my core, making it ache as I rubbed my hips against his hardness, seeking a release. I tugged on his neck, pulling him closer and gasped when he nipped my lip.

His hands moved between our bodies and unbuttoned my jacket and dragging it away from my chest to my sides. His palm was startlingly cold when he slid it beneath my wool sweater. I gasped at the sting on my skin and felt my nipples harden in reaction to the chill coursing over my torso.

Then he stilled and glanced up at the sky. I followed his gaze to where it was fixed on the full moon that sent cold rays straight down at us. I blinked at how bright it was, almost blindingly white.

"We need to move Kay." His voice washed over me, sounding like water bubbling over stones.

"M-move?"

He stood up and bent to lift me into his arms. I lay against his chest as he carried me to the stone slab that he had fallen on.

"Did you bring the consecration ashes?" he asked hurriedly.

I looked up at him and jerked my face as a snowdrop fell into my eye. "W-what?"

"The ashes. We need them for the bonding," he said with an urgency I was starting to feel too. I was also starting to get hot and shrugged out of my thick winter jacket. Dropping it on the ground, I reached for my sweater and hauled it up and over my head.

"Kay." His voice lowered as he gazed at me. "So lovely." His hand skimmed over my collarbone and down to my bra. I hissed out a needy breath as his thumb traced my nipples beneath the plain white cotton. They were so hard and achy, the material felt rough against my skin. I started to take it off but his hands stopped me.

"Wait, not now, soon, Kay, soon. The time is not upon us."

Shaking my head, I tried to make sense of what he was saying. "I'm sorry. What time? How can you know what the time is? You don't have a clothes, never mind a watch."

He shook his head. "I don't need a watch. I can feel it." Then, he stared deep into my eyes. "As can you."

"I can?" I ask worriedly.

"Yes, you can. It's in your blood." He smiled like that explained everything.

"I… what?" I was so lost by what he was saying I was starting to come out of whatever fog he'd put me in. I searched the circle and sighed hopelessly when no sign of a rescue appeared. None would either. I was alone on this isle, or I'd thought I was.

"What do you want with me?" I asked and reached for my discarded sweater.

"Kay, my love, do not fear me." His urgent voice brought my eyes back to his face. "Kay, my heart. You belong here, with me. Always."

I backed away. "Look mister, I-I don't know what crazy game you are playing here, but I'm not your love or your heart. I certainly don't belong here forever! I have a life… a job… friends…"

"But, no love." He looked into my eyes and it was as if he could see my life. "Never. You have always been alone… untouched. Sacred."

"How…?" I gasped. "Sacred?"

"To me." He stepped closer and took my hands, then placed my right one on his chest above his heart. I felt the strong, steady beat of it, pulsing beneath my palm.

"I don't understand this… any of it. How do you know all these things about me? I don't know you. I-I mean do you even have a name?"

"It's Eideard."

"What's that? Your name? Is that like Gaelic or something?" I asked curiously. "Can I just call you Eddie?"

"Yes, it's Gaelic, and yes, you can call me Ed, not Eddie." He stared at me, and we seemed to hang suspended in time. I swallowed then licked my dry lips and that broke the spell. Ed groaned softly and pulled me to him. "The ashes, Kay, where are they?"

"I... do you mean my gran's ashes?" I asked, suddenly realizing that was what he meant. "But h-how do you know that she died?"

He glanced at the moon again. "Kay, we don't have time to discuss this now. I need those ashes."

"Okay, okay," I muttered and turned and pointed at the sentinel stone. "It behind that one, in my backpack."

"Fetch it, please." His tone was suddenly brusque, almost curt, but he let me go, so I did as he asked. Once at the stone, I glanced back as I grabbed my pack. He was bent over brushing the snow from the flat stone with methodical precision. Could I make another run for it? Would I be fast enough, or would those long muscular legs of his just eat up the distance between us, before I could make it through the small outcrop of trees surrounding the circle of stones.

I shook my head; it was a waste of time. He was too big and too fast, he'd proven that already. Besides...my mouth dried up as I ran my eyes over his body. I wanted him... somehow, I knew that's what this was all about. I had to give myself to him...

willingly. Maybe afterwards, he'd explain everything else?

When I returned to the center of the circle, I opened my backpack and pulled out gran's urn. I felt my hand shake as I passed it to him. He smiled in thanks, then cupped my cheek. I closed my eyes and leaned into his touch. It was more than comforting; it set off a whole host of butterflies in my belly. His hand slid away and I opened my eyes to see him facing the stone.

He raised the urn and spoke in what I could only assume was Gaelic, then he pulled off the lid, tipped the urn and scattered the contents carefully. The ashes fell in a soft cloud and when he was finished they covered the top of the stone.

When I looked closer, I saw that there was a pattern incised into the stone and the ash followed it in a soft, gray mist. The pattern looked somewhat like a tree, and strangely familiar. When I held my palm over it I felt... energy? Something very odd. I shook my head, sure that my mind was playing tricks on me.

"What now?" I asked when he turned to me.

His eyes gleamed with renewed hunger, making my core clench. "Now it is time."

"For what?" I searched his face as he reached for my bra straps and slid them off my shoulders, then he unclipped the fastening and my breasts spilled free. I shuddered and waited. His fingers ran slowly down my chest and stopped at my jeans.

"You need to remove everything. You have to be bare for the bonding."

"B-bare? What, even my boots?" I gasped. Why was I worried about my feet when the rest of me was going to be bare assed naked? He chuckled like I had amused him and I probably had.

"Yes, the boots, too. Here, let me help." He knelt quickly and undid my laces and then slipped the boot and the sock off of my right foot. I was surprised when he tucked the sock inside my boot. He did the same for the left, then undid my jeans and stripped then down my legs. I should have been freezing by now, talking through chattering teeth but I felt warm... hot even.

"So... beautiful," he said reverently.

Then Ed pushed up from the ground, trailing the fingers of his right hand up the inside of my calf, my knee, my inner thigh and stopped just below my sex. I stared at him, willing his hand to go higher. To touch me where no man had ever touched. I was shaking all over as his eyes found mine and he smiled triumphantly.

"Ed, please," I begged, desperate for him to do... something... anything.

His lips covered my mouth in a sensual kiss, drawing me closer until I sighed and sank against his chest. Only then did his fingers move and skim my outer lips, so softly it could have been a ghost. I shivered but not from the cold.

I never even noticed him lifting me or laying me down on the stone. I didn't feel the chill beneath me or how hard the stone was. All I felt or saw was Ed. His lips, his touch, his body as he lowered his to mine. I arched my back and then his fingers slid over my folds and parted them, pressing far enough inside to make me whimper and tremble. I rode those fingers like the inexperienced virgin I was. I stared into his eyes as he gazed at me with a tenderness so unexpected it brought a pang to my heart.

"More. I want more, Ed!" I pleaded, breathless with wonder and longing. He smiled at my entreaty as his mouth covered my lips in a hard, bruising, powerfully addictive kiss. I kissed him back, biting his lip in my aching need to be fulfilled.

I sighed in relief when he moved backward, kissing his way to my breasts. His tongue drew a circle around one nipple, then the other. Then his teeth grazed my sensitive skin forcing a hiss of desire from my mouth as he suckled hard. He drove me insane with that mouth and tongue as I grew wetter and more desperate to feel him inside of me.

My hips arched and I rubbed my core against his shaft, making him groan with pleasure, which reverberated inside my body. He shifted lowered to my belly dragging his fingertips along my skin. Then his hands were pushing my thighs apart. My breath hitched in anticipation but when his lips touched my folds, I trembled and grabbed his hair. His tongue flattened against me then licked upwards and my back bowed.

"YES!" I screamed in approval. Then I felt him chuckle against my slippery flesh and I answered with a sigh.

He licked my slit harder, pulling more sensations out of me until I was writhing in a delirium of longing. His tongue delved into my center and licked my juices with fervent care. I bucked beneath his expert ministrations and cried lustily as his tongue finally made contact with my clit.

"Oh… my god… Ed," I whimpered, gripping his hair tighter and pushing my clit into his mouth. He sucked and I jerked upward. "Yes! Yes! Yes!" I felt like Meg Ryan in that old movie gran used to watch. Only my orgasm wasn't pretend, it was surging inside me ready to break out. "YES!" My body convulsed, twisting back and forth on the hard surface.

Ed's eyes burned with pride when he lifted his head and gazed up at me from between my thighs. I gazed back with my heart in my mouth.

"My love." He whispered the endearment with a smile.

"My heart." I whispered back, making his smile even bigger.

Then I felt it. His cock at my entrance, seeking admittance. "Yes, Ed. Yes, take me. Make me yours."

"Mine!" He echoed and his eyes lifted to the sky. I tipped my head back to follow his gaze. The moon was even brighter and shone straight down at us. "Now…" He entered me in one strong thrust.

I screamed, expecting pain, but it never came. Heat blasted from my body as pleasure surged to my extremities, swirling around in a maelstrom of sensations. I cried out in rapt delight.

"Ed! Ed!"

His teeth sank into my neck hard enough to draw blood. I hissed sharply from the sting of his bite.

"Shh, mark me." He instructed, lifting my hand to my neck. I stared at him as he used my blood and fingers to mark the skin above his heart.

"Your turn," he said softly and leaned close so that I could bite his neck. I wasn't sure I could do that but then he dug his nails into my hips. I squealed with the pain and snapped my teeth shut over his skin.

The coppery taste of blood dripped onto my tongue and I jerked back. Blood leaked from his neck.

"Oh, god, I'm so sorry!" I gasped, shocked to have hurt him so badly.

He smiled, then gave me his hand. I took it and smeared his finger in my blood, then he rubbed our joined hands over my heart, marking a mark just as I had done.

His smile was predatory as he lowered his chest to mine, pressing our bodies together. Then he started to move, pumping his hips rapidly as his cock sank in and out of me. His fingers tunneled into my hair as he began kissing me so hard I could barely breathe.

Our bodies slammed together as he pounded into me, getting faster and harder. I screamed with the need to come, locking my arms and legs around him, jerking my hips up to meet each of his thrusts. His head lifted and he stared down at me with an almost feral look in his eyes.

"Mine," he grunted as his body tightened and he rammed into me so deep I was sure there would be a hole in my back. It hurt and I winced with the pain. His eyes softened when he heard my whimper of discomfort. "Sorry. I got carried away."

He moved slower for a few seconds until the pain eased and I cupped his jaw. "I'm okay, really."

"Good," he murmured and ran a hand down my stomach and between my legs. His thumb found my clit and flicked it gently making me gasp. I worked my hips, circling around his thumb and within a few minutes my body was on the verge again.

"I'm going to come!" I cried and clutched his neck. "Ed… I'm going to come."

"No, wait." He stopped and quickly pulled out, making me whimper with regret at his loss. "Get onto your hands and knees," he urged softly.

I looked up at his face warily. He smiled to show there was nothing to fear, so I slowly changed position.

His fingers smoothed over my shoulders, down my back to my ass and cupped my bottom in his big hands. He made my backside feel small even though I knew it wasn't. I trembled as his fingers found my pussy and stroked it over and over until the hardness of the stone beneath me was forgotten. I felt his thighs brush against mine and then his cock was sliding between my buttocks and into my slippery folds.

"So hot... so wet," he praised me. "So... tight."

"Oh, Ed... you feel so good!" I shuddered from the words he murmured in my ear, then arched my back as he licked the shell then nipped at the lobe. He pounded into me harder and harder as I thrust my ass in the air. His hands fisted in my hair as he leaned back and pulled me up against his chest. I could feel every single thick inch of him in this position. He was so big, so thick and I loved it. My juices flowed out of my core and slid down my thighs.

"So wet, I can feel you all over me," he muttered. "So tight, you hold me in your caress. Ride me, Keita, take me, all of me."

"Oh, Ed," I thrust my ass into his hips as hard as I could. "I'm coming."

"Yes, my love, now, come for me now." He groaned lustily.

My body thrashed in a convulsive climax. As he tensed, the muscles in his arms became like iron bands as they held me up and he pumped his hot seed inside me. I whimpered as it filled my channel and set off an aftershock that made my inner walls clench around his thick shaft.

"Mine, Keita. Forever." He released me carefully and I dropped down onto my hands then a sharp pain between my shoulder blades made me round my back. Ed stroked his hand over me.

"Don't fight it, my love," he said gently. "Let them free."

"What?" I gasped as a bone crushing pain shot through me. I dropped to the stone and curled into a ball feeling as if my body was getting smaller and my bones were breaking. I closed my eyes and my fingers clamped into fists but my nails were so sharp I had to loosen them.

"Ed," I croaked. What did that sound like? A bird's cry? Not my voice! I shook my head and tried to sit up, but my hands weren't working. They must have become numb from kneeling so long. I stuck my arms out and flapped them wildly trying to get the feeling back into them.

Suddenly, I felt as light as a feather and opened my eyes to see the ground far below me. I shrieked with fear but all I heard was an owl's cry.

Follow me –

Goodreads –

https://www.goodreads.com/author/show/13493975.Cee_Cee_Houston

Facebook –

https://www.facebook.com/AuthorCeeceeHouston/?fref=ts&ref=br_tf

Lunar Gets Some Loving

A Purian Empire Short

By Crystal Dawn

Lunar Gets Some Loving

His second, fifth, and sixth officers were off duty. He needed them to be rested so they could take over when he and the others went off duty. That's when they would be needed. When they were aboard ship, twelve-hour shifts were common. It wasn't like there was much else to do. He had ten thousand personnel on his ship but less than three percent were female. There were a possible three hundred and eighty-two happy males on board, unless some females doubled up, which he had heard some rumors of. The rest of his males were aggressive and ready to blow after several lunar cycles in the outer edges of the known worlds. If they survived this trip, he would have to look for a place where his males could find some relief.

Colonel Lunar was looking for a way to blow off some steam himself. Lt. Evory was looking good for a night or two. She wasn't a female he would consider for a long-term relationship but he didn't really do long-term anyway. Someday, he might find his mate but until then he was a male with a male's needs. The mate he wanted someday was one of the reasons he hesitated to dip his wick in a local spot. The problem was they had been out for so much longer than usual and he thought his cock might fall off from the blue balls he carried around with him.

Lt. Evory was bending over, unnecessarily picking up an item she had probably dropped on the floor purposely. Lunar wasn't the only one staring at the cheeks of her ass where the bottoms showed under her barely there panties. He held his breath as his cock hardened while she lingered in a bent over state. It was something an officer could get reprimanded for, but he had to admit he'd enjoyed the show.

Maybe he should require the females to wear pants instead of allowing them the choice between pants and skirts. He'd always enjoyed the view immensely since the female crew members were attractive, each in their own way. They had a variety from short to tall and almost boyish to curvaceous. While they were all attractive, none had turned out to be his mate. Glancing at his com, he saw he had only minutes to go before his replacement would arrive. Maybe some self-help in the shower would take the edge off. Damn, his hand was tired of doing the deed but he had no choice.

His second came to take his place looking relaxed and happy. The SOB was fucking one of the sergeants in weaponry. She was an Amazon with a high sex drive according to the rumors spread by past lovers. If he didn't look satisfied something would have been very wrong. It was almost enough to make him reconsider his personal rules but he didn't want his ship littered with former lovers. Sometimes that could cause embarrassment and ill will among the crew, not to mention problems once he found his mate.

Lunar went over everything with Scott quickly so he could get away. All over the bridge his people were switching off duty as their replacements arrived. It was hard on all of them since they did twelve on and twelve off without a day off in cycles. They were on a high watch level with the neighboring empire threatening the peace. He wasted no time getting to his suite. His job was that of a captain, even though his rank was higher, so he had the second best room on the ship. The best was reserved for high ranking visitors like the Emperor or ambassadors.

As soon as the door to his suite closed he began to strip while he walked to the bathroom. He breathed a sigh of relief as his cock popped free from its fabric prison. It was purple and hard as a rock from the need that had grown until it was like a volcano about to erupt. Turning the water on, no sonic shower for him, he decided to wait a moment until it was warm before stepping under it. A sound caught his attention and he considered getting out of the shower to see what was going on but decided it must be someone out in the hall. If they were knocking they would have to wait until he handled his personal needs before they had a chance to talk to him.

Taking himself firmly in hand, he stroked from root to tip closing his eyes to fully enjoy it. A scent hit his nose; female! His eyes opened in shock as he took in Lt. Evory standing right in front of him, naked as the day she was born. How had she gotten in? She reached out grabbing his cock and dropped to her knees. As her lips wrapped around his thick length, he decided to wait until later to punish her. She sucked in hard, hollowing her cheeks as she sank all the way to the base. Unable to prevent it, he groaned his pleasure.

The female was talented and she sucked the seed out of him in moments, even though he tried to hold back to enjoy it longer. His shaft was still thick and hard, his need barely dimmed. She jumped to her feet and threw herself on him. Her arms wrapped around his neck as his hands grabbed her ass cheeks, squeezing them and holding her against him. Sliding her around he inserted his length fully inside her and she moaned in delight. Turning so she was pressed firmly against the shower wall he began to bump and grind against her. He devoured her mouth as she rode him. His cock went deep into her hot, wet folds as he drove harder, deeper, and faster.

Water splashed on them but it was sweat that beaded on his forehead from his exertions. His balls itched to dump their load and he felt a tingle run down his back signaling his coming release. A growl broke free as he stiffened. Evory dug her nails into his back as she let out a sound like a scalded Scurcat. Her body clasp around his, the muscles of her channel squeezing him like a vise. There was no way he could hold back another second.

Hot, white ropes of cum filled her greedy pussy which sucked it up like a desert absorbed rain. It amazed him that not one drop rolled down the inside of her thighs. Even though he shot out a large load of cum, his underused cock still didn't go down any noticeable amount. The bitch was here and wanted to be used, so he would wear out that already well-used pussy before he sent her on her way. Once her channel quit grabbing his shaft, he loosed his hold on her, letting her slide down his body.

The blonde-haired orange-eyed Thomasiny grinned with satisfaction; she was enjoying Lunar putting the meat to her. He could admit he was enjoying it too and as long as she had no expectations they would be fine. Getting out of the shower, he dried off then threw her the towel to dry off too. Lunar was just getting started. Once she'd dried off, he pulled her out to the bedroom and pushed her on the bed. On her hands and knees in front of him, she was positioned for what he had in mind. Kneeling behind her he pushed her legs apart then drove into her. She slammed back against him, hungry for more.

The greedy wench couldn't get enough. He squeezed her small breasts, pinching her nipples until she moaned with pleasure. This was a female that liked a sting of pain with her delight. Maybe even more than a sting, but that was all she would get from him. Lunar impaled her on his impressive length over and over. There was no problem holding out longer and fully enjoying the ride this time. Moving his fingers to her clit, he strummed it like a finely tuned instrument. Her keening warned him she was about to explode. That was alright because he was near his bliss as well.

She screeched loud and long as she found her release, making his ears hurt but not enough to interfere with his climax. He pumped into her several times before he was dry. Now he rolled her over and his hand brought his staff back to full attention in just a few strokes. He was in this with her and he would get every bit of pleasure out of her before he evicted her from his room. How she got in here was another mystery to be solved later.

With her on her back, he rolled over on top of her. Hooking her legs over his arms he pushed her knees even with her ears. Now she was spread out beneath him. He impaled her on his impressive shaft, sinking balls deep inside her. Lunar pumped in and out furiously. His body became slicked with sweat as he pounded her pussy hard and deep. She moaned enthusiastically and he'd bet she would be sore tomorrow but he didn't care. The female was getting just what she wanted.

Thomasinies were an especially lusty race. Evory was one of the lustiest of them all, taking care of more than her fair share of his crew. Were it not for the intensive medical care, birth control and vaccinations against most known sexually transmitted diseases, he wouldn't touch her. She had targeted him when she first came aboard his ship but he had resisted her at every attempt until now. Being stuck out on patrol for several cycles, something unheard of before all the border skirmishes, had taken its toll on his resistance. He had a feeling regardless of her reputation and the large number of lovers she had, she would have expectations now that she was fucking him.

He drove in harder drawing another moan out of her and pushing her over the edge. Her pussy squeezed his cock hard, pulling out his cum in streams. Admittedly it felt wonderful after being denied his pleasure for so long. Rather than fall on top of her, he fell to the side to take a moment's rest; Evory didn't like it. She rolled over wrapping her lips around him once more. Lunar was a Garonian and they were pretty lusty themselves but they were also picky. Okay, they were usually picky and Evory wasn't his type. It was just being denied so long was hard on a male. Someday he would have his mate, his fated other half, but for now he had to sate himself with whatever female was handy.

Lunar groaned lustily as Evory sank all the way down his shaft to his base, swirling her tongue along the vein on the underside of it. It felt heavenly bringing him close to shooting his load but he held back as long as he could. Her hands grabbed his balls gently but firmly massaging them. Whatever else he had to say about this particular Thomasiny, she certainly knew how to use her mouth and hands expertly. She hollowed her cheeks as she drew back from the base working her way to the tip of his cock pulling all his semen out. This time his dick deflated and would need time to rise to the next occasion. Resting, he would wait until he could service her one more time before he sent her on her way. That would only be fair since she had given him such good service.

He drifted off for a short while as he rested. Once he was done with her he was sure he would sleep like a baby. It was hard to stay awake as it was. Jerking awake, he glanced at his clock, noting it had only been a short time. Evory had fallen asleep, worn out by her exertions. Maybe he should be grateful but he didn't even particularly like the female. She was a high maintenance kind of lover, which was the last thing he needed. The rumor was the chief of the mechanics was in love with her. That didn't seem to slow her down any. If she cared about that male at all, it didn't show.

All he knew for certain right now was he needed to wake her to finish this tryst so he could get some sleep before his next shift. They were headed to a zone that was unstable. Their presence would hopefully calm things but lately they'd had the opposite effect on the nearby Grecians. Lunar thought it was a sign that war was headed their way. Meanwhile, he'd best wake her. Reaching over he shook her lightly. She rolled over away from him unwilling to wake.

"Evory!" He spoke in his colonel voice.

He hid his smile when she jumped and fell out of bed. Lunar wasn't being mean because it was really funny. She jumped to her feet. "Sir?"

"You're awake," he observed with a smile. Stretching out on the bed with his cock pointed to the ceiling, he motioned for her to come to him.

Enthusiasm radiated from her as she rushed around to his side of the bed and climbed onboard. Holding his cock to guide it, she slid it right in because she was slippery from their previous bed play. Evory paused a second once he was fully seated, no doubt enjoying the full feeling he gave her. She started to rock, rolling her hips at the same time. He couldn't deny it felt amazing. The female was good at sex, but to him it was nothing but sex. Her speed picked up as she rocked harder. His body came alive as energy and pleasure flowed through him.

Both their bodies were slicked with sweat and he held out long enough that she was breathing heavily. He could tell she was about to climax since the muscles of her channel were gripping him harder. Her moans were louder as her body moved faster. Evory erupted in a flurry of motions, screeching louder than ever before. She jerked hard as her muscles tightened around his shaft pushing him over the edge as well. Hot cum poured out of his cock filling her channel. This time some dripped out onto her inner thighs.

Once they were both passed the throes of their climax, Evory dropped down on him, embracing him like a lover. He pushed her off of him and got up. It was time to send her on her way, take a shower, and get some sleep. "It's time for you to go now."

"Why? I thought perhaps you would want me to stay. We both know there is a shortage of females onboard. You enjoyed this time we spent together. This is something we could do every night. Your place is big enough for two."

"No."

"No? It is a big place." She spoke hesitantly, as if she couldn't understand what he meant.

"No, I don't want you to move in here. It was enjoyable, but it's not going to happen again."

"But you liked it. I know I'm not ugly and I know how to please a male. I know how to please you."

"I didn't say you didn't. I said it's not happening again. How did you get in here anyway?"

"You left the door open."

"We both know that's not true. It locks automatically."

She shrugged and started to get dressed. It looked like she wanted to keep her secrets. Lunar would find out eventually. Evory strutted to the door shaking her ass like it would change his mind. It didn't. When she opened his door, she turned to give him one last chance. The look in her eyes said it all. Lunar shook his head. As she walked out all he felt was relief. It was good that she had gone. He was a little surprised she had left so easily.

He turned to walk back to the shower. Now that she was gone and he was alone he felt the need to get clean. Setting the water temperature as hot as he could stand, he stepped under the water before he got some soap and lathered up. His sexual appetite was sated for now so no need to jack off. That would be needed plenty later if they stayed out on patrol.

Standing under the steady stream of water he relaxed and wondered when he would find his mate. Sometimes he could almost imagine what she would look like but the vision would disappear. His kind didn't always recognize their mates right away, but after being around the females onboard for months there was little doubt that none of them were his. Some of his kind found mates among their own kind but lately more were finding them among the other races they mixed with.

It made him wonder if his mate would be a Thomasiny like Evory, a human like his second, or even a Yukonder like his third. With hundreds of races in the known worlds and others not yet known that were being discovered all the time, the possibilities were endless. When he'd been a youth, he'd enjoyed his sexual liaisons. Now he was older and he found that he wanted his mate. He'd seen many of his kind mated and there was something exciting about watching the interactions of fated mates. They were just so damned happy.

Tomorrow he would deal with Lt. Evory and they would head into potentially hostile territory. Tonight he would get some sleep and hopefully dream of his destined other half, wherever she might be. He got out of the shower, dried off, and went to bed. Sleep found him as soon as his head hit the pillow. Dreams followed soon and his future played out in them. He would remember nothing when he woke but he would be rested.

crystal_dawn_author@aol.com
amazon.com/author/crystaldawn
http://crystaldawnauthor.wordpress.com
http://www.youtube.com/watch?v=94o8Yy0dcEo
http://www.facebook.com/pages/Crystal-Dawn/378841472210002
twitter.com/crystaldawnauth
www.tsu.co/crystalauthor
thebookreviewsblog.tumblr.com
https://www.facebook.com/books2revue
https://www.goodreads.com/author/show/976311.Crystal_Dawn
https://app.mailerlite.com/webforms/landing/h9z1q5

Disclaimer:
Any resemblance to persons living or dead are strictly a coincidence. While some actual places may be named, they are used only in the context of imaginary events. The story is strictly created from the author's imagination and all of the events are fictitious

Deployment – Dalliance

By

EJ Christopher

Four times. Four damn times she'd been sent to the Middle East. Jessie loved her country, loved being in the military, but there was honestly a limit to the amount of time in the sandbox that people could handle. She'd lost friends to suicide bombers and suicide, she'd seen relationships falter and disintegrate. On the other hand, she'd made numerous new friends and actually stood at a couple of weddings. Deployments sucked but Jessie had to admit they did have their good points, too.

Jessie sighed to herself as she helped the rest of her unit unload duffle bags from the underbelly of the plane. It was hot and cramped, but they quickly formed an assembly line and before long the duffles and rucks for a couple hundred soldiers and Marines were on the blacktop. Fortunately, someone had the foresight to keep the gear separate first by military branch, then by unit. Jessie found her gear, fell in with the rest of her unit, then played the hurry-up-and-wait game.

They were a Quartermaster unit - they supplied gear to the other people who needed it so the odds of any of them seeing any type of combat or anything were very low, but that didn't mean they didn't get a lot of the same training. Jessie glanced around at her comrades - some were playing cards, others - the newer guys - were reading the cultural pamphlets and quick guides, a few were on their laptops (probably watching porn, she smiled to herself), but most of them slept. Damn near 24 hours on a plane and even though she slept for most of it, Jessie thought the soldiers checking their eyelids for holes had the right idea. She leaned against her bag, pulled her cap over her eyes, and dozed off.

It wasn't long before a caravan of MRAPs and Rhinos pulled in. Everybody rousted their friends, reformed the assembly line, and got the gear all loaded onto the vehicles. After a quick headcount, they were off, headed to the Green Zone - or what was left of it. The U.S. had been steadily handing control of Baghdad back to the Iraqis, which mean that, with any luck, there would be no reason for troops to be there.

Jessie listened as her comrades spoke quietly amongst themselves, comparing the current climes to their last trip over. Some of the more 'seasoned' vets were regaling the newbies with tales of what to expect during their time there. It wasn't long before the topic of discussion was the infamous 'desert goggles' and everyone was joking and placing bets about how long people would last before others in the group would start to wear them.

The young woman just grinned and shook her head. She'd have been lying if she said she hadn't messed around on any of her previous trips, but she managed to keep the same standards in men here as she did in the States. She'd never had a fling with a married guy and she never had a fling with anyone that, after she got home, she looked back and thought, "What in the actual FUCK was I thinking??"

A young PFC met them as they disembarked from the vehicles. After grabbing all of their gear, she escorted them to a huge tent and apologized, explaining that they would have to sit through a lot of the same PowerPoint stuff that they saw before they left the States. There was a collective groan and a lot of eye-rolling, but for Jessie and the other 'old pros', this was nothing new. As was expected, dozens of chairs were set up toward the back of the tent, facing a projection screen. Jessie grabbed a seat in the middle and did some people-watching while waiting for the show to begin.

In addition to the usual military folk, there were quite a few people in civilian attire - nothing out of the ordinary since civilian contractors had to go through a lot of the same in-processing as military personnel. Also, there were some of the intel folks who were authorized to travel in civvies. Jessie's eyes zeroed in on one such person - she couldn't be certain whether or not he was military since the intel guys were allowed to disregard the regs when it came to their appearance. This guy, though....

He was about six feet tall and the blue from his polo shirt made the blue in his eyes pop even in the dim lighting of the tent. The sleeves were snug against his biceps and his pecs were well-defined against the cotton material. His jeans left little to the imagination, clinging to the curve of his ass and hugging his thighs. His hair was dark brown (or maybe black) and longer than regs allowed by barely brushing the tops of his ears. He very much reminded Jessie of one of those guys who, if in a bar, was being hit on by every chick in the place. To say he was hot was an understatement.

"I wondered when you'd see him," her friend Alex said, nudging her shoulder. This was Alex's second time to the desert and she and Jessie had bunked together the last time. They got along very well, which came in handy when either of them wanted to have a discreet dalliance. They gave each other privacy when it was requested and they covered for each other whenever anyone asked questions.

"He is a looker, isn't he?" Jessie said, giving the man another hungry appraisal before turning back around. "He'll make the women very happy wherever he winds up, that's for damn sure."

"What, you don't think he was lucky enough to win an all-expenses paid trip to sunny Baghdad?" Alex laughed.

"I wouldn't be that lucky," Jessie smirked. She leaned back in her seat and talked to Alex about what was probably going to be covered. "Death by PowerPoint," she laughed, and she was almost right.

Four hours and countless slides later, they were released for the day. The next three days were more of the same - paperwork, cultural sensitivity training, more paperwork, PowerPoint presentations, more paperwork - punctuated by meals, PT, discreet naps, and the occasional sighting of the still-unnamed hottie.

Jessie and Alex spent their downtime doing what soldiers do - going to the gym, watching bootleg movies, checking out whatever show the USO had booked, and sleeping. Jessie knew that some of the guys in the unit were already busy getting their freak on - some of them decided to see how many different girls they could fuck while they were deployed, some of them just wanted to take care of the itch that Rosie Palm and her five sisters couldn't quite scratch. Jessie's mindset was if anything came along, she wouldn't turn it down, but she wasn't going to actively look for a roll in the sheets. After they'd spent a total of nine days at the in-processing station, they packed up their gear and made their way to Baghdad.

The first week at their new post was spent with the outgoing unit, learning the ins and outs of the job. More importantly, it was spent learning the outgoing personnel's contacts - who could get you what and what kind of favors they looked for. That was the thing about being in a supply unit - you had access to a lot of stuff other people wanted and that could be used to get you stuff that other people needed. It was a little harder to do in the States with checks and balances and all, but Jessie knew how the game was played. Especially over here.

The second week was spent with the old unit tying up loose ends and getting ready to go home. They were technically supposed to stick around to make sure Jessie and her fellow soldiers were familiar enough with the job to seamlessly take over for good, but she knew that kind of thing seldom, if ever, happened. The person training Jessie, though,

Aravelo,, said he had very little to ship back, so he was in the supply cage quite a bit, making sure she knew who to call for things she'd need.

One day, she and Aravelo were taking inventory, getting ready for her to sign for the things she'd be responsible for, when they heard a tentative voice call, "Hello?" They looked at each other and Aravelo nodded for her to attend to whomever had walked in.

"Yes? Can I help you?" Jessie rounded the corner and saw Tall Dark and Handsome standing at her counter. He was wearing another polo shirt - beige - and a pair of Dockers. She had to really fight to keep from rolling her eyes when he smiled and showed off a perfect set of gorgeous white teeth. *Could this possibly get any more cliché?* she thought to herself. *Tall, gorgeous, perfect teeth... seriously, it's like something out of a damn predictable romance novel or something.*

"Hey, I just transferred in and was told that you were the person I needed to talk to to, uh, well...." TD&H nervously rubbed the back of his neck and smiled sheepishly at Jessie.

"To...? Get 'things?'" Jessie smirked as she did the air quotes.

"Yeah. Things." TD&H shrugged. Jessie thought his cheeks were turning a bit pink.

"Well, I have a lot of 'things'," Jessie said, waving her arms around the cage. "What kind of things are you looking for?"

The man stuck his hands in his pockets and said, "Well, I need things to use to barter with the locals."

"Ah," Jessie said, grinning broadly. The mystery man worked in the intel sector - using cash and goods to get information. She'd dealt with this kind of thing before. "Well, you know the forms I need and if there's something I don't have, I'll have to see what I can do."

"Right. Forms. I knew that," he said, shaking his head. "RIght now, I'm just familiarizing myself with where everything is, so...." He gave another small shrug.

"Well, I'm Jessie," she said, offering a handshake. "Sergeant Mills, if you have to be formal about it."

"I deal with enough formality on the job. Jessie is fine. I'm Zane." His handshake was firm and Jessie would have sworn that she felt him rub his thumb along her hand.

"Zane. Pleasure to meet you," Jessie said quietly. *Is it me or did it just get hot in here... Jesus, he's just shaking my hand!* "I'm still learning the ropes, but I'll do what I can to help you out. Provided you have the proper forms and stuff."

"Right. Well, I'll see you around." Zane looked at their hands for a moment before (reluctantly?) pulling away. He gave her another smile before turning to walk out.

She heard Aravelo clear his throat from behind her. "I worked with the guy he's replacing," he said, pushing himself off of the cage. "Damn shame."

"Shame? Why? What happened?" Jessie had a feeling she might already know - same thing that happened to a lot of people here, especially the ones who dealt directly with the locals.

"His convoy got ambushed," Aravelo shrugged. "He had only been here about 2 months, too. These guys rotate out every 6 months so they don't burn out. Their job is pretty stressful."

"I can imagine," Jessie murmured, looking at where Zane had walked out. She'd worked with intel people on her previous deployments, though not near in the direct capacity she'd have on this trip.

Two days later, Aravelo and the rest of his unit shipped out to start their journey home, leaving Jessie, Alex, and the rest of the new guys to pick up where the old unit had left off. They were kept busy, making sure all of the incoming units had what they needed and the outgoing units turned in what they were supposed to. The monotony of the day was broken up by visits from the various intel people, including Zane.

Zane would show up - sometimes with a partner, but usually alone - hand over his forms, get what he needed, and make a little small talk before he left. As the days, then weeks, went by, he would linger a bit longer, their conversations delving into home life and downtime activities. It wasn't long before the flirting began and their conversations took on a more personal tone. They'd bump into each other at the mess hall, where he'd lean closer than he had to when reaching for something. Or the gym, where he'd press against her as he squeezed past to get to the weights. At first, she chalked it up as an extension of the flirting they did but as it continued, Jessie would find her breath catching in her throat and she'd have to bite her lower lip to keep from whimpering. To make matters worse, she made the mistake of telling him what her favorite cologne was and the bastard started wearing it. All. The. Time.

Jessie gave as good as she was getting, though. She'd run her fingers over Zane's hand when he was signing for things or press her chest against his back as she would squeeze by him in line at the PX. She never knew, though, if she was having the same effect on him that he was having on her. She did know that she wanted to fuck this man in the worst way possible before he left.

About four months into the deployment, Zane invited her to the weekly poker game that he and his buddies had. He casually mentioned, too, how strict his unit was about the military's fraternization policy. Jessie wasn't sure what his point was because immediately after, he brushed his hand across her breast while reaching for some silverware. If everything thus far had been heavy flirting, she was ok with that. Disappointed, but okay. She'd continue to follow his lead, though - as long as he flirted, she'd give it right back.

Jessie frowned when Zane explained that attire for the games was civilian. She explained that she didn't have any civvies - she and the rest of her unit, hell, pretty much everyone in the Green Zone, were supposed to be in some type of uniform at all times.

"Well, the PX sells civvies. And you can order something from the internet. You can wear your PT uniform there and change in my room or something. But if you'd rather just wear your PTs because you don't want to get in trouble, I'm okay with that."

Jessie nodded and Zane said he'd pick her up that night around 7 - time for her to lock up the cage, get some chow, and change from her duty uniform to her PTs. She didn't realize she had a grin plastered to her face until Alex said something about it.

"So... you look like the cat that just ate the canary. Spill," her roomie said as they walked back to the barracks.

Jessie explained about the poker game. "I was hoping that maybe I'd finally get some action out of that man, but then he turned around and said about how his unit really enforces the 'no fraternization' thing."

"Yeah, but you guys aren't even in the same unit. That policy shouldn't apply," Alex stated.

"And you obviously weren't paying attention to the in-briefs when we got here. No sex here. Period. Anyone getting caught is risking an Article 15. It's just that some units have leadership that understand human needs and are a bit more lax about enforcing it. Zane's unit apparently is not like that," Jessie sighed. "Maybe I can get him to come here or we can squeeze in a quickie in the cage or something."

"Oh, not the cage. I mean, the Captain said he didn't want to know what we did in our spare time. You'd be taking a huge risk doing anything there," Alex disagreed.

Jessie knew her friend was right. There had to be something she could do, though. She loved the flirting and the physical contact and she'd been hoping it would lead to something more physical. She really didn't want all of it to be a dead end.

Zane was prompt and the ride to his unit's compound was innocent - Zane couldn't travel alone so there was someone else in the car. Once they arrived, introductions were made, beer was offered (which Jessie had to regretfully decline), and cards were dealt. Zane sat across from her, occasionally running his foot over hers and up her leg. She returned the favor as discreetly as she could, again letting Zane take the lead.

She was one of the final three people in the game, outlasting even Zane, who'd bragged about his poker skills (and then said his loss to Jessie was 'beginner's luck'). She didn't win, though, and said her goodbyes as Zane rounded up someone else to travel with them back to Jessie's unit.

The next several weeks went like that - the usual flirting, the poker games, the reminders about how Zane's unit didn't play around about them having sex while deployed. Jessie did break down and buy a couple pieces of civilian attire from the PX. She'd throw them in a bag and change in Zane's room prior to the game starting, then change back to her PTs for the ride back. And finally, she decided she would get a new outfit just to wear to torture Zane.

She ordered everything online - hip hugger shorts from one place that barely covered her ass, a bustier from another, and a pair of sandals to tie everything together. When everything arrived, she tried it on and Alex let out a whistle. "Girl, if that doesn't get him in you, I don't know what will," her friend stated. "Seriously. That shit is hot. I'm getting turned on and I don't swing that way."

Jessie laughed and folded everything up, carefully placing it in her bag, thankful that it had all arrived in time for that night's game. She kept smiling to herself as she waited for Zane to pick her up and when he asked what she was smirking about, she simply said, "Oh, nothing. Just some stuff I got in the mail today."

She followed Zane to his room and quickly changed. Jessie didn't mess with make-up or anything like that. The point of the outfit was to get a reaction out of Zane - one that would hopefully end with the two of them fucking. She couldn't help but grin, too, when she walked out of his room and saw the look on his face; 'reaction' was an understatement.

"You... wow... you look... just... damn," he sputtered, his jaw agape.

"You like?" Jessie did a slow turn in front of him.

"Very much," he growled and took a step closer. Just then, one of his buddies poked his head around the corner to remind them to hurry up. Jessie gave Zane an innocent smile and sauntered out ahead of him to the common area where she was greeted with several whistles and comments about how she needed to dress like that more often.

The poker game was long and torturous. Zane made sure to sit next to Jessie - something he never did before. His hand would squeeze her thigh, his fingers gradually making their way further up her leg. When she'd head to the kitchen for another drink, Zane would follow shortly behind, standing close behind her, brushing his nose along her ear and neck but never saying a word. It didn't help any that he was wearing that cologne that just drove her nuts, either.

When Jessie finally lost all of her chips, she waited until the end of the hand to nudge Zane and tell him it was time for her to head back. He followed her back to his room, making several comments under his breath about the view. He reached around her, opening the door for her and taking a chance to let his hands briefly wander over her body. He finally stood aside and as Jessie walked past, she grinned at him slyly and said, "Would you like to stay & help me change?"

She had a feeling he'd say no, so she wasn't surprised when Zane sighed quite audibly and said, "As much as I would love to, I can't. The guys will start asking questions."

Even though she knew that would be the answer, she couldn't hide her disappointment, especially after the mini grope-session he just had. Still, she slid up to him, running her fingers along his bicep and he flexed just a bit, enough to make her shiver and smile. "Come on, you know you want to," she said, her voice husky with want. She looked up at him and raised an eyebrow and started to lift her shirt.

Zane's jaw flexed and his eyes darted for the door. For the briefest moment, Jessie thought she'd finally get to score with the intel hottie who'd been haunting her dreams. Instead, he cleared his throat and blushed just a little. "I shouldn't," he stammered and walked out the door.

Jessie watched his retreating figure with confusion and frustration. He'd always been so confident and assertive when they talked and flirted, always taking the lead, and now he seemed awkward and shy, even.

Jessie turned back around, sighing. *Damn it! I knew he'd say no, but I thought I'd get more out of him than that*. She lifted the bustier over her head and felt someone grab both of her wrists over her head and a hand went over her mouth.

"Shh," she heard Zane whisper. "I am going to have you. Right here, right now. But you have to be quiet, these walls are thin." Jessie nodded and Zane moved his hand from her mouth to her breast. He massaged the smooth flesh, pinching the nipple between his thumb and finger, eliciting a soft whimper from Jessie's mouth. His other hand kept her hands pinned together over her head. His lips found the sweet spot on her neck and he kissed and nibbled along the sensitive skin, paying extra attention to her jawline. Jessie squirmed under his touch as warmth bloomed in her stomach.

He whispered, "You looked so good tonight. You have no idea how hard it was, sitting next to you, not being able to do anything with you or to you. I'm going to fix that right now." At that last word, he gently bit her neck and smiled at the sharp gasp Jessie let out. He lowered her arms in front of her, but kept her wrists pinned together. He slid his free hand down her breast and over her stomach, leaving behind a trail of goosebumps.

Jessie's breaths turned to quick pants and her jaw quivered. A wanton moan slipped past her lips when Zane's fingers found their way inside her shorts and he wiggled his knuckles around, stretching the material to give him some more room to move his fingers. He chuckled wickedly as Jessie squirmed against him when he stopped just above her clit. Jessie bucked her hips, trying to get his fingers where she wanted them.

"Oh, no," he said as his fingers skirted along her folds. "We go at my pace. I know you still have time before you have to get back and I told the guys that I had to step outside to make a phone call." He slid his hand back out of her shorts and worked them down over her hips a bit. Jessie gasped when the cooler air in the room hit the hot skin between her legs. Zane's fingers quickly found their way back to her cunt and he teased his fingers along her slick hole, chuckling as she writhed against him.

"I'm going to bend you over this bed and fuck the shit out of you," he whispered gruffly. "I've been thinking about that for the last two hours." He then slid his finger into her ready opening, humming at how wet she was. "It looks like I'm not the only one who wants to fuck," he murmured. His finger thrust slowly in and out of her, making Jennie moan and quiver. Zane curled his finger against her walls, while working his thumb over her clit. He pressed his hips against her backside, pressing the bulge in his pants against her backside.

Jessie struggled against his grip, desperate to run her fingers through his hair, over his arms, anything. His fingers continued to glide to and from her cunt, slowly adding to the warmth still spreading through her belly.

"Where do you think you're going?" Zane asked, tightening his grip and pausing in his ministrations.

"Nowhere," Jessie stammered. "I just wanted to touch you."

Zane said, "This isn't about what you want. It's about what I want. And what I'm going to get." He then moved her wrists to behind her back and slid her shorts down to her ankles. Using his grip on her wrists to control her, he pushed her over the bed.

"You have no idea how I want to make this last. To tease you mercilessly. But I just don't have time." Jessie heard Zane unfasten his pants and drop them to the floor. She felt the head of Zane's cock tease around the opening to her pussy. God, she was so wet; she wanted him to fuck her in the worst way.

Finally, he thrust his hard cock deep inside Jessie's cunt, burying himself deep inside her in one swift movement. Jessie pressed her lips together to muffle a pleasured moan as he stretched and filled her.

Zane grabbed a handful of Jessie's hair and used that, along with her pinned wrists, as leverage to impale Jessie on his cock over and over, each thrust ending with a muffled cry as Jessie kept her lips pressed shut. The combination of Zane being in control on top of the weeks of merciless flirting had her quickly approaching the edge. She felt herself get wetter with each powerful thrust and struggled yet again against his grip.

Zane released her hair and bent over her, continuing to drive his throbbing, stiff dick deeper and deeper into Jessie's pussy. Reaching around with his free hand, he began teasing her clit, rubbing it in rhythm with the thrusting of his cock. Jessie felt her orgasm creep ever closer, making her want to moan and cry out, but she didn't dare. She clenched her jaw and tried to keep any noises she made as quiet as possible.

"You like this?" Zane asked. "You like it when I fuck you like this, don't you?"

"Yes," Jessie said, a little louder than she had wanted to. "God, yes. This feels so good."

Zane's thrusts got harder and deeper, his finger continued to tease at Jessie's clit. Finally, he brought her over the edge; her muscles tensed, but she could barely move anywhere because Zane's grip was so tight. He growled as her pussy muscles spasmed around his cock. "Yes," he said. "God, you feel so good when you cum and you get all tight."

"How good?" Jessie panted, her hips still bucking reflexively against his.

Zane grunted and forcefully thrust against her once… twice… three times before digging his fingers into her hips and pulling her tight against him. Jessie could feel his cock twitch as he spilled his seed deep inside her. Her own orgasm was starting to unwind - her vaginal muscles still contracting against his cock. She couldn't help but grin when he gasped at the sensation.

The stayed like that for a few moments, breathless and sweaty. Zane rested his forehead on Jessie's back and he slowly slid his spent member from her cunt. He released her wrists, wrapped his arms around her, and said, "I hope I didn't hurt you."

Jessie lightly traced her fingers over his forearms. "I'll be fine. Maybe a little sore tomorrow, but nothing major."

"Good," he said, kissing her neck. "Just wait until next week's game."

This book is a work of fiction. People, places, events, and situations are the product of the author's imagination. Any resemblances to actual persons, living or dead, or historical events, is purely coincidental.

Fruit, Veg & Starfish.

By

T.L Wainwright

"Can I help you with anything?"

"I'm fine thank you," I reply to the young wisp of a girl standing beside me.

"It's just that..." she mumbles shyly. I wait for a response but all she does is nervously shuffle from one foot to the other.

"It's just what? Come on spit it out," I respond a tad harsher than I intended.

I take a moment to peruse her. A petite little thing with over bleached hair and sky blue eyes that would be stunning, if it wasn't for the overloaded eyeliner that makes them look almost... piggy. The standard issue supermarket uniform is far too tight, but with a figure like hers, I guess it's intentional. I can't say I blame her, I'd do the same if I was packing it like she is. Her pert little tits must have been wrestled into submission to get into the two cup size, too small bra she's wearing, making her cleavage look like over plump, creamy pink, marshmallows. The zip front of the dress is worn a little too low. Who am I kidding, a lot too low. I know I'm in the fruit and veg section but hell, there is way too many melons going on here.

"I'm sorry madam but the store is about to close," she mumbles. "Could you please make your way to the tills?"

"I haven't finished," I fake smile at her. She's lucky she got that. Annoying bint, with her perfect boobs and ass. My eyes linger on her tight little waist. Biiartch!

"I sorry madam but we announced it over 15 minutes ago." She starts to look a little flushed. "The stores closing."

"Tough!" I snipe back. "I haven't decided what I want and until I do, I will take as much time as I need."

"I'm off to get the manager," she squeaks now close to tears.

"You do that little girl," I snigger. "Go on, scurry off little mouse." She trips, almost going arse over tit as she makes a hasty retreat. "Go get your precious manager, as if that's going to make the slightest bit of difference!" I shout after her. A feeling of guilt lies solid in my gut for being such a nasty cow. O hum!

With my handbag hooked over my shoulder, I rest the handle of the shopping basket in the crook of my arm. Picking up a bunch of grapes, I let the individual green pearls sit in the palm of my hand. I pluck one from the stalk and roll it between my finger and thumb, gently testing the firmness of the skin.

"They are extremely juicy," a voice rasps just behind me. I jump and the increase of pressure on the little bead of flesh causes it to pop. Sticky nectar runs down my fingers. "And sweet," he adds.

I turn with great expectations towards the owner of the deep and incredibly sexy voice and I'm not the slightest bit disappointed.

So many times you find that the voice doesn't match the body or visa versa. However, not in this case. From his perfectly groomed, slick backed hair to the dark tan laced up, slightly pointed, brogue shoes, everything in between is mesmerising. Perfection even. I inhale deeply trying to increase the oxygen levels to my dizzy head.

"You made me jump," I say, lazily licking the delicious residue from my hand. I let my tongue slip between the V of my fingers. His eyes are immediately drawn to my mouth and I increase the suggestiveness of my display. I slide the tip of my tongue up and around my index finger before taking it into my mouth. I suck hard before releasing it with a pop. "I've tasted better."

His focus remains on my lips so I take the opportunity to assess his face. What was probably a clean cut chin this morning, was now covered with a sprinkling of 5 o'clock shadow against his otherwise clear complexion. A nose that is slightly too big for his face, but is strong, straight and certainly does nothing to diminish his impeccable good looks. What sets him a par from the rest of team hot men, are those dreamy chocolate eyes and perfectly lush, full mouth that is currently turned slightly up at one side.

"Are you checking me out?" he questions while giving me with a lop-sided grin.

"No more than you were me," I counter claim.

Inquisitive eyes roam down my body. In my head, I praise myself for going with the just above knee, slightly flared black skirt showing my legs off perfectly. The soft lemon, short sleeved cashmere jumper, clings to my 36C's. Nipples visible and aroused simply from his gaze, or possibly from the nipple rings that have teased the button of flesh into standing to attention. Gradually his eyes raise to meet mine as he licks his lips before spluttering a small cough in an attempt to regain composure.

"Is there something I can help you with?" he asks.

"I don't know is there?"

"Are you looking for anything in particular?"

"That," I skim over the badge that is pinned to his shirt, picking out his first name, "Daniel," I reply while gently placing the grapes back onto the display, "is my dilemma."

"Allow me to assist you," his voice rumbles from his soft moist lips. Moving closer towards me I take a step back. Only the one, as that is all I'm able to take before my butt hits the display unit. His hand reaches past me. As he has now invaded my space, I have to look up to make any connection. "We have oranges." He holds one close to my face but his eyes don't flicker away from mine, not once, fused, as if trying to read me. "Feel the texture of the slightly puckered skin."

"Is the juice sharp?" I ask keeping my eyes locked to his while I run the tips of my fingers across the citrus fruit.

"So sharp it makes your taste buds tingle."

"No thanks," I shake my head dismissively. "I already have some at home. I'm looking for something... a little different."

"Mr Rossi," Perky Tits appears from nowhere, interrupting our little flirty exchange. "Me and the guys, well we are um, we're wanting to go home."

"Of course Shanice." His eyes drop to the floor in frustration, but only for a moment. "Let me come and lock the door behind you."

"But what about..." she nods her head in my direction. "Her, Mr Rossi?"

"I will make sure the lady leaves here with total customer satisfaction." The way he glances back at me with a wickedness in his eyes makes me quiver. "If you could kindly wait here Madam, I will be back in just a moment."

His walk has a hint of military as he guides Perky Tits towards the front of the store where the others have congregated. I can't help but take in the firmness of his arse cheeks under the grey pinstriped fabric. He has the type of bum that you'd love to sink your red shellac, manicured nails into, gripping on for dear life, while he's banging you hard with all the enthusiasm of a drill sergeant.

Shanice glances back catching me ogling him. I stick out my tongue in an exaggerated childish manner. Fuck her and her young, superior lady lumps.

I look over the array of finery laid out in front of me. It's only a small store, so everything in the fruit and veg category is pretty much close at hand. The sound of muffled voices followed by the noise of metal hitting metal distracts me and I glance back towards the store front. I can see the shutters begin to slide down with a slight judder accompanied with the whirring sound of the mechanical motor. The front of store lights go off along with the florescent tubes that illuminate the cash out area, plunging the front part of the store into total darkness. My eyes try to adjust to the blackness, but it's not long until he bursts into the light like a man on a mission, walking towards me again, getting up all close and personal.

"Now let me see if I can tempt you to something else," his hand goes behind me. "Why don't we make this a little more fun," he whispers close to my ear. "Close your eyes."

"Ahh, but can I trust you?" I question.

"Isn't that part of the thrill? Not knowing what comes next."

"What if I don't like what comes next?"

"Then just say the word and I'll stop," his voice thickens as he moves in, his lips skim the shell of my ear. "Trust me."

As he steps back and looks deep into my eyes I blink once, twice, on the third time, I keep them closed and whisper "I trust you."

I tense up as I feel the sudden softness of fabric fall across my eyes.

"Easy, it's just my tie," he soothes. "We don't want any cheating now do we," he laughs softly. "You can tell me to stop at any time if it gets too much."

"What if I don't like the dark?"

"Then I will show you a different kind of light."

I can hear him moving around but everything becomes a little disorientated.

"What shall I call you?" he asks, which brings me back to reality as now I have to think. Do I give him my real name or some sexy alias?

"Delilah," I mumble then giggle, as shit knows where that came from.

"Mmm, Delilah," he almost groans. "That's fucking sexy. In fact...you're fucking sexy. Now. Open your mouth."

Within seconds I present him with the perfect O, the tip of something round pushes through my lips. I run my tongue across it before sucking it part way in and pursing my lips around it.

"Bite it," he growls.

As I follow his order, the sweet berry smell hits my nose as the watery juice runs down my chin.

"Strawberry?" I mutter. "I'm a little disappointed Daniel. I thought you would have been a little more adventurous than that."

"Forgive me," he sighs. "Clearly I underestimated you." I feel his mouth against my ear, his lips against the lobe, a small little tug. "I can see that I need to up my game if I'm to impress you." He moves away and I immediately miss the closeness. "Let me see. Ahh yes."

The sound of ripping plastic reaches my ears at the same time as the mix of different fruity smells, mingled with the already heady aroma, hits my nose. As his hands grip my upper arms gently holding me, my body shivers from the unexpected touch. Slowly he coaxes my body forward towards him.

The mixture of sweet and tart hits my mouth, but its only seconds, before his soft lips cover mine. Using his tongue he pushes the small piece of pineapple further into my mouth. Eagerly I swallow the fruit without chewing and wrap my hands behind his neck, reducing his chance of escape, as I begin to play a sensual game of tongue tag with him.

His hands cup my face holding me firmly as he increases the force of our play. And God love him, he bloody well knows how to kiss. Holy fucking fanny flutters!

"Fuck, I should have known pineapple was your thing," he breathes out when he eventually comes up for air. "I want this off," he says tugging at the hem of my jumper.

"I want to see your face," I counter as I put my hand up to untie the make shift blindfold. He beats me to it, slipping the knot and it slides from my eyes. With a little squinting and blinking, I regain my focus and the sight that greets me is outstanding.

Standing in front of me is the most gorgeous, shirtless body I've ever had the pleasure of casting a glance over. Gym work is evident but not too much as to make you feel over conscious of your own body. His muscles are defined but not bulging. Cut but not cavernous. Naturally tanned and certainly not orange!

"Now your turn." He pulls the jumper roughly over my head. If it wasn't for the bobble keeping my long hair back in a high pony tail, it would've been a whole lot of head mess.

"Do you know that if a guy eats enough pineapple a couple of hours before sex, you can taste it in his cum?" I blurt out.

"Is that right?" he shakes his head and seems a little taken aback by my bizarre allegation.

"Do you want to try it out?" I pant. "Personally I think it's a load of tosh but in the name of science, I'm willing to check it out."

"Maybe later," he replies, but his attention is on other things. Two to be exact.

Running the palm of his hand across the sheer yellow fabric of my bra he raises an eyebrow when hitting the hard knob at the tip.

"I need to see your tits... like right now!"

I help him out by reaching back and releasing the catch. I wiggle my shoulders allowing the straps to slowly slide down my arms, keeping up the tease, before casting the garment to the floor.

"Pierced?" he asks looking a little shocked.

"No just nipple rings. They make them stick ouuuuuwwww..." I growl as he covers one with his mouth.

Swirling the tip of his tongue around the circumference he then takes the metal loop between his teeth and teases it off. It causes the most erotic sting as it grazes the sensitive surface. My clit begins to purr. So that's why it's called a pussy.

He takes the ring from his mouth and pockets it, before giving the other nipple the same treatment. Now clear of any additional embellishments he proceeds to bite, suck and generally worry the hell out of the little buddies.

There's an urgency about the way I fumble with the belt of his trousers, it's an emergency. I need to get my hands on his dick. Belt – Check. Hook – Check. Zipper – Check. As the heavy buckle hits the floor with a thud, a sharp intake of breath can be clearly heard. Commando – Double check.

I push him away from me, not that I wasn't enjoying the tit attention, but I need to see the full package. It's hard, thick and perfectly pink with the exception of the almost purple round head complete with glistening pre-cum drop peeping from the eye.

"Your cock is impressive," I gasp dropping to my knees. "It's so smooth like a freshly cut-throat razor, baldy-head." I wrap my hand around the shaft and stroke, only a couple of times, before I lean in and scoop up the bead of moisture with the point of my tongue.

"Delilah," his voice is so deep and horny that it plucks a string in my chest that vibrates tenfold, making a bee line for my clit. Only stopping for a pit stop half way, leaving a kaleidoscope of butterflies partying in my stomach.

I work my tongue from the bottom of the shaft to the very top, following the line of the vain all the way, before me popping the whole kit and caboodle into my mouth.

"Delilah, ohh, ohh, Delilah."

Pushing aside the thoughts of Tom Jones that are trying to permeate my head, I squeeze the tip of his cock with the back of my throat before sucking hard. Cupping and massaging his full heavy balls, it's as plain as the hairs on his testicles, that them there boys need to dump their load before they implode. Me, being the considerate person that I am, feel that is only right that I offer up my services.

My plan of action is briskly thwarted, as he removes himself from my mouth with a clear and precise pop of the cock.

"Stand up," he commands but softens the abruptness by holding his hand out to assist me. I turn to watch him as he starts moving the various produce around, pushing it to each side, making a clear area on the display counter.

"Get your arse up here," he growls patting the now empty space.

"Is that a cucumber in your hand or are you just pleased to see me?" I snigger while throwing him a questionable glance.

When he realises that he still has a firm grip on the green phallic symbol, he tosses it over his head in no particular direction. Launching himself at me he effortlessly lifts me, turns me and sits me on the counter. Pushing up my skirt he hooks his thumbs under each side of my knickers and pulls.

"Woah, what are you doing?" I gasp, putting my hands on his; stopping him going any further. "What about the produce?"

"Fuck it, it's past its sell by date," he rasps whipping off my pants like a magic trick. "Unlike you," he growls and falls to his knees. Putting both his hands on the inside of my legs he slides them up, pushes them apart, giving him a full view of my newly pampered pussy.

"Oh sweet baby Jesus," he hisses when he sees my hairless essentials. "My first ever visit to Hollywood."

With a feather like touch his fingers move over each side of my outer lips. "So smooth on the outside." With two fingers together he strokes along my slit from top to bottom, each time becoming more arousing, causing my normally hidden clitoris to peek through from where she was hiding. A finger slides in burrowing into me. "Oh baby, I can't believe how wet you are." A second digit joins in with the welcome intrusion, curling inside, rubbing and teasing that magical spot with the capital G.

"O! O Daniel," I whimper as his mouth joins the assault on my nether regions.

"God you taste so sweet yet..." he looks at me while licking his lips. "A little salty. Fucking delicious."

"O Dan!" I squeak. "Dan. Dan, can I call you Dan?"

"You can call me anything you want baby, as long as you're screaming it when you come.

"That could be sooner than you... Oh fuck...DANnnnnn!"

The come down is slow as he continues to lap up my juices.

"Clean up on aisle one," I giggle breathlessly and still slightly dazed.

He lifts his head from between my legs, lips glistening, mouth grinning as he stands. Like the cat that just got the cream. Or maybe I should say Dirty Dog!

Putting his hands in mine he pulls me to my feet before kissing me. I can taste myself on his lips and yes, it's sweet, a little salty and fucking sexy.

"That was amazing," I pant into his kiss.

"Baby, you better take a few deep, deep breaths," he warns. "Cos I ain't finished yet. Now turn around and let me take a look at your arse."

"Holy shit with sugar on!" I blurt out as he spins me around and bends me over. Whoop there goes my skirt again as I come face to face with a punnet of plums.

"This is one perfect little arse." Both hands caress a cheek a piece, stroking softly then gripping hard, fingers sinking into my supple skin. "My cock is like a fucking rock, so open your legs and stick your arse up I need to get to that gorgeous pussy of yours."

I stretch up on my very tippy toes with my legs as far apart as they will possibly go. Grabbing my hips, he moves my butt up and towards him. With one hand on my hip the other guides his cock across my entrance, teasing my clit, before plunging into me. So deep, so hard, so fucking full.

"Fuck me, you feel so good," he growls as he slowly pulls back before pushing back into me.

"No," I whimper back. "Fuck me and fuck me hard."

A cracking sound echoes and bounces off the walls as the palm of his hand comes down hard on my bare flesh. The pain of it leads me to let out a deep guttural moan of pure pleasure as he soothes and strokes away the sting.

"Do you like being spanked Delilah?" He doesn't wait for my response before his hand provides me with an encore as he increases the speed of his trusts.

"Yes," I declare with each trust and moan with each spank.

"Oh baby I'm so close, put your hand between your legs and touch yourself." His voice is thick with arousal. "Rub that hard little clit of yours."

My fingers slide into the wetness and roll over the sensitive bud as Daniel pumps faster and harder causing our skin to slap against each other. When his thumb slides into the entrance of my little puckered starfish, I'm gone.

Not once, twice or even thrice do I scream out his name but over and over again with each and every blissful wave of ecstasy.

The sound that escapes his mouth when he hits his own frenzied euphoria is almost feral. Deep, throaty rasps of release.

Pulling me towards him and enveloping me within his arms, we slide to the floor exhausted and sexually sedated. We sit for some time and he nuzzles into my neck, kissing and brushing his lips against my skin, holding each other, until our bodies return back to a modicum of normality.

"I really need to go," I say with a heavy heart.

"I know," he replies but his arms squeeze me even tighter.

"This was fun." I turn my face towards him and smile. "Ohh, ohh, ohh Delilah?" I giggle. "Was you expecting me to throw my knickers at you?"

"Haa! Haa!" he rewards me with a breath-taking smile. "Whatever! I still got your knickers even though I had to remove them myself." His hand waves the said item in front of me. I go to grab them. "Naa they are mine now," he laughs as he gets to his feet. "Call it a memento, a little something to remind me of this night." I graciously accept his outstretched hand and he pulls me up to meet him.

I quickly clean myself up. Thank God for pocket packs of baby wipes. Retrieving our clothes, we dress in only minutes. When finished, we stand in silence, just looking at each other. We slam into each other's arms and kiss.

"I really need to make a move," I let out a sigh as I look into those deep pools of chocolate that are looking at me with so much feeling it's scary.

"Thank you for tonight," he kisses me deeply and it's like being hit in the face with a ten-pound lump hammer. A total sensational knockout.

I force myself to pull away from him, even though I so want to stay and just bathe in his loveliness.

"I better go." I look around at the carnage that we've left behind. It looks like there's been some sort of veggie revenge by the Meat Lovers R Us group. Squashed satsumas, lacklustre lemons and an unexpected new line of mixed veg. "I'm sorry I can't stay and help you tidy up but if I don't get home to the kids and your mum misses her Bingo night, they'll be all hell to pay."

"I know," he nods and laughs in his adorable way.

"Happy birthday darling." I kiss the lips I know so well. "I hope your fantasy was everything you wished for." We walk toward the exit door at the back of the building where I'd parked my car before the start of our little sexy charade.

"And more baby, much, much more." He opens the door before stealing another kiss. "I love you more than words can say," he murmurs.

"I love you more and more each day," I sing back.

"Hey!" I shout back at him as I get to my car. "You do know it's my birthday in a couple of weeks?"

"Yeah!"

"Maybe we should book a hotel for the night." I give him my best seductive wink. "Test out the pineapple theory and do a more in depth investigation into the puckered starfish."

The end.

XOXO

Other books by T.L Wainwright

NAUGHTY BUT RICE – Book 1 (Reed and Rice Series) available now on eBook

RICE BACK AT YOU! - Book 2 (Reed and Rice Series) available now on eBook

NAUGHTY BUT RICE/RICE BACK AT YOU! - both together as one Paperback available via Amazon.

A HOLE LOTTO LOVING – available now on eBook and Paperback.

DEACON. Soldier. Fighter. JACKass! – available now on eBook and Paperback.

Coming soon 2016/2017:-

60 Minute Love Affair – Short Story.

Petra and Cade's Story - Book 3 (Standalone spin off from Reed and Rice Series).

Nessa and Axe's Story - Book 4 (Standalone spin off from Reed and Rice Series).

Tomek and Allie's Story – (Standalone spin off from Deacon).

To connect with TL Wainwright visit her facebook page

T.L Wainwright (Author)

https://m.facebook.com/profile.php?ref=m_notif¬if_t=group_comment_reply

https://m.facebook.com/tlwainwright/?ref=bookmarks

Or email ttdwainwright@gmail.com

Twitter: @wainwright_tl

Instagram: tl.wainwright

3

An Eden Rose Short Story

Chapter One

I've always enjoyed wearing a dress without underwear on. There's something sensual and exotic about it. The thought of me being able to lift my skirt up to show everyone my freshly waxed pussy has always excited me.

Which is why my husband and I are at the bar right now. I'm not entirely sure that he knows I'm not wearing any underwear and I'm not going to tell him. We are at the bar to see if we can find a third for our "Save the Marriage" operation. Joe and I are stretched along the plush seats of the bar and I'm busy scanning the crowd.

"Baby, did you find anyone?" Joe whispers in his sultry voice. I look over at my husband of six years and smile. His excited brown eyes are glimmering in the low lighting of the bar but the way he fills out that Armani suit us fucking hot.

I shake my head and comb through the crowd again. Shit, it's the exact same lame people as earlier. "Are you sure you are okay with another man?" I'm asking, because guys are super sensitive about having their dicks out when there is another man in the room.

Such babies.

He scans the crowd again before he finds someone that he likes. "Jill, what about her?" He points off into the bar crowd but I don't see who he's pointing to just yet.

"Who?" I ask and search through the bodies of half-naked women and men who are all here for the same thing.

Joe places his hand high up on my thigh and I can feel the warmth through the fabric. "The pretty redhead wearing the black dress. I think she's here by herself. Why don't we go and talk to her?" He whispers these words into my ear and my body shivers from anticipation.

"All right," I stand up to go talk to her.

My heels are making my walking a little wobbly. Or maybe it's the tequila I have consumed.

This was Joe's idea after he told me in therapy that he's missing something in our relationship. Talk about a slap in the face. I'm still not sure how to take that bombshell. Our therapist is the one that suggested we go to a group meeting for couples that have hit a dry spell. When we went, someone gave Joe the information for this.

We have been married for six years but have been together since middle school. Hell, I haven't even kissed another person. I have only ever been with Joe. We went to the same high school together and then college. I doubt that people even know our names separately from each other.

By the time we walk through the crowded room, I see the woman Joe picked out. She makes me feel a little uncomfortable as if I'm not nearly as sexy as she is, but I suck it up and walk up to her. Up close, she's even more beautiful and I want to hate her on sight.

"Hi, uh, my name is—"

The redhead starts laughing and then shakes her head. Dumbfounded, I look up at her and see she's laughing at me. "What?" I ask.

"You must be new. You don't just go up to someone and ask them to fuck. You need to get to know them and make sure they are right for you and your husband. And by the way you are holding your hands, I'm guessing you aren't attracted to women. Do me a favor and run along."

I'm pretty sure that my face is beet red and I spin on my heels to go back to Joe. Once I'm there, I feel tears of embarrassment leaking out of the corner of my eyes.

"What happened, baby?" he asks, and puts his arm around my shoulders. Once I'm close enough to put my face in his neck, I feel the tears coming harder and faster.

"I want to go home," I say.

By the time we get to the car, I have stopped crying and he's holding my hand. "What did she say to you?"

"She knew I've never done anything like this and told me this wasn't how it worked."

Joe squeezes my thigh and then lifts his hand to brush against my pussy. Sex is the last thing on my mind and all I want to do is go inside and sit in the tub.

"Stop," I whisper and let the tears fall more. Suddenly, I feel bad for rejecting him and turn to look at his profile. His firm jaw is clenched and he looks pissed off. "I'm sorry. We will find a way..."

Chapter Two

I'm in a meeting at work and all I can think about is how to find a third for our bedroom. I try to be discreet as I pull my phone out of my purse and open up the web browser. In the search bar, I type in: *swingers in Oakland County Michigan* and then hit search.

There are several websites that come up for dating sites and all of that, but that's not what I'm looking for. I'm looking for a website that introduces married couples with others who are wanting to do the same thing.

Finally, an ad pops up and I click on it. There are scrolls of couples and their photos that are surrounding the page. The title says: "Are you looking for something to spice up your relationship?" I click yes and then am directed to a questionnaire that is asking me questions about what I'm looking for.

"Jill?"

"What?" I ask as I set down my phone. I am looking at the heads of the company and they are staring me down.

One of the head honchos looks at me from across the table and I can see he's looking curiously at me. "Jill, please put your phone away."

I do what is asked and slip it under my thigh. I survey the room and see everyone is looking at me. There are several people that are older than me but I never realized that Brandon, the head honcho, is actually pretty cute. His body fills out the suit that he's wearing and his gold cuff links shine and twinkle in the light.

My pussy clenches at nothing and I shift in my seat.

About an hour later, and an hour's worth of inappropriate thoughts about my boss, I leave the room before I can embarrass myself anymore. Once I'm in the hallway, I beeline for the bathroom and lock myself into the stall at the end. I don't have to go to the to the bathroom, but I sit on the toilet and take a deep breath.

Holy shit. I feel like I just got caught doing something totally wrong, but I didn't. I'm trying to save my marriage and I'm doing what I need to do to save it. If that means I have to watch him with someone else, I guess I'll have to deal with it.

Chapter Three

When I get home, I'm beyond ready to be there. I park my car and reach in the back to get my briefcase. As soon as I'm inside, I kick my shoes off in the corner and then begin to strip.

This is my daily routine because I hate wearing a bra. I feel like I'm suffocating in it. I'm a natural 42 DD and every time I take it off, I have lines from the underwire across the outer-tit.

"Jill? Baby? Is that you?" Joe calls from the den.

I walk through the mudroom and into the den. This is Joe's space and he's decorated it in University of Michigan colors.

"Hey." I lean over him and kiss his lips gently. "I joined a swinger website."

He puts down his phone and looks over at me. "I'm sorry—"

"Stop. I don't want to hear you apologize about voicing what you are not getting in our relationship."

I pull out the app and hand my phone over to him. He scrolls through the profiles and then types out a message to one of them. "Now what?" I ask and he shrugs.

"We wait."

When he hands me my phone, I read his message.

ME: Hi, my name is Joe and I'm looking for a third person for my wife and I. We are an adventurous couple who is looking to spice up things in the bedroom. We are open to you meeting us for dinner first and then we can see how things go. My number is 248-555-5555. Please text me or call with any questions. We look forward to hearing from you. Thank you.

I'm not going to lie, my insides did a little flip and my pussy contracted against the emptiness in it. Damn, I never thought this would happen. I'm actually excited about this.

I set the phone down and place my hand on Joe's hardening cock. Once I'm gripping it, I squeeze a little tighter and it makes him moan. "Let me suck you off," I whisper as I undo his zipper.

Quietly, I slide down and situate myself between his thighs. Joe rubs his fingers through my loose blonde hair and then grips it at the scalp. "Damn, baby. I love looking at those heart shaped lips as they get ready to suck my dick."

Feeling praised, I do just that. I don't do a warm up, but I swallow him whole into the back of my throat. I relax my throat muscles to accommodate him and hear him groan. That groan is my motivation and I pull out the nasty kit in the back of my mind that I hold for these moments.

I love feeling like a goddess and knowing that I'm the one that is doing this to him. With my throat muscles massaging his head and shaft, I slip my hand off of his thigh and rub his balls.

"Holy fucking shit, baby!"

With my other hand I grip his shaft. Joe shoves himself farther into my throat and his pubic bone smashes my nose. The lack of oxygen is making me feel dizzy but it's empowering.

I fight against his hands in my hair and then pull off of his dick. There are strands of saliva that are connected between my lips and his dick. I lick my lips and then look up at him with lust-filled eyes. I love that he looks like this; I love seeing his cloudy green eyes as he watches me with wonder.

"Put me back in your mouth. I'm going to come all down your throat and you are going to take every fucking drop. Aren't you? You're being my dirty girl tonight. I fucking love it."

His dirty talk is making my thighs squeeze and I do just what he asked. I suck his head and lave around the mushroom head with my tongue. I love sucking his dick. He's got the perfect size; not too big but not too small. Just the right size for me to suck him into the back of my throat.

The bite from Joe's fingers in my hair is making me swallow him all the way into my mouth. Shit! "Take it, baby. Take everything I have to give you. I love you. I love that you are being my dirty girl tonight."

I suck his head and shuttle my hand up and down his shaft and he groans.

"Fuck! I'm coming!"

The first splash startles me. I jump a little and open my eyes to look at him. His eyes are squeezed shut but he looks beautiful. When the last drop hits me, I pull off of his dick and then lick my lips as I look in his eyes.

"Fuck, baby."

I smile and climb off the floor to start dinner.

Chapter Four

While sitting in my meeting the next day, I notice that my phone buzzes repeatedly under my thigh. I do my best to pay attention to the big wigs complaining about how the pens that they want are twelve cents more but they write better. Blah, blah, blah.

I pull my phone out because I couldn't take it anymore.

BANKER: I got your message and I'm interested in meeting with you and your wife. I'm married and willing to do a swap. I want to be in the room with you when you're sleeping with my wife, though. Let me know what you think.

Holy shit. Granted, I was well aware that Joe would be with another woman or be there when I'm with another person... But this is getting very real. Jesus. For the next five minutes, I try to think of what to say and I can't think of a damn thing.

Finally, I forward the message to Joe and he writes me back instantly.

JOE: Message him back and ask them to go to dinner with us. We can discuss everything there. Does that work for you?

ME: All right... I'm nervous.

JOE: You won't have to do anything that you don't want to do. If you don't want to do this, we don't have to.

His text makes me feel better but I can't help thinking that if I back out, he might do this behind my back. I sure hope not, but he told the counselor that he's missing something. He kept saying that it had nothing to do with me, but he's wanting something more sexually.

Decision made, I tap out a message to him.

I take a deep breath and look around the room to see everyone continuing with the meeting as if I'm not contemplating my life.

ME: Yes, that's fine. Would you like to meet for dinner? My husband and I work downtown but we are available to meet whenever works for you.

BANKER: Let me talk to my wife.

Before I message him and ask what the hell, I set my phone down and concentrate on the remaining part of the meeting. I look over at Brandon, who is rubbing his bottom lip, and he has a slight smirk on his face. Damn, he's pretty.

BANKER: Seven tonight? At Spruce?

I wilt a little at the mention of the most coveted restaurant in Oakland County. Anyone who is anyone eats there and it's expensive. Damn. That's going to be pricey. I shake it off and message him back telling him okay. I also text Joe and tell him what we decided.

Chapter Five

I smooth my hands down my only nice dress and slip into a pair of torture devices; I mean, heels. Self-consciously, I fluff my hair to make it look beachy with waves. I straighten my wedding rings and then spray some perfume on.

I feel like I'm going on a date and it's making me crazy. By crazy, I mean excited. I guess this is considered a date since we are going out with another couple.

"Are you ready?" Joe asks as he leans against the entryway to the bedroom. He's dressed in his slacks that are fitted perfectly to his body and a button down shirt that is molded to his torso.

What he sees in me, I will never know.

I nod and bend over at the waist to grab my purse. I'm wearing an off-black dress that has capped sleeves on my shoulders but is fitted loosely on my body. I love this dress because it makes my tits look perfect.

Joe wraps his arm around my shoulders and then leans in and whispers, "You look absolutely beautiful."

"Thanks. Let's go."

The whole way there, I'm debating jumping out of the car. Straight tuck and roll out. I'm so nervous that my thighs are sticking together and I'm worried that I'm going to stink. This is not cool.

When we get to the restaurant, I'm not calm at all. I'm straight up freaking out. What happens if they don't like me but want to sleep with Joe? Is this like a two-for-one deal?

He parks the car and hands the keys off to the valet man that is waiting. The other valet opens my car door and holds his hand out for me. Once I'm standing, my nerves come to a head.

Fuck me!

"You look beautiful. Your husband is a lucky man," the valet says and I look at him with flushed cheeks. He's about eighteen years old with a baby face; he's adorable.

"Thank you," I murmur and then Joe comes over to me. I slip my hand from the valet and tuck it in Joe's elbow.

We walk with stride into the restaurant and the hostess is smiling as we enter. I don't know if she knows what we are doing, but I feel like I have HARLOT written across my head. "Hello, how may I help you?"

I speak up and then see Brandon and the redhead that shut me down at the bar. Holy shit. I begin to recoil inside as I see them walking over to me. No, no no! This is not happening.

I back away from Joe but he holds onto me and squeezes me tighter. "We aren't doing anything wrong, baby. We're just having dinner. Brandon won't even know."

"I don't believe you! They are coming this way!"

"Joe and Jill. Our table is over here."

Quickly, I yank my arm out of Joe's and look at my boss. "Are you fucking kidding me?"

Brandon chuckles and the redhead from the bar steps forward and thrusts her hand out to me. "I'm Whitney. It's nice to meet you."

Am I dreaming? This is not happening. What the hell is going on? What the actual fuck?

Chapter Six

We walk to the back table and I consider walking out of here. What the hell is going on? Since when is Brandon into this?

"Am I being fired?" I ask as we sit down. The waiter pours me a glass of wine and I snatch it out of his hand and down the liquid courage.

Brandon laughs and shakes his head. "No. I saw your profile online and showed it to Whitney. She told me she saw you guys at the bar."

Whitney giggles and places her hand on Joe's; I wince with jealousy. Looking at the attraction in her eyes, I also feel a sense of pride that she's interested in my husband.

The restaurant is beautifully decorated with red and gold. Our table is lit by candlelight and there are real flowers in the middle of it. It's a circle shaped table with captain chairs surrounding it. I'm seated in between Joe and Brandon and I shiver in anticipation.

Joe looks over at Brandon and nods his head. "This was actually set up ahead of time. I knew that Joe was looking for something to spice up your relationship and I knew we could help. Whitney and I are part of a swinger community and have been doing this for years."

I grab Joe's glass of wine and down it as well. "Are you even attracted to me?"

Did that seriously come out of my mouth? What the hell is wrong with me?

Brandon places his hand on my thigh and squeezes it. "Yes. Whitney and I are attracted to both of you. We are both bisexual and interested in both you and Joe. I know that Joe is straight, but I want to see him fuck my wife. Is that okay with you?"

"So how do we do this? Just meet up and fuck in the conference room?" The words fall out of my mouth before I can catch them.

Whitney giggles and looks over at Joe with longing. "No, we meet some place where we are comfortable and just let it happen."

"How do we find that? What's going to happen with work?" I ask because I'm too afraid Joe and I are going to lose our jobs because we decided to get a little freaky.

Whitney's smoky eyes calm me and she looks as beautiful as a siren. "Sweetie. Trust me. There is nothing we will do that will ruin your job."

Chapter Seven

Two weeks later, Joe and I are getting off of a plane in Chicago. We all decided that we wanted a vacation out of this so we could enjoy being together without having to worry about people knowing who we are or what we are doing.

Joe is the first one to step up to the baggage claim and he picks up our suitcase. Once he's got it, he holds his hand out to me and I take it.

We are about to have swinger sex.

How do we do it? Do we just get naked and pick which husband to fuck? Am I going to be okay with seeing Joe with another woman who is more attractive than I am?

"Are you sure about this?" I ask Joe as we slide into the cab.

My husband leans over and kisses my cheek. "I'm positive, baby. You are so great. Thank you."

We ride in silence until we are brought to a big hotel that is hidden in the back surrounded by woods. It's a majestic looking hotel that is shrouded with erotic secrets and my pussy clenches. When we get to the front, Joe pays the driver and I pull the suitcase out of the backseat. Once it is standing next to me, Joe walks back over and leads me to the front of the hotel.

In all the years we have been married, I have never seen him this excited about something. I'm not going to lie: it makes me jealous that he is not happy being with just me.

I shake off my insecurity and take in the expansive and impressive hotel. The inside looks like a resort with a fountain in the middle that is as big as my master bedroom and master bathroom combined. In the pool part of the fountain, there are different lights that shoot gold and silver through the water.

The counter is to the side and there is a big fish tank next to it filled with exotic fish. I have never seen a fish tank this big before—it's bigger than a wall at home. The concierge in the front is a young woman with big breasts that are sticking out.

God damn it. What is it about this place that is making so jealous of everyone?

"We are Joe and Jill Baxter. We have a reservation," I say to the woman. I stand up straight and flip my hair back in a nervous habit.

She types something and looks at us expectantly. "Your party has arrived. I will show you to your room."

When she walks in front of us, I place my hand in Joe's and squeeze. I'm not this brave. I have no idea what I'm doing here and I'm so freaked out that this is going to ruin my marriage completely. What if he likes her more than me?

The hallways are dimly lit but the designs on the walls don't need that much of a display. They are beautiful with little swirls that are strangely exotic.

Everything about this place is exotic.

"Everything is going to be fine. Don't worry about a thing," he says to me and kisses my cheek.

That's easy for him to say. This was his idea from the beginning. I'm just here for the ride. And hopefully a few orgasms.

The room that we are being led to his behind a thick wooden door that is dark. Or maybe it's the light. "Right this way. Enjoy your stay with us." The woman leaves and Joe lightly knocks on the door.

Chapter Eight

The room is the biggest thing I have ever seen. There is a fire place that is roaring in the background and I can feel the heat off of it and it's making me sweat. There is light music in playing and I can hear the sound of water running.

"Holy shit," I murmur and look around some more.

Paintings upon paintings are lining the walls and then there is a little kitchenette in a cubby at the back. There is a glass wall standing in the middle of the room, and I walk over to it. The sound of the running water is louder coming from over here so I peek behind it.

Holy fucking shit. There is a pool in the middle of the room with a waterfall flowing into it.

"Joe!"

Whitney and Brandon are in the hot tub that is in the middle of the pool and they are naked. I can see from where I'm standing that she is sitting on his lap with her thighs spread. My pussy is drenched as I think about this.

"Come on in, guys," Brandon says and Whitney looks up from him.

Here goes nothing.

Before I make it to the hot tub, Joe comes up behind me and grabs my hips. He thrusts his hard dick against my ass and then whispers: "I love you and only you. Let's spend the next few days getting crazy."

Can't argue with that logic.

Chapter Nine

I walk over the hot tub and kick my heels off to the side. From here, I can see Whitney's perky tits and Brandon's hard dick. Shit, I'm not sure where to look or where I'm allowed to look.

Whitney must see my dilemma because she giggles and holds her hand out to me. Like the siren that I'm thinking she is, I place my hand in hers. "Get naked and come sit in the tub."

Joe comes up to my front and then unbuttons my dress from the front. When he gets to the last button, I hold onto the sides of my dress. "It's okay, baby. You can keep it on."

My husband strips out of his clothes and I gulp when he sheds his boxers. His dick is impressive. Whitney must think so because she's staring at it.

"At least come to the edge, baby," Whitney says, patting the side.

Joe is already submerged into the water and he's sitting next to Whitney. I watch with fascination as he trails his fingers down her back and she shivers. I close my eyes, strip out of my clothes as quickly as I can and go to the tub.

As soon as I'm in the water, Joe swings over to me and places his arm around my shoulders and strokes my nipple. "How does this work?" I ask.

"If you don't mind," Joe begins, "I have been fantasizing about this for a long time. In order to make Jill comfortable, I'm thinking that we can focus on our own spouse and then when we are primed and ready, we can switch. Does that work?" He directs the last question to me. I nod and look at the other two.

Brandon has his hand tucked between Whitney's pussy lips and I can't see it ut I know he's stroking her clit. "Yeah, that works for us."

My husband slides between my legs and places his hands on my tits gently. I moan when his fingers lightly graze my nipples. "Does it make you horny when I touch you in front of them? Are you going to show them my dirty girl tonight?"

"Yes," I moan and then I hear another moan coming from Whitney. I look up and see her sitting on the edge of the tub with her thighs spread and Brandon's head between them. "Does it... does it feel good?" I ask her with cloudy eyes.

"Oh shit. yes. He eats the best pussy."

The tip of Joe's dick slides between my lips and I scream out when he slides all the way home. In a matter of three thrusts, he has me laying on the edge of the landing around the tub with my legs still in the water. He's got his hands gripping my thighs as he slides in and out while he is still in the water.

My eyes roll to the back of my head when he hits my spot continuously but I can't stop the scream that comes from the back of my throat.

And then suddenly, Joe stops. My legs are dropped back into the hot water and I look up to see Brandon. He's gloriously and beautifully naked standing in front of me with his dick at full attention. "Do you think you could be with me like that? I don't want to pressure you, but I think you're so beautiful."

How can I say no to that?

I nod my head and then look down to see him scanning my body before settling at the spot between my thighs. "Did you like watching me eat Whitney's pussy? Did you like knowing that I was sucking on her clit while Joe was fucking you?"

"Jesus Christ!" I yell out as Brandon's mouth falls to my clit and sucks it into his mouth. He purses his lips and captures it into his mouth. My head thrashes from side to side and I can't help but scream.

I look up past Brandon's brown-haired head and over to Joe. He's making out with Whitney and she's straddling him. I wish I could say that there was a stab of jealousy but there isn't. I feel a sense of accomplishment that my husband is able to make her feel as good as her moans are telling me.

He vibrates his lips against my clit and my thighs shake as they wrap around his head to hold him in place. There's pressure in my lower muscles as my orgasm comes crashing down on me with a force that brings tears to my eyes. I'm crying out from ecstasy and I squeeze my eyes shut.

Whitney moans and then screams. I open my eyes to see Joe's mouth attached to her pussy too.

Brandon sits up, tugs on his erect dick and looks over at his wife. "She can't come too much; we still have a long night ahead of us."

I'm pretty sure that the men haven't come yet but we are sitting next to each other while we eat a light snack after the hot tub. We are all still naked and it's freeing. It's freeing to be this comfortable with everyone. I'm loving it.

Chapter Ten

About an hour later, Whitney and I are laying on the bed completely naked while Joe and Brandon are talking in the corner and looking over at us. "I want to kiss you," I say to her and then look down at her lips.

"Okay, darling. Go ahead."

I lean over and then push myself up to my elbow and cover her gently. With my other hand, I stroke the side of her face before I press my lips against hers. She moans into my mouth and then parts her lips to lick my lips. I part mine and our tongues caress each other's until I'm sliding my body on top of hers.

Whitney's body is hard but soft at the same time. The exact opposite of mine, but I'm loving how she feels.

"Don't stop, lovelies."

I turn to see Joe and Brandon standing at the other end of the bed and they are watching us as we stroke and kiss each other. I'm so wrapped up in kissing Whitney, that I don't feel hands grabbing my hips and pulling me off of her.

Before I can look over, I see Brandon behind me but his eyes are on my ass. "I'm going to fuck you while you kiss my wife. And while you're doing that, Joe is going to fuck Whitney. Can you do that?"

Hell yeah!

"Yeah, hurry. I feel so empty."

Joe groans and then ducks his head down to capture Whitney's nipple in his teeth. I continue to kiss her and massage her tongue with mine as Joe settles between her thighs and then thrusts in her. Brandon takes this time to slam all the way home inside me and he is buried to the hilt.

"Not empty anymore, sweetheart. You are tight as shit. Do you like it rough? Tell me how you want it."

I don't answer but I shove my hips back into him and he grabs my ass cheeks and spreads them. "You like it rough. You like it so fucking filthy you won't be able to walk out of here."

Joe takes his lips off of Whitney's chest and leans over to pet my clit. "Yeah, she's my dirty fucking girl. Aren't you, baby? You love being so dirty. I know you do."

Brandon pushes him off of me lightly and then takes one hand to slip in between Whitney's thighs. "Baby, you are so perfect. You know that? So perfect. I love you," he whispers to Whitney.

She breaks our kiss and I can see the love in her eyes as she looks at Brandon's. "I love you, too."

Joe takes this time to slide out of Whitney and then nudge Brandon. "Let me have my wife back."

"She's all yours until later." He slides out of me and lightly pushes me down so I'm flat on my stomach.

My husband picks me up so I'm cradled against his chest as he carries me off. "We're going to go to the pool and make love in the waterfall. Would you like that?"

I nod and I allow him to carry me through the hotel room. Once we are behind the glass, he walks us into the beach-way opening until we are behind the waterfall. There's an embankment there and he lays me down on top of it.

"You are so wonderful. Thank you."

"I love you," I whisper and he slides into me gently and lovingly. His thrusts are shallow at first before they go all the way in me and makes me gasp. "Oh, Joe. That's so good," I moan and then sit up on my elbows so my tits are shaking. "Let me get on top."

He slides out of me and then lays down where I was and holds his hands out for me. I adjust myself so that I'm on top of him and take him down to the root.

I swivel my hips against him, rub my clit against his pubic bone and it makes me shatter into a million pieces. There's no slack in his hands as he holds me up and I use them to hump him to an orgasm right after me. He took the condom off before he got into the pool with me and he's shot his come into my hungry pussy.

I collapse on top of him and he holds my body to him as we catch our breaths.

"What now?" I ask, once I've caught my breath.

"Now? Now we go back inside and take a shower together and see where the night takes us. Does that work?"

I nod and squeeze his dick with my pussy muscles. "Don't do that, baby! I'm too sensitive!"

"Don't be a baby and fuck your wife so we can watch!" Brandon yells from the side of the pool as he wades through the water to us with Whitney in his arms.

Want more Joe and Jill? Stay tuned. You might just see what they are going to do for the next two days!

Thanks for reading!

XOXO,

Eden

Dedication:

To all of those married couples who are trying to make their marriage work. It's hard work.

Delayed in Ecstasy

By

Tiffani Lynn

Chapter One: Lizzie

My ponytail slides across my bare shoulder as I turn my head, looking into the emerald depths of Beckett's eyes. The same eyes that had stolen both my attention and my heart six months ago when he stepped in front of me blocking the afternoon sun. My first response that day was to yell at whoever it was to stay out of my sun, but when I opened my eyes, the broad shoulders and trim waist outlined by the sun he was blocking, made me sit up and take notice. A deep vibrating masculine voice queried, "Can I join you for a second?"

I'd been so stunned by his forward nature that I sat up, scooted back and slid my sunglasses on top of my head. Green eyes, like the grassy meadows in Ireland, were trained on me, taking note of my reaction. He smiled at me while I gaped like a fish out of water. Embarrassment still weighs heavy on my chest when I think about it, even now.

"I'm Beckett," he'd stated. He'd paused, waiting for me to reciprocate with my name, but I was frozen for a few seconds.

My brain finally snapped in to place and I responded, "I'm Lizzie." My voice had been quiet and unsure.

"Nice to meet you, Lizzie." His deep voice rumbled through me and the panicky sensation I got around men bubbled to the surface.

"I've been watching you since yesterday. I'm sorry if that sounds creepy, but I couldn't help myself. I wondered if I could take you to dinner tonight?"

I'd breathed a sigh of relief as I realized I had an easy out. "Thank you for the invite, but my flight leaves in four hours. I'm trying to catch a few more rays before I head back." I gave him my best apologetic smile and waited for him to leave. He surprised me with a bigger grin, like he understood I was nervous and liked making me that way.

"Well, it was nice meeting you, Lizzie. If you change your mind and decide to extend your vacation, please let me know. I'm in room eight twenty-three. The offer doesn't expire." He was so charming and unbelievably handsome.

"Thank you, but I have to be back at work by tomorrow morning so unfortunately, this is the end of my vacation."

He flashed me one more smile before he got up and strutted away with more confidence than an Armani model at Paris Fashion week. The muscles in his back rippled and flexed as he moved and my swimsuit bottoms dampened at the thought of him without his swim trunks. I pulled my sunglasses back down over my eyes, hoping to mask the fact that I watched as he rejoined a group of men all about his age. He was obviously taking a ribbing about me shooting him down. Instead of appearing angry though he turned to look at me one more time, shared that sexy grin and leaned back in his chair.

****

Hours later I sat in the lobby of the posh Miami hotel staring at my phone. My flight had been cancelled due to blizzard like conditions with no option to re-book until the storm was over. According to weather reports, that could be up to forty-eight hours. What the hell? I have no idea why I didn't check the weather at that time of year since I was returning to Chicago, a place notorious for bad weather. I stood and pulled my suitcase up to the desk and questioned the clerk, "Can I rebook my room? My flight was cancelled indefinitely."

A mask of concern crossed her face as she replied, "Ms. Martinson, the hotel is booked solid tonight. I think everyone had the same issue you did. Let me make some calls to other hotels and see if we can get you booked."

"Oh, I can do that myself. I'm sure you are far too busy for that," I told her.

"No, no, no, I'll be glad to help you. Give me a few minutes. Why don't you have a seat in the bar and I'll come find you once it's done? I'll keep your suitcase, too."

"Well, I could use a drink so I'll take you up on that. Thank you for your help."

Ten minutes later I was half way through a Long Island Iced Tea when someone propped up against the bar next to me. I glanced over and blushed realizing it was Beckett. My heart flipped and my stomach dropped when he flashed me a wicked grin. "Snowed out?" he asked.

I tilted my head wondering how he knew that. As if he understood my unspoken question he answered, "One of my buddies was flying to Kansas City and had to come back to the hotel because his flight was cancelled. That's the only reason I can figure you're not on your way back home now."

I sighed. "Yes, I should have looked at the weather and left a day early, but I was too busy enjoying the Florida sun. I'm screwed. I'm going to be so far behind at work." I took a slug of my drink in a very un-lady-like fashion.

"So where are you staying? My buddy is crashing with one of the other guys since there were no rooms available."

"I don't know. They're calling other hotels to find something for me. I can't believe this. I feel like an idiot."

He reached over and pushed a loose hair behind my ear and I involuntarily shuddered. His lips kicked up on the side before he asked, "So, can I take you to dinner once you're settled in your new hotel?"

"Um, I..." I stuttered as I attempted to get the right words out.

Men make me nervous; I've never been able to keep my cool around them. According to my parents I should've been married off to some big time banker or senator or something by now. I just happen to be terrible with the opposite sex so I stopped accepting date requests a long time ago to avoid the embarrassment that came with that stuff.

Before I could finish my response, the desk clerk approached me with a look of dread on her face. "I'm sorry, Ms. Martinson. I can't find a single hotel that has a room available. Between the flight issues and a dance convention in town everything is full. I didn't try any one or two-star facilities, but I can. I didn't want to do it without talking to you first." I still remember the dread settling in my gut at the thought. I'm not a snob by any means, but staying in a sub-par hotel in a sketchy part of town by myself sounded like a terrible idea.

I tapped the bar behind me. The bartender glanced up at me as he continued filling a beer stein. "Can I have a double shot of tequila?"

He nodded once and poured it, setting the lime and salt next to it. I shook my head and slammed the double shot back relishing the burn as it traveled to my stomach. Then I turned back to the desk clerk and said, "I can get online and book one of those. Thank you so much for your help."

She appeared uncertain and I knew it was because of my status, my family, that she was afraid to upset me. I'm not like them, but their reputation is known far and wide as snobbish, entitled, and privileged. I'm glad Beckett didn't ask my last name or seem to notice when the clerk used it. The knowledge might have sent him running before I got one of those smiles.

"It's okay. I appreciate all you've done. I can handle it from here." She nodded as she chewed on the inside of her lip. I gave her a small smile to reassure her. She turned and clicked on her heels back to the reception desk.

Chapter Two: Lizzie

I looked back up to find Beckett still standing there with the same sexy smirk on his face. "Ready for a solution?" He rested his elbow on the bar, laced his fingers together and I couldn't help but follow the motion. He had large, rugged, real man hands. The kind you want to caress you from head to toe in the dark of night.

I knew I shouldn't ask, but couldn't help myself. I took another swig of my drink. "What kind of solution?"

"You can let me take you to dinner and then you can share my room." The look on his face told me he thought this was a seriously viable solution. My mouth dropped open and I'm sure the look was similar to the fish gape I had by the pool earlier in the day. He didn't break eye contact and I realized that the light green polo he was wearing made his eyes more lethal than before.

"I'm not saying you have to have sex with me, but I am offering you a place to stay. The only price is you having dinner with me. I promise I'll be a complete gentleman."

"I don't think that's a good idea. I don't even know you. You could be a serial killer or a rapist or something along those lines," I argued.

"You're right, I could be. But I'm not. I'm a building contractor, not a serial killer. I've never had to force a woman to have sex with me. If fact, I don't even usually initiate sex." His smile never left his face and I was mesmerized by the combination of the eyes and smile and the hint of a dimple I saw on his left cheek.

"Come on, would you rather attempt a one-star motel in a shady part of town to avoid dinner with me or stay in this lovely establishment where you're safe and have dinner with me. I promise not to bite."

I pounded the rest of my drink, licked my lips and replied, "What happens if you decide during dinner that you don't like me? I won't have anywhere to stay and it'll be weird." That was a real possibility if you looked at my previous dates over the years. However, the liquor was running through my veins full throttle and I realized my inhibitions were dropping because it suddenly didn't sound like a bad idea anymore. I tapped the bar again requesting a single shot this time. When I was done he pierced me with his eyes and explained, "If dinner doesn't go well, I'll find somewhere else to stay and you can have my room." There is no way this guy was for real. I blinked at him a few times while I processed what he'd said.

Between the alcohol and the idea of sleeping in a crappy motel the choice was made easy. "Okay."

"That's a yes?" he probed.

I nodded. He called the bartender over and told him to put the drinks on his room and pulled me by the hand back to the desk. "She'll be staying in room eight twenty-three with me. Can you have her bags sent up?"

The desk clerk blushed and replied, "Yes, sir."

He propelled me toward the elevator and pressed the eight button once we were inside. On the second floor more people got on the elevator so he tugged me back against his incredibly firm body and wrapped an arm around my waist securing my position. I took a deep breath and let it out slowly, trying to settle my nerves. We exited and walked to his room with his hand on the small of my back. The contact sent chills down my spine.

Not the luxury suite I vacated earlier, but his room was adequate, although it only had a king sized bed, not two queens like I expected. His balcony had a beach view. A knock on the door signaled the arrival of my suitcase. He took my bag from the bellhop and tipped him.

"I'll leave you to get ready. Is an hour sufficient?"

"Um... I probably only need a half hour to be honest. I showered before I went downstairs earlier."

"Okay, I'll pick you up in thirty minutes. Do you have any preferences for dinner?"

"No, I eat anything."

"See you soon." He grinned as he closed the door and I stood staring at his retreating back wondering what in the hell I was doing. My mother would've had a heart attack if she knew about that arrangement.

****

Thirty minutes later I was standing in a little black dress and black strappy heels inspecting myself in the mirror when the door opened and he appeared. "Hey, I need to change. Give me five minutes." He collected something from the closet and a few things from his suitcase and disappeared into the bathroom as I applied my lipstick.

He strolled out of the bathroom in a charcoal tailored suit with a black button down shirt. He was ridiculously hot and I felt the strip of lace between my legs dampen in response.

"You look amazing," he complimented me.

"Thank you. You too."

At dinner conversation was easier than it had ever been with a man for me. I don't know if he sensed my awkwardness and tailored the conversation or if it was the level of alcohol in my system. After dinner he laced his fingers in mine and said, "Let's take a walk. The weather is beautiful here, a novelty this time of year for us Midwesterners."

"That sounds nice."

We walked for fifteen minutes, not saying much, just holding hands, when he asked, "Do you feel better about sleeping in my room?"

"I think so. This all seems weird to me. Like the part of a movie where the woman says yes when she clearly should have said no and later regrets it as she's locked in a small cage with a dog collar and a freak wielding a whip."

His laugh was hearty as he squeezed my hand. "The desk clerk knows you're staying with me. If you turned up missing she'd be the first one to point the finger in my direction."

"Oh yeah. I forgot about her." My body settled in an instant and a grin appeared on my face. "In that case, yes, much better." He chuckled and shook his head.

We came to the end of the sidewalk and he asked, "Want to walk on the beach or go back to the room?" The wind tussled his midnight colored hair giving him a boyish appearance and I melted a little more. Now that I felt a little safer my mind began to loosen up and let some more interesting things in. My eyes shifted to his lush lips unable to look at anything else all of a sudden. The night air was charged with an electricity I couldn't explain. He closed the gap between us and his warm breath traveled across my lips. "Room or Beach?" he questioned again, his tone quiet.

Unable to help myself I pressed my lips against his, noting that those were the softest lips that had ever touched mine. His hands grasped my cheeks holding me in place and he tilted his head, thrusting his tongue inside my mouth. The kiss was all consuming and the hottest thing I'd ever felt in my life. Our tongues tangled and stroked against the other and I had an insane urge to hike my leg up on his hip and grind against him. Instead I pulled away and said, "Room. Take me to the room, please."

The smile he gave me was different than the others. It was spectacular and slightly predatory. My nipples beaded and poked into the fabric of my dress. He grabbed my hand and pulled me to the curb. Stepping out from the curb he hailed a taxi that whisked us back to the hotel.

The cab ride was used as a teaser of things to come as his fingers stroked the inside of my thigh and he whispered naughty things in my ear. In the elevator he pulled me against him, my back to his front, his erection pressed into my back and the heat of his breath against my ear as he bent to lick it covertly. My knees shook with pent up desire. By the time we reached the room I was a hot puddle of goo.

When the door closed to the room he spun me and slammed me against the wall as his mouth came down on mine in a punishing kiss. I lifted my leg over his hip like I wanted to earlier and rotated against him. The pressure was so good a deep groan escaped my lips. He reached under my legs and hiked up so that both my legs were up. I wrapped them around his waist and kissed him harder. He spun again and stalked to the bed, depositing me in the middle. Tossing his suit coat to the floor, he unbuttoned his shirt. The muscled planes of his chest were exposed by the open shirt, drawing a sigh from my parted lips. He knelt between my legs...

"Lizzie," Beckett interrupted, whispering against my ear. I shake my head as I work to come back from the memory of our first time together. He tugs on my ponytail and asks, "Where'd you go? Your mind slipped off into la-la land, I think."

I giggle a little leaning back, seeking the heat of his naked body against mine. The water droplets roll between us, while spray from the shower continues to coat his back. He pumps some shower gel on his hands and rubs them together before he washes me, starting at my neck and working the muscles as he goes. "Seriously, what's on your mind?" he questioned.

"I was just thinking about the first day we met and how your eyes melted my lady parts."

Chapter Three: Beckett

I knew when I first saw Lizzie stretched out on her lounger by the pool that day she was the type of woman who was strung tight on a regular basis but would go off like a fire cracker when touched just right. Some women are like that; thank God she's one of them.

I think about our first night together more often than I should. She'd been so fucking perfect, laid out in front of me like a raven haired goddess. Her eyes were clouded with lust, her hair fanned out around her head and shoulders. Black lace panties peeked out at me from under the hem of her dress which was still hiked up around her hips from my attack a second before. Her lips were swollen from the kisses we'd shared and she was panting in anticipation. So damn hot! I knelt in front of her and pushed the dress higher, searching her eyes to confirm consent. She nodded her head and I shuffled the little black panties down her shapely legs and tossed them to the floor.

I ran my hands up the inside of her thighs and pushed them open all the way. Her pussy was bare and glistening with the evidence of her arousal. My cock pushed painfully against my boxers. I reached down and unbuttoned and unzipped my slacks hoping to provide some relief. I adjusted myself and dipped my face down against her sex, inhaling the sweet scent of her. Unable to help myself, I swiped my tongue on the smooth lips and then reached up to part them. Peeling the folds back like the petals of a flower, I examined the swollen tissue before I licked in soft strokes. Her hips lifted, moving to place me right where she wanted me so I pinned her to the mattress and said, "I need to taste all of you, be patient. I promise I'll take care of you."

The sexiest little mewl came out of her mouth and her muscles relaxed. I smiled against her sex as I continued to work her. She was so responsive to my touch, to my tongue, to my words. She still is.

When I realized she couldn't take any more I sucked her clit between my teeth and flicked the nub with my tongue. She came off the mattress and bucked wildly as she came, screaming my name. "Beckett, Beckett, Beckett!" It echoed off the walls and my chest swelled with satisfaction. I released her and waited while she caught her breath. She was the most beautiful thing my eyes had ever seen; still is, if I'm being honest. I crawled up her body, hooking her knees with my forearms as I went, spreading her wider, leaving her more vulnerable.

My rock hard cock bobbed between us, smacking against her skin as I moved into position. I lowered my hips into the cradle of her pussy adding pressure to the sensitive tissue. She cried out at the contact as her eyes rolled back into her head. Her body shuddered uncontrollably again. I remember the look on her face as I watched her body break apart and rebuild for me. "Beckett," she whispered as she found herself again, the word enough to ignite an inferno within.

I sat back on my heels and reached for my pants, ready to be buried deep, pulling a foil packet out of my slacks. I tore it between my teeth and rolled it down my length. She was up on her elbows watching the process with hooded eyes.

I readjusted her legs to rest on my shoulders and lowered myself until we were skin to skin, the head of my fully primed cock rested at the entrance of her channel. I rolled my hips so slowly I ached with need, entering her an inch at a time. Once I bottomed out I realized that I'd never been wrapped in a pussy this tight or this hot. I ran baseball stats through my head in an attempt to settle my balls which had pulled up tight, ready to blow with the slightest movement. By the time I was through with the '69 Mets roster I was settled as she squirmed under me, ready for more.

I lowered my head and tugged the top of her dress down with my teeth and said, "Let me see them." She complied, peeling the dress down and lifting her full, round breasts from the cups of her bra. Her dusky nipples pebbled in the cool air of the room. I swiped one with my tongue, swirling before I gripped lightly with my teeth. She whimpered and I repeated the process on the other breast, rocking into her through it all.

She lifted up, capturing my mouth with hers in a kiss meant to entice and consume all at once. I looked down between us to where our bodies met and watched my shaft disappear into her glistening sex. "So fucking sexy," I growled as I pumped into her harder, faster, her breasts bouncing with the movement. Her body arched up and I nipped at her nipples, harder this time, working to get a reaction from her.

I lowered my head into the space between her shoulder and her ear and said, "Your pussy is so fucking tight. So good. Grip me harder." She squeezed her walls around me and I groaned louder than before. I slammed into her over and over and over until my back arched, head thrown back, eyes clenched shut, hips thrust forward and exploded inside her. She screamed my name again and I slipped her legs down to rest on the mattress, collapsing against her.

After several minutes I peeled myself away from her and dumped the condom in the trashcan. When I returned to the bed I removed her dress and bra and tossed them to the floor with my coat. I rolled, pulling her on top of me as my body recovered wondering why a woman like her was alone on vacation.

Just thinking about that night has me hard as a fucking rock.

Chapter Four: Lizzie

After our first time together, I rested with my head on his chest right below his shoulder, sprawled on him like a starfish. I was limp, sated, and happy all at once for probably the first time in my life. All the insecurities that I always carried with me slipped away along with any inhibitions, somewhere between dinner and bed. A small smile spread across my face as I realized this was the first time I'd slept with someone that I didn't know prior and hadn't been dating for an extended period. My total number of sexual partners is only five. I'm so awkward there weren't many opportunities for more. I usually scared my suitors away before the end of the first date. The pretty face fed their assumption that I had my shit together, but once alone with me for thirty minutes it became obvious I wasn't what they thought.

His hands grazed over my back, down over my ass and across the backs of my thighs. I could feel the goose flesh rise in the wake of his motion. His hands were everything I expected and he was so gentle with me that I melted against him. I'll never forget the quiet of the room, his heart beat the only thing I could hear.

He broke the silence by asking, "Are you seeing anyone back home?"

"No," I said, thankful that it was true.

"Why not? Did you just come out of a relationship or something?" His question seemed genuine so I answered with the truth. It wasn't like I was going to see him after this anyway.

"I'm not quite a hot commodity at home."

"I find that hard to believe." Disbelief colored his tone.

"It's true." I turned my head to rest on my hands so I could see his face. "I'm sure it's obvious to you, but I'm not very smooth. I tend to be uncomfortable in dating situations so I avoid them. Humiliation is not something I want to relive often."

"You seem a bit shy, but it didn't take much to overcome that."

I didn't say anything because he was correct. I didn't have a problem overcoming that with him. Anyone else? Well… that was a different story.

We spent the rest of the next two days in bed. It was during that time I found out he lived on the opposite side of Chicago. When we said good-bye in the hotel lobby I thought that would be it. Although we lived in the same city we were about an hour apart and it was a little vacation fling. He surprised me by showing up on my doorstep two days later, coming straight from the airport.

Bringing me back to the present again he smacks my ass in a playful gesture. I brace my hands on the shower wall to keep from falling forward. He takes advantage of the moment by kicking my feet farther apart, shifting soapy fingers between my legs to coax my clit out of hiding. "Are you still thinking about that first night?"

I whimper and answer, "Yes."

"Keep your hands on the wall. If you take them off, I'll stop and I know you don't want that. Time to bring you back to the present and keep you here."

I wiggle my ass at him in impatience. He smacks me again, the sting drawing a moan from somewhere deep inside. His fingers massage between my legs until I'm a throbbing, whimpering mess. They circle my clit hard and fast. I throw my head back and moan, "Oh god! I'm coming, I'm coming, don't stop!" He increases the pace as the fireworks burst behind my eyes, my legs rubbery. He holds me to him until I come back to myself.

Once I can see again, I twist in his arms and lower to my knees at his feet. Pressing my palms inside his thighs I urge him to spread his feet slightly. His cock is hard and thick, hanging heavily in front of my face in all its glory. Instead of placing my lips on it, I lift it out of the way and run my tongue up the seam of his sac. He shudders and groans. I hear his hand thump against the tile next to him as he braces himself.

I grip the sensitive flesh in my hand and pull one nut into my mouth, humming softly as I stroke with my tongue. His body shakes as I release it and switch to the other one. He gasps as I hum louder this time. The tender flesh slips from between my lips and I palm his heavy sac, massaging as he adjusts his feet further apart, allowing me more space to work. I release with a pop of my lips and grip his shaft, directing the mushroom head of his cock to my lips, sucking it hard. I bob up and down until my throat is crammed full.

His fingers thread into my hair and grip tight. He flexes into me and I gag a little. "Relax your throat, Lizzie, you can take more. I'll go slow, but you're going to take it all." I stare up at him as a tremor of fear, oddly followed by excitement, rushes through me. I continue to keep my eyes on his as I pull away and slide back down again, swallowing him slower as I approach my stopping point.

"Take a deep breath and concentrate on relaxing those muscles," he commands. The fire in his mossy colored eyes encourages me and I do my best to comply. I gag again and force myself to relax. He slides in deeper and the feral sound that escapes his throat makes me want to do this for him. His fingers tighten in my hair and I swallow and breathe in through my nose. I pull out, murmuring encouraging words as he pushes in and pulls out, not going as deep. I cup his balls and massage with gentle hands.

"Lizzie, fuck, Lizzie, so fucking good." He praises me and I work harder for him. Bobbing deeper each time. His already thick shaft swells, throbbing against my tongue, and I swallow the head as far down as it can go as he explodes, coating my throat in his hot sticky seed. I drain him and then allow his softening cock to slip from my lips. The look of satisfaction that settles on his face as he reaches for me makes me feel like I've won the lottery.

I clasp his hand and stand. He squeezes the water from my hair never shifting those sexy eyes away from me. He turns off the water and wraps a towel around my shoulders and then one around his waist. We step out of the shower and he leads me across the room in front of the vanity and takes the towel off to wipe me dry. Then he motions for me to sit in the chair and face the mirror.

"Brush," he requests, placing his open palm out toward me. This is my favorite post-shower ritual with him. He runs it through his hair and then brushes mine in long soft strokes.

"I think about the day we met at least twice a day, every day," he says, his voice deep and soft.

My eyes shift to his in the mirror, wondering where he's going with this conversation. "You do?"

"Of course. How could I not? I found the most beautiful, intelligent, sexually satisfying woman ever that day. I was on a guy's vacation, not hoping for anything but some fun with my buddies and then I saw you. I knew that I had to have you and when you said you were flying out in a few hours I almost begged you to stay. When I heard the Midwestern flights were cancelled I prayed one of those was yours. When I saw that you were still at the hotel, I was ready to do anything to have you. I didn't realize then just how lucky I was."

A single tears slides out of the corner of my eye and trails down my face. I never thought someone would feel that way about me, much less someone as amazing as him.

"Beckett," I whisper, afraid to say more.

"I love you, Lizzie."

My breath catches in my throat and I spin around on my chair to stand in front of him. "You do?" I ask, flabbergasted. I'd been too afraid to share those same feelings up to this point even though they'd been building inside me for months. Afraid that it wasn't the same for him, afraid that I was moving too fast. I jump into his arms, consuming him with my mouth, tongue, and teeth. My legs lock around his waist, and both of our towels drop to the ground. He takes two steps and slams me into the wall.

I grip his hair and pull him away from me, both of us breathing like we've run a marathon. "I love you, too. I've known for a while but I was afraid to tell you."

His wild eyes search my face for a moment before he crushes his mouth to mine and carries me to the bed. He lowers me, changing gears from rough and frantic to soft and sweet. He spends the next hour showing me with his actions how happy he is that I feel the same.

*** Connect with Tiffani Lynn by visiting her official website at tiffanilynn.com or on Facebook at https://www.facebook.com/Tiffani-Lynn-884746684907421/

Yearning For Desire

The prequel to Desired

By

Amanda O'lone

Chapter 1

"Have you ever hooked up with anyone from Facebook?" I'm lost in my thoughts when I feel a thud in my shoulder. "Alli!"

"Huh? Ouch! What did you hit me for?" I ask, rubbing my arm where Jennifer punched me.

"Because I'm talking to you and you're not even here in the room. I asked if you had ever hooked up with anyone from Facebook?"

I blush, smirk and look away.

"Ooooh, you have! Shit Alli, when? Tell me!"

Damn, where do I begin? "Okay, but no judging!"

She shakes her head and I begin telling her how Jake and I first met.

I couldn't sleep so I decided to get up and searching around on Facebook. Not much was happening so for shits and giggles I decided to check out a BBW (Big Beautiful Women) chat group. Within minutes I was accepted and was scrolling through looking at the pictures posted. It all seems tasteful enough, so what the hell. I post a pic of myself and thank them for the add. I immediately get responses. All telling me I'm gorgeous, cute and pretty. Really? Are you all crazy? I'm 5'3 and a size 28. I'm a fucking beach ball.

I start getting friend requests by the dozens and I even started chatting with a few. Eventually, I'm getting dick pics and guys begging for nudes of me. The Innocent Shy Girl who has been told she is fucking ugly as sin, who never gets the hot, built men is thinking 'yeah, they just want the pics of the fat girl to plaster around the internet and make fat jokes about her.' But then there is the deviant side of me that is becoming more dominant lately. If they were going to really do that, wouldn't they have done it to other women by now? Wouldn't these groups be shut down by now if men were just using the pics to make fun of the women.

The women seem to all be comfortable in their skin, they know they are beautiful and proud to be who they are. Do the men really love big women? Those men really exist?

So I go for it. I send a tit pic to a few. Then they ask for a pussy pic. Wow, am I really thinking about giving one? Hell yes, I am. So I take a pic and I edit it so none of my rolls are showing. Fuck, they are eating these pics up like they have never seen tits and pussy before. They ask for a full body nude pic and that's where I drew the line. I'm not ready for that. Yeah, I know, pretty fucking stupid since the pics I just gave out shows everything, but showing my flaws in detail is just not something I'm ready to do.

I shut down and go to bed for the night. I wake around noon the next day and decide to go back on Facebook to see if there were any more comments on my pic. Holy fuck! 288 likes and 111 comments! Shit. Even women have commented telling me I'm hot. Then I see I have 13 friend requests. I check them out and the majority of them are from the guys that I have already talked to. So I friend them. There are a couple of the woman who friended me as well and I accept. Then there is one that I have never talked to. I check out the profile and see that there is nothing much there. Only two friends and that they are from Pennsylvania and work at Wal-mart. I don't friend anyone with a profile like that but something is telling me to do it. So I do. I log off and head downstairs to hear my parents fighting over the usual shit. Jim's drinking, Kathy's moods and aggressive behavior. I am so tired of hearing it. Ever since Annie left home I have noticed the crap here more than before.

I'd always assumed that Annie had brought a lot of the drama onto herself, but now I see that it was all directed at her. Since she isn't here to have it directed at her, they are fighting with each other. Even I get hit with the insults at times and I never did before. I was a daddy's girl, but not now. He's been calling me a whore and a slut, telling me I need to stop eating or I'm going to be fat like my lazy sister. Hell, my sister found the love of her life by running away from here. She has sent me text messages and pictures of them. I have to say, my brother-in-law is fucking hot. Tall, built and covered in tats. He could be a fucking model and he loves big women. His best friend is also tall, built and hot and loves big women. Are the men around here just shallow or are they like undercover BBW lovers? I don't get it. I grab my keys and head out the door, shutting the yelling in as I walk out the door. I get in my car and drive to work. A couple hours into my shift I get a message from a guy named Jake. I open it and comment back.

Jake: Hi

Me: Hi

Jake: How are you?

Jake: I see that I'm not your type

Me: I'm good. How do you know you aren't my type?

Jake: I was looking at your profile and see that you like cowboys and country life. That's not me. I'm a city hip hop kinda guy.

Me: I like all :-)

Jake: Oh really?

Me: Yep

I'm smiling to myself and I hear someone clearing their throat. It startles me and I look up to find Todd standing there. Fuck me. I sigh. "What do you want, Todd?"

"What has you so happy?" he asks with a grin.

"Nothing. Just reading a book. What are you doing here?"

"I came to see my girl. Is that a crime?"

"I'm not your girl anymore, Todd. How many times do I have to tell you that? We broke up weeks ago. I don't want to be with a guy who plays with my emotions, who is only around when it's convenient for him. Now, please leave."

"Baby, come on. You know you want to go out with me tonight. We can go to the movies and then to that club you love so much." He walks over to me and wraps his arms around my waist. He kisses my neck because he knows that's my weakness. My eyes roll closed and I let a soft moan out. He hears it and takes the next step. He kisses, sucks and licks the spot up to my ear. I start going weak in the knees.

"Is that a yes, baby? I know it is. You are getting wet aren't you, baby girl? Feel what you do to me." He grips my waist and thrusts his hard cock onto my ass and grinds. Okay, the man does have a nice big cock and hell, it's cock. I'll take it.

"Okay, fine. But this doesn't mean we're back together, Todd." He lets go and heads to the door.

"I'll pick you up at 8pm." And he walks out the door.

If the man didn't have a seven-inch dick, I would have no problem telling him to fuck off. He is dull and repetitive in bed. As far as the relationship goes, he's a home body. We never went out anywhere. No dates, no hanging out with friends, nothing. If I wanted to go out, it was alone because he refused to go. So I broke up with him. Now he's wanting everything to do with my life. I shake my head and go back to my phone to see if Jake is still there.

Jake: So what do you do for fun?

Me: Um, what do you mean by fun?

Jake: Like hobbies and shit.

Me: Not too much. I live in a small-ass town, not much to do here. I read a lot.

Jake: Oh, cool. What do you like to read?

Me: Dirty sex novels lol

Jake: sex is good, very good

Me: Yes, yes it is. So what do you do for fun?

Jake: Well, I don't have a lot of free time just now. I'm in construction. I also have a weekend job. But I mostly just like to go with the flow, chill with friends.

Me: Construction? I though your profile says you worked at Wal-mart?

OK, maybe I shouldn't trust him, he has lied either to me or on his profile.

Jake: Yeah, I don't like my business to be known. I don't trust anyone.

Me: So that's a fake profile?

Jake: Pretty much. I mean if I trust you then you will get to know the real me. And yes, I am trusting you.

Me: Okay. So what do you do in the construction business?

Jake: I'm just a worker, building the buildings. I put in long hours and then work as a clerk at a gas station on the weekends. What do you do for work?

Me: I work at the local bookstore.

Jake: Oh cool. So are you seeing anyone?

Me: No, are you?

Jake: Nope. Have you ever been with a black man?

Me: Nope.

Jake: Oh really? Well, welcome to the dark side, baby!

Me: You saying you want to be my first? lol

Jake: If the chance comes up, hell yeah, I do.

Me: Well, I need to let you know I'm not looking for a relationship. I'm just getting out of a bad one and I don't want to get into another anytime soon.

Jake: I feel you, I'm not wanting into a relationship either. Just want to get to know you, see where things go.

Me: Um Okay, but I'm in Maine and you're in Pennsylvania.

Jake: Yeah, I'm actually in Massachusetts. And If we do decide to meet, I will travel to you.

Me: Okay, but let's just talk more. I'm not going to jump into anything right away.

Jake: Sounds good to me. I really like you and want to get to know you more.

Me: Me, too. Listen, I need to get going for now. I will message you later.

Jake: Okay, love, talk to you soon.

I put my phone down on the counter and take a deep breath. Alli, you need to slow shit down, girl. Don't jump into another relationship like you did with Todd. Now you can't get rid of the loser. Although it doesn't help that I keep hooking up with him at least once a week. I grab the feather duster and head out to start dusting off the shelves and straightening them up. Two hours later I'm headed home to get ready to go out with Todd. He shows up at 7:50 p.m. Ine good thing about him, I guess, is that he's always on time. He and I head out the door and I'm getting into his truck when my father comes out and starts his shit.

"Alli, don't be going and getting yourself knocked up like your sister did!" he yells from the porch. Todd gets in and we drive to the movies.

"You ever think of having babies, Alli?" he asks out of nowhere.

"Um, no. I'm 20. Why the hell would I be thinking about babies right now?"

"Just asking, babe. I would someday like to make a baby with you."

I burst out laughing. "Todd, we will never have a kid together. We're not even a couple anymore. I don't want to be with you romantically. As a friend, sure, we can be that, but nothing more. We really need to stop the fucking, too."

"Okay, if that's what you want, we can just be friends. I can wait for you." He reaches over grabs my hand and kisses the back of it. "You're worth the wait, baby." He winks at me and I pull my hand back.

We reach the theater and as soon as the truck is in park I hop out and head into the building. Todd catches up and wraps his arms around my waist as we wait in line. I loosen his grip, pull out of his grasp and turn to him.

"I'm going to go to the bathroom, I will meet you in there." And I hurry to the bathroom. Once in there I pull my phone out and text Jennifer.

Me: Girl, I have got to get away from this place! Todd won't take the hint we are done!

Jen: Stop fucking him and maybe he will leave.

Me: Yeah, I know, stfu! Lol. We're at the movies and then going to club 9....meet me there PLEASE

Jen: OK, I'll get Mandy and Tessa to go too.

Me: Thank you! Love ya, see you soon.

I head back out and find where Todd is sitting. I sit down beside him and he puts his arm around my shoulders and pulls me into him. Fuck it, we are stuck here for a couple hours, might as well get comfortable. Against my better judgment I slouch down and lay my head in the crook of his shoulder and he grips me tighter.

Chapter 2

We get to the club and the girls are standing outside waiting for us. Thank fuck. I need away from Todd. He had been trying to make out and was all hands throughout the whole movie. It seems to turn him on more every time I refuse him, so you can imagine how worked up he is now. There is no way I will be dancing with him tonight. He will rub that hard cock all over me and before I know it we will be out here in his truck fucking like rabbits. Wait, what's so bad about that? I really could use a good fuck. Oh yeah, that's what's wrong with it: he isn't a good fuck. It's the same every time. I blow him and then he fucks me doggie. I fake it 90% of the time just to get it over with. Then I'm pissed for a day or so for even getting involved with him in the first place. Todd puts his arms around my shoulders and we walk to the door. Thank you, Jen! As soon as we get to them she grabs me out of his grasp and pulls me along with her.

"Hi, Todd! Bye, Todd! Alli will be fine with us!" Jen announces to him. We all giggle and run up the ramp and into the club. We get inside with our trusty fake ID's and head to the bar.

"Where's Luke?" I ask Jen.

"Over there playing pool with his friends. Why?"

"Um, we're all drinking, so how are we going to get home?" And right on cue there he is again.

"I will make sure you get home safe, baby. Go. Have some fun with your girls. I'll go see Luke for a bit." He kisses my neck with a little nibble and walks away. I let out a soft moan and he grins, knowing he just confirmed we will be fucking before daybreak.

"Yes, Todd, go!" Jen says as she shoves him to leave.

"Have fun, baby." he says and walks over to the pool tables where Luke and a bunch of other guys are. I watch as they all give their man hugs and hi-fives. I roll my eyes and turn towards the bar and get my usual Mike's Hard Strawberry Lemonade. Once the girls all have a drink, we head out to the dance floor.

"Alli, you really need to deny him your va-jay-jay."

"Jen!"

"Well, you do. He is going to continue to keep coming back to you if you give in to him."

"I know, I know. But, well, I need my needs met too!"

"Honey, we all do—get a dildo." The four of us laugh hysterically.

"What I think I really need is something new. Something that I never even considered before," I say, chugging down half of my drink and heading back to the bar for another. The girls follow on my tail.

"Wait! You can't just say that and walk away! What are you talking about?" Mandy asks.

"I am talking about a big black cock!" Tessa and Jen spit their drinks out and Mandy's jaw drops. "Yes, you heard me right. I want a black dick."

"Well, let's go find you some black dick." Tessa says grabbing my hand and pulling me out to the dance floor.

"Wait! I didn't mean tonight!"

"Why not tonight?" Mandy chimes in. "Then you won't have to go home with Todd."

"Oh, yeah! I like that reason. Get my girl some black dick, Tessa!" Jen shouts just as the song ends and a slow song starts. The people in our near vicinity are grinning or giggling at us.

I walk to the restrooms and lock myself in a stall. What the fuck am I doing? Why the fuck did I just tell them that? It's not like I will ever get it. I sigh.

But I want it. I want Jake and that is wrong on so many levels. I just met the man. On Facebook, no less!

"Alli? Honey, I'm sorry, I didn't mean to shout it." Jen says.

I unlock the door and come out. "I know. It's not that. I just don't know what I'm doing lately. I need to stop being so desperate for a relationship. I need to just let one find me."

"Aw, Alli. You will find someone. There is a man out there right now thinking the same thing you are and you know what, that's your soul mate. He is your happily ever after." Jen hugs me. Tessa and Mandy come in and hug us as well.

"We all will find our prince charming," Tessa says.

"Okay, prince charming? That's just a little cheesy." I giggle. We all laugh and head to the mirrors to freshen up.

"Okay, let's get back out there and just dance our feet off." Mandy says holding the door open. We all exit and head to the dance floor.

Chapter 3

I am woken up the next morning to a message from Jake. When my eyes focus and see that it's from him I get butterfly's in my belly. I go to sit up and realize there is an arm draped over my waist. Fuck! I look behind me and yup, there is Todd. I slowly remove his arm and sit up in bed.

Jake: Gm beautiful

Me: Morning

Jake: How are you doing?

Me: I'm okay, a little hung over lol

Jake: Oh really?

Me: Yeah, went out last night with some friends. And judging by the guy lying next to me, I got pretty hammered lol

Jake: Ohh, the walk of shame. Been there too, love.

Me: Yeah, I have done it a lot lately. It's my ex. He won't give up and I don't know how to say no.

Jake: You just need to know your worth, love. You deserve to be happy.

Me: Yeah, I know. That's what my friends keep telling me.

Jake: And they're right. Man, if I was there, you would definitely know your worth.

Me: Really? And how would you show me that?

Jake: You would feel loved, know you're loved. You would see love.

Me: Jake...

Jake: Yes, love?

Me: Can I get a pic of you? I'd like to know who I'm talking to... you know, make sure you aren't a chick lol

Jake: Of course, one sec...

A couple of minutes later I receive his picture. Damn, he is hot. I love his eyes. And he is built. Ugh. He is not gonna want to see me. Damn it.

Jake: Love, I wanna see a full body pic of you please.

Fuck.... I can't show him. I don't want him to be disgusted.

Jake: Alli, you are a sexy, beautiful woman. I absolutely love big women. The bigger the better. They are fucking hot!

Me: Okay...

I get up out of the bed and head to the bathroom. I take care of the necessities first, brush my hair and jut take the picture. I hit send and wait, biting my nails, scared as shit he's never going to talk to me again.

Jake: OMG!!! You are fucking hot! Mm, damn girl.

Me: Seriously? You aren't just saying that so you don't hurt my feelings?

Jake: Fuck no. Girl, my dick is hard as fuck looking at you.

I groan. Oh god, I want to see that.

Me: Show me.

Jake: Mm, if I show you, you have to show too, sexy

Me: Okay. What do you want to see?

Jake: All! I want to see that sexy ass, your juicy pussy and those big tits.

And just like that I get a pic of his huge hard cock. Oh my fucking god! That's big and thick! My pussy starts tingling. I get started taking the pics for him. My nipples are hard as a rock. I am getting so fucking turned on doing this. I get all the pics taken and send them.

Jake: FUCK!! Lemme suck that clit. Mm, I need to get behind that ass and put in some work, love. I need to spank and fuck that ass hard, baby.

Me: Mm, yea? You want me?

Jake: Love, I want you so fucking bad.

Me: Oh yea? Then come get me.

Jake: I'm working on that now, love. You free this weekend?

Shit, shit, shit! What am I doing? You know what? I'm gonna do it. I deserve to get what I want and do what I want and be with whoever I want. And right now I am wanting that fine looking man right there.

Me: I am. Do you want me to meet you half way?

Jake: Nope, I will come to you. Do you have your own place or should I get us a hotel room?

Me: Yeah, we will need a room. I still live with my parents.

Jake: No problem. I will see you in a few days, love. I need to get to work now. I will message you later.

Me: Okay, talk to you later, Hun.

Chapter 4

I am sitting in my car in the parking lot to the hotel where he told me he was going to get a room. I'm starting to get the feeling he isn't going to show up. I'm such a fool for falling for a prank on the internet. I start the car and just then a truck pulls in the lot. A tall dark man steps out. He removes his hat and it's him. Jake showed up, but he hasn't seen me yet. He walks into the office and I get out of my car. I stand next to it, waiting for him to come out. I watch him as he talks to the clerk. He is so hot; muscular arms, big broad shoulders, a tat on at least one of his shoulders. He turns to look out the window as the clerk is entering his info into the computer and he spots me. He smiles. God, he has a beautiful smile. I smile back and his attention is brought back to the clerk. He gets the key, heads out the door and starts walking over to me. Once he reaches me, he embraces me and I hug him back. Damn, it feels good to be in his arms. It feels right. He kisses my neck and my head lulls to the side to give him better access.

"Mm, I need to get you into the room now, love."

"I second that."

He grabs my hand and walks us to the room. He unlocks the door and lets me in. Once inside he grabs my bag and places it down in the chair along with his.

"Come here, sexy. Show me that fine body." I walk over to him, he grabs my shirt, lifts it up over my head and throws it to the bed. I reach behind and undo my bra so he can cup my breasts. Oh my God, that feels so good. I look down and see his big brown hands squeezing my tits and it's fucking hot. Ebony and ivory. We just mesh beautifully together. I look into his eyes and they are so dark, full of lust; he really wants me. I see it in his eyes. He leans in and kisses me. Damn, he tastes good. I deepen the kiss. Oh so good.

"Damn, baby, I love the feel of your skin. So soft. Take that skirt off. I want to feel that ass."

I pull my skirt down over my hips, he gets down on his knees and pulls it down all the way. He kisses my thighs and grips my ass, hard. Then he starts nibbling towards my pussy.

"Oh, god!"

"Yeah, you like that, love? I'm going to worship this body. Every inch of you. Sit on the bed and open those legs. Let me see that pretty pink pussy."

I do as he asks and he gets naked. FUCK! That cock is huge! I feel my pussy growing wetter by the second looking at his naked body. He turns to do something and I see he has a huge tat on his back. Shit! I am soaked now. Why are tats my weakness? My pussy is aching so bad now. I squeeze my legs together to try and alleviate some of the ache but it doesn't work. So I reach down and start rubbing my clit lightly. I close my eyes, my back arches and my head falls back. I feel him running his hands up my legs. He picks them up and spreads them open. I continue rubbing my clit.

"Yeah, love, get that pussy nice and wet for me. I want to taste that juicy pussy. It looks so fucking good. I can't wait to sink my cock deep into it, to feel you gripping my hard cock... to feel you cream all over it many times before I bust deep inside you."

"Oh, please, please, Jake. Fuck me please! I need you now!"

"After I taste you, baby. Give me that pussy." He wraps his arms around my thighs and pulls me up to his mouth.

"OH FUCK!! Oh god, yes! Right there."

"Damn, this pussy tastes better than I imagined. So fucking good."

"More, more! Jake, I need to come."

"You will, love. Relax, just feel me." Shit, I need to come so fucking bad! He stands and I lean up and dive for his cock. I need to suck that massive dick. It's so big that I can barely fit it in my mouth.

"Oh damn, girl! Shit, that feels good. Suck it. Mm, you like that cock, don't you?"

"Mm hmm," is all I manage as I am working hard to get this cock all the way in my mouth. I want to deep throat this big boy.

"Yeah, suck it, babe. Mm, yeah, oh shit." He pulls me off his cock and picks me up and bends me over the bed. "Spread them legs, love. Show me that pussy. Ass in the air and head on the bed."

I do as he asks and he groans. "Mm you ready? You want this big cock in that tight pussy?"

"Yes! Please, fuck me now, Jake!" He slides in and I lose it.

"OH MY GOD YESSSS! Mm, yeah, right there, harder. Oh god, I'm gonna come, don't stop!"

"Shit, your pussy feels so good. Damn. Come on my cock, love." He grips my hair and pulls it back.

"Ohhhh, fuuucck! I'm coming!"

He slaps my ass and I come so hard I see white stars. He pulls out and lays me on my side.

"Move up on the bed some, love."

I move up and he climbs up on the bed as well. He then lifts the leg that is on top and bends it up towards my chest and he straddles my other leg as he slides back into me. God damn!

"Oh shit! More!" I'm gripping the bed so hard my knuckles are turning white. This man knows how to fuck! He reaches up and pries my grip.

"Relax, babe, it's okay." He kisses my neck. "You like this cock?"

"Oh god, yes." He continues kissing. "Mm, I'm gonna come again...Aaahhhh."

"That's it, love, come on my cock. I love feeling you gripping my cock."

"Shit! Jake, I'm coming... Mm, fuck yessssss."

"Damn, I love that pussy. Shit, it's going to make me come too... Oh fuck, you ready for this nut, baby? You ready to feel my cum deep inside that pretty pussy? Here it comes, love! AARRRGGGG—fuck yeah! Shit!" With him coming, it pushed me into another orgasm. "Shit, baby, you are amazing."

"I can't move. Holy shit, that was incredible."

"Yeah, you enjoyed that?"

"Oh, hell yeah." I kiss him. "Let's do it again." He laughs and rolls me to my back so he can kiss me. I wrap my arms around his neck and my legs around his waist and pull him into me. He leans down and takes a nipple into his mouth. I gasp and throw my head back. I reach in between us to stroke his cock and I'm surprised to find him already hard again.

"That's what you do to me, baby. God, you are so fucking sexy. Slide my cock in your tight pussy, baby. I want back into that hot juicy wetness." I rub his head on my clit and then place him just inside and he slowly slides in; we both groan. He pulls out slowly and slides back in. God damn, that feels amazing. Then he adds the roll of his hips and OH MY GOD! He hits all angles and I am on fire. I bite at his neck and that sends him flying. He grabs my hands and brings them up over my head and holds them there as he starts picking up speed, getting in hard and deep. After a couple of minutes, he sits up and brings my legs together and up onto his right shoulder and wraps his arms around them and starts pounding me hard. He flips me around, gets on one knee behind me and puts his other leg up next to mine and slides back in. Shit! Just when I don't think it can get any better he adds a new position and it feels even better. It definitely beats Todd and only doing it doggie style.

"Oh my god! Jake, fuck me harder, ooooh, I'm so close, please, please I need to come again."

"Damn, baby, I'm gonna bust too! Grip my cock, milk it—make me bust with you." And just as I'm told, I let it go and I come so fucking hard it knocks me out.

Chapter 5

The next morning, we wake in each other's arms. It feels like heaven lying here in his arms and I never want to move, but life awaits us. I have so many thoughts and questions running around in my head. Where do we go from here? Is there an *us*? Will I see him again? I'm falling for him and I can't. I don't want to be in a relationship. I roll over to face him and he's smiling.

"Morning, love."

"Mm... morning." I give him a kiss. "I don't want to move."

"Me either, but unfortunately we do. I have to get to work. I told them I would work this afternoon."

"Oh, okay."

He gets up and heads to the bathroom. I hear him peeing and then turning on the shower. He opens the door. "Wanna join me?" he asks with a grin. I grin back and hop out of bed, hurrying into the bathroom to hop in with him.

"Mm... slippery and wet. Just the way I love you." He pulls me in for a hug.

"Jake, where are going from here? I mean, are we going to continue to see each other?"

"Of course we are. I want to see you every chance I get. I'm hooked, love."

"I am too, babe."

"Well, then it's settled, we are hooked and gonna see each other again."

I smile and reach up to kiss him.

"Good. Now wash my back." I turn and wiggle my ass at him.

"I'll do more than wash that back, baby." He slaps my ass and bites my neck. "Mm, one more fuck before we have to part."

"Mm, make it hurt real good—I want to feel you for days." I moan. He lifts my leg and slams into me, fucking me into next week. God, I hope to hook up with him again because I am definitely falling in love with this Adonis.

THE END

More of Alli and Jake to come in DESIRED Book 4 in The Chances Series coming out summer 2016

Printed in the United States of America

First Printing, 2016

Amanda O'lone

Newport, VT